WWW○GOD

One Man's Journey
Toward Wholeness

*To Anne
With a lot of love
and esteem Bob*

ROBERT A. KELLER

Introduction by
Robert A. Johnson
Illustrations by
Peter Scott

CHICAGO SPECTRUM PRESS
LOUISVILLE, KENTUCKY 40207

Gratitude to: Princeton University Press for permission to reprint quotations from Carl Jung's letters; Wilfred Meynell Estate for permission to quote the last lines of Francis Thompson's poem, "The Hound of Heaven"; *U.S. Catholic* for permission to quote from Carl Rahner's article, "Christian of the Future"; Springs Studio of Alpena for permission to print photo of Fr. Bob's first mass; Photographer of Joplin for permission to print photo of Madolin and "The Nifty Nine"; Stephen of Louisville for permission to print photo of Kate and "The Treasured Three."

Printed in the U.S.A.

10 9 8 7 6 5 4 3 2 1

ISBN: 1-58374-009-0

Cover illustration by Peter Scott, Professor, School of the Museum of Fine Arts, Boston, MA

Memory cannot fully recall nor paper adequately record the names of people who should be mentioned here. This book is gratefully and joyfully dedicated to four groups of people:

1. Those whose names and pictures appear in the book.
2. Those who are mentioned generically — relatives, friends, teachers, real and composite schoolmates, parishioners, cursillistas, students, Journey companions.
3. Those with whom I have interacted in some way over my lifetime — neighbors, health care professionals, bankers, lawyers, energy suppliers and distributors, service people, media folks, administrators and assistants, and public servants.
4. The individuals responsible for the immediate production of this book — daughter Joanie who set me in motion, wife Kate who taught me how to shift and accelerate, Dr. and Mrs. William Oldham, Rich, and brother Jim who convinced me that my story was worth telling when I had shifted into reverse, and Dorothy and Wanda who took my scattered pages and made them look like a book.

Thank you all.

God is a circle whose center is everywhere and whose circumference is nowhere.

CONTENTS

INTRODUCTION 7

Chapter One
GOD'S COUNTRY 9
Chapter Two
A CORNER ON LIFE 20
Chapter Three
SEASON TICKETS 26
Chapter Four
LEARNING LIFE'S LITTLE LESSONS 34
Chapter Five
SOUL SAVING SACRAMENTS 45
Chapter Six
ONLY SHOW IN TOWN 56
Chapter Seven
ONWARD CHRISTIAN SOLDIERS 69
Chapter Eight
PUBESCENT POWER PUZZLE 77
Chapter Nine
CRUNCH TIME 96
Chapter Ten
TO SOW OR NOT TO SOW 107
Chapter Eleven
THE MEXICAN WAR 118
Chapter Twelve
MAKING MAJOR MOVE 127
Chapter Thirteen
THE REAL PRIEST FACTORY 137
Chapter Fourteen
PRIESTHOOD OR SACERDOTAL START 148
Chapter Fifteen
BROTHER MARTIN 159

Chapter Sixteen
IT HAS TO BE YOU 165
Chapter Seventeen
THE SHORT COURSE 172
Chapter Eighteen
SHEPHERDING IN THE ASPHALT JUNGLE 181
Chapter Nineteen
TACKLING TOUCHDOWN TOWN 191
Chapter Twenty
JUMPING OFF THE ESCALATOR 197
Chapter Twenty-One
INSTANT FAMILY 205
Chapter Twenty-Two
FROM PREACHER TO TEACHER 211
Chapter Twenty-Three
MADOLIN'S TREE 222
Chapter Twenty-Four
THE CRYSTAL BALL THING 234
Chapter Twenty-Five
IMAGES OF GOD 246
Chapter Twenty-Six
END OF THE ROAD 257

INTRODUCTION

One of my favorite words is the verb "to saunter." Webster's definition is "to wander about idly, stroll, wander, roam . . . Saunter suggests a leisurely pace with an idle and carefree mind." Some time ago I discovered the literal meaning of the verb. It comes from the two Latin words, *santa* (holy) and *terra* (earth). So the word really means to walk on the earth with reverence for its holiness.

"Saunter" is not just a favorite word of mine. Sauntering over the holy earth has been my favorite activity since I was a young boy. I have sauntered extensively in the United States and Europe. For over twenty years I spent my winters sauntering throughout India. My current source of contentment is sauntering in the desert near my home.

A short time before his death, Joseph Campbell, the renowned mythologist, was asked how the rivalries, antipathies, and hatred that now exist in most parts of the world can be resolved. His response shocked his audience with its simplicity, tourism. Touring at its best is sauntering.

Among the great benefits of wandering at a leisurely pace with an idle and carefree mind is a better understanding and reverence for the people who live on the face of the holy earth. Adjustment and adaptation to place and time is called culture. Every culture is an unique experiment, one society's particular way of existing and surviving on the holy land. It is wrong to think of cultures in comparative terms, as if there is only one correct way of adjusting to place and time. All cultures are valid and merit our examination and respect. In each culture there is an abundance of useful information for living "wholly" that can be garnered by sauntering and wandering leisurely with an open mind.

It is true that the world is getting smaller as communication and means of transportation improve. Sadly, a large number of people do not have the means to exploit these technological advances, but that does not mean that other cultures cannot be explored in less expensive and complicated ways. Migration has continued to distribute and mix cultures across the globe, even as close as our neighborhood where it should be easy to saunter. The difficulty, or course, is our reluctance to take the time and open our minds.

There is even a simpler and cheaper way of sauntering through another culture, reading. There are libraries filled with the fascinating works of anthropologists and sociologists that deal with specific cultures. Then there are biographies. Every life is a mini culture, the adjustment and adaptation of one individual to time and place. And just as we can learn from the collective adaptation of a whole society, so also there is much to learn from the adaption, the story, of just one individual.

And so I am recommending to you *WWWoGod*. It is a fascinating and humorous story of one man's adaptation to a total institution, religion. He asks questions and gives answers that are worthy of serious consideration. He speaks to modern people who are trying to balance older Theology with newer Sociology and Psychology. I'm certain that sauntering through this book will bring you much enjoyment, cross-cultural understanding, and a clearer perspective of the world of religion.

Finally, I recommend this book because I sincerely believe in Bob Keller. He energizes me. In fact, I believe in him so firmly that I recently asked him to be my fictive grandfather. Happy sauntering!

–Robert A. Johnson, Jungian Analyst
Author of *He; She; We; Balancing
Heaven and Earth;* and *Contentment*

CHAPTER ONE
GOD'S COUNTRY

The Rock — the main character of this story — was born on the fourth of July, 1929. It was a hot day in an ominous year. Just as he was about to begin his traumatic descent into life, Beezo Couture who lived next door, shot some fireworks onto the roof of his parents' home and shingles were ignited. The Rock and the fire department arrived simultaneously. To this day, the Rock is reflexively agitated when he hears a siren, and is occasionally awakened in the middle of the night by the acrid smell of burning wood. To top things off, three and a half months after the fire, Black Friday depressed the country.

The Rock's place of origin was Alpena, Michigan. It is a small town on Thunder Bay of Lake Huron. Many of the people who were born there call it God's country. Some visitors have been heard to comment, "Only God would want it." Alpena is about one hundred miles south of the Straits of Mackinaw. No doubt you have heard of the Big Mac bridge that joins the two peninsulas of Michigan. If you check out the national weather during the winter months you will frequently see Alpena featured as the coldest spot in the country.

Cement was the big industry in Alpena and everything in the town had a gray dust on it most of the time. It was particularly visible in the winter when it snowed. Winter lasted for six months up there. When it snowed or rained everything also got crusty and heavier. A lot of people walked with stooped shoulders. There is still a significant number of Alpenaites who claim that the plaque that they have in their arteries is half randomly inhaled, semi-cured, ready-mixed concrete.

The little town was neatly packaged. Most residents were working class folks. There were a couple of semi-wealthy families with big houses on the lake shore, and a small aspiring middle class on the blocks just off the shore. The town also had its ratio of famous and infamous people. The man who shot President McKinley learned his violence there. The great Nebraska cornhusker Bob Devaney did his first coaching at Alpena High, and Chris O'Toole, the Rock's cousin, went to Rome and became the Superior General of the Congregation of the Holy Cross — the religious order that runs Notre Dame.

The principal variable that stratified the population was religion. Numerically, the Catholics were dominant. They had three large parishes, two with grade and high schools, and one with only a grade school. The Lutherans were in second place with two small parishes, both with only grade schools.

Historians and social commentators say that during the heavy immigration years just before and after the turn of the century, national churches served as good pressure cookers for immigrants and helped them integrate into a pluralistic society from a position of strength. That certainly was true for the Rock's clan.

Out in the west end of town where 9th Street was the main artery, a large number of French immigrants settled around St. Anne Parish. Two houses from 9th on Tawas Street was a plain white house with a large wrap-around veranda. It was the home of Robert and Cornelia (LeBlanc) Martin. Their eldest daughter was named Genevieve. Her mother was a dignified lady and a top flight seamstress. So Genevieve ended up being a ribbon and bows lady, or a legitimate quail, the local idiom for foxy.

Four blocks further South on 9th Street was another small, plain house. It labored to contain the Frank and Barbara (O'Toole) Keller family of seven sons and a daughter. Number three son was named Andrew Arlie. Most people preferred to call him Arlie. Early pictures indicate that he was handsome and family stories indicate that he was viewed as highly eligible by the quail in the neighborhood.

One afternoon in the summer of 1924, Genevieve trotted over to the local grocery on an errand for her mother. Fortuitously, Joe Couture's store on the corner of 9th and Saginaw Streets was half way between the Martin and Keller residences. On this particular day, Arlie and one of his buddies, both certified quail hunters, were out in front of the store. Arlie had been eyeballing Gen for some time, but had never been properly introduced. Leo, his buddy, who was dating Gen's best friend, seized the opportunity to introduce them, and the show got on the road.

Their courtship was interesting. Like a lot of fathers, Robert Martin was very protective of his eldest daughter, and with good reason. Arlie had a reputation for being unpredictable, with a red hot temper. Even his brothers were afraid of him. So Mr. Martin assisted his daughter by establishing a formal dating pattern.

Arlie and Gen, 1950

Gen and Arlie dated for about two years and almost always on Saturday evenings. Arlie would drop by Gen's house, and along with her younger sister Gina as chaperone, they walked downtown to Howe's music store. There they would pick out a few sheets of music to try out on a piano in one of the small cubicles available for this purpose. It was here, no doubt, that they got to do a little private cuddling and smooching when Arlie bribed Gina with money to buy candy at the nearby Woolworth store.

Once they had selected and purchased some music, they headed back to the Martin home where Gen would play the piano and Arlie would sing along. Gina patrolled as a vigilant nuisance. Gen always dated the sheets of music and added appropriate and insightful commentary on the front page. There is a lot of great music in the collection, pieces like "Poor Papa," July 3, 1924, and "It Takes a Long Tall Brown-skin Gal to Make a Preacher Lay His Bible Down," Sept. 14, 1925. This style of courting was declared the neatest bit of male domestication ever seen in that neighborhood. When the relationship finally got certified in St. Anne's church on May 16, 1926, the event was viewed as a modern miracle.

It didn't take Arlie and Gen long to demonstrate that they knew what the primary purpose of marriage was. On March 9, 1927, Gen gave birth to a cute, little, curly headed, left-hander whom she named Martin Francis. Curly, as he was soon nicknamed, had a peaceful and loving disposition. Gen and Arlie

Rock, Curly, Joe, and Jim, 1940

were so thrilled with their first production that they decided to savor this gift from heaven for a couple of years before trying again. Two years and four months later a second son arrived . They named him Robert Andrew after his grandfather and father. This new baby did not resemble Curly in any way. Grandpa Martin soon dubbed him "the independent firecracker."

You have probably noted that Gen had an interesting way of keeping her family names alive. She pinned her maiden name on her first born, and then added her father's first name to her second son. A few years later she got her oldest brother in the act by naming her third son James, and her fourth son was named Joseph for her second brother. Foxy lady in more ways than one, right?

In December of that year, as the Depression deepened, Gen and Arlie and the two boys regrouped at Grandpa Martin's house by the depot. There were now three families of four crammed into a small three bedroom house. Only Grandpa had a job. Early on "the independent firecracker," Robert Andrew, gave signs of being environmentally precocious. Aunt Winnie, who lived across the hall with Uncle Jim and their two daughters, still teases him about re-cycling his food. Imagine the worst and you've got the picture. With that kind of intro-duction is it any wonder that the kid developed a dark brown

The Rock, 1932

outlook on life? Early photos exhibit him with nose rolled up, eyes half closed, hair disheveled, and clothes in disarray. Arlie often said of his second born, "That kid would just as soon hit you over the head with a hammer as look at you."

As the Depression lightened in the early 1930s, Arlie was able to pick up odd jobs here and there to help supplement Grandpa's railroad salary. Then in mid 1932 he got a steady job operating a drill out at Thunder Bay Quarry. A nickel an hour was not a big wage, but it was enough for Arlie and Gen to move into a rented house and manage their own affairs. Those affairs, however, had to be managed in the context of a large extended family.

When "the firecracker" was about five, his cousin Blackie hung a new and life-long moniker on him. Blackie had a flair for this. He renamed about three quarters of the neighborhood during his long tenure as firstborn of the second generation. Seems like "the firecracker" took a shine to the Jack Benny radio show and was caught up with Rochester, Benny's sidekick. Thus Robert became Rock or Rocky. That early affection for and affinity with Rochester had an enduring impact on the Rock's adult life.

The number one value and priority on both sides of the Rock's lineage was kinship loyalty. Every Sunday after church, the Rock and Curly visited both sets of grandparents. While discharging that duty they generally got to visit with most of their aunts, uncles, and cousins who were doing their family duty. If you went away, even for just a couple of days, it was expected that you visited everyone to say good-bye and tell them where you were going. When you returned you visited again to say hello and tell them what kind of trip you had.

The Rock doesn't know a whole lot about his Grandpa Frank Keller. All that Arlie could recall was that his dad came from a little town in Germany named Berne. He spoke English, German, and French. Arlie often said that his father's French was better than that of the local "frogs." All of which could lead one to think that Grandpa was really Swiss. Berne, Switzerland is

Grandma Keller, 1960

Grandpa Keller, 1900

Grandma Martin, 1900

Grandpa Martin, 1960

not a little town, but it was and is home to a lot of Kellers. A lot of Swiss are also tri-lingual in the same way that Frank was. The Rock has to check that out one of these years.

Grandma Keller was another story. She was a farm girl and married Frank in her late teens. They brought seven sons and a daughter into the world. Frank supported them by making beer at the local Beck's Brewery. Sadly, however, Frank died in the flu epidemic of 1918 and left Barbara with a very young family, with the oldest , fifteen and the youngest an infant.

The distressed young family was poor but industrious, fun loving, and close. As late as the 1940s they all lived within six blocks of each other, four families on one corner alone. Every Sunday after church Grandma fed the whole clan, had a beer or two with the adults, and played cards with super gusto. She could knuckle the table as loud as any of her thick fisted sons. Grandma had a special formula for charming warts and healing minor infirmities. Almost every Sunday people sought her out and later they commented that her free treatment was more effective than that of the medical people in town. She also had a talent for witching water and travelled all over the territory telling people where to dig their wells.

Cornelia LeBlanc, the Rock's maternal grandmother, died of cancer when he was eleven years old. He remembers that she loved to sing and was a strong member of the St. Anne choir. She taught him a number of French hymns. Curly and Rock stopped at her house almost on a daily basis on their way home from school. She fueled them with cookies, fresh bread, apples, rhubarb, and a lot of TLC. She was a cultured and loving lady, and she treasured her grandchildren.

Grandpa Martin was the grandparent that the Rock knew the best and admired the most. He had a big impact on the Rock's story. Robert Martin was a feisty, self-made man who spoke and wrote both excellent English and French. He was an engineer on the Detroit and Mackinaw railroad, although in actuality, the railroad went to neither place. Robert was very active in the railroad brotherhood. Fr. Charles Coughlin, the popular Detroit radio commentator of the 1930s, was his patron saint. On Sunday afternoons all physical activity in the neighborhood was curtailed for an hour when Fr. Coughlin came on station WJR. Depressed adults chewed on his stuff well into the evening.

The Rock well remembers the Sunday when the pastor labeled the railroad brotherhood a bunch of Bolsheviks. Mother was very embarassed as she saw her father march up to the sacristy at the end of Mass and she tried to get Curly and the Rock out of church as quickly as possible. Sensing that a skirmish was in the making, the Rock slipped quietly up to the front and proudly witnessed his grandpa head-butting with Fr. Bouchard.

Although Grandpa Martin had little formal schooling, education was a high priority as far as his children were concerned. He filled his home with classical works of literature, urged all of his children to play and appreciate music, supported all four through high school, and two sons through college. That was the 1920s and 1930s, mind you.

The Rock's early and prevailing image of his grandpa, garnered from the Huguenot innuendoes of his French relatives, was that Grandpa drank too much and that from time to time he looked admiringly at other women. When the Rock was about 40 years old, he had many conversations with Grandpa, and had to rewrite a lot of family history based on what he found out.

One bit of advice that prompted this revision was Grandpa's theory that life is a brown sandwich. It happens. Everyday, he said, you have to take a bite or two, and it's wise to modify the taste a bit with a little hot mustard or a tasty potion. He also added, that if the time came when you had to eat the whole sandwich in one day, then it was time for a more radical change. All things considered, the sandwich got to Grandpa from time to time. He was a tough old dude and died at age 92 with a pint of Old Fitz and a package of Lucky Strikes on his nightstand.

When Rock was about six years old the little family almost lost everything. Arlie was involved in a serious construction accident, and because of the inadequate state of medicine in Alpena at that time, gangrene set in and he lost his left leg and some movement in his left arm. His artificial limb never slowed him down, however, and no one ever viewed him as being handicapped. He wouldn't allow it. He worked hard all his life, first as a drill operator in a limestone quarry and then as a molder in a gray iron foundry. About the only activity he didn't return to after the accident was roller skating. In fact he claimed an advantage in swimming because his stump floated, and in drop kicking a football because his wooden leg gave him greater clout.

Genevieve was a tiny lady, about five foot three and weighed not much more than a hundred pounds. To this day the Rock marvels that such a tiny and delicate creature could give birth to four larger than normal offspring. She kept a very clean house, tried to keep the boys just as clean, sewed and patched a lot, and provided adequate food for all of them. During those Depression days there wasn't much to go around.

Early in life Gen unfortunately learned that the best role for her to play in life's game was that of the helpless one. It started out, no doubt, because of her size. Arlie always protected her and did a lot of the household chores because he thought they were too much for her. The boys followed suit and soon Arlie's phrases were regularly echoed around the house. " You can't do that, Let me take care of that, Get out of the way and let me handle that, Why don't you just sit down and I'll get that taken care of in a couple of minutes."

There is a sociological axiom that one becomes what one is expected to be. Soon Gen came to believe that she couldn't do anything. Her response to just about everything was a worried look, a wringing of hands, and the comment, "What am I going to do?" It was too bad that this behavior was reinforced because every year Gen became a little less self-reliant and independent. Caring for her became quite difficult for Arlie in his retirement and for the boys when Arlie died. Too late did these well intentioned knights realize what they had helped to create.

From l932-1968, the Rocks' family lived at 401 8th Street where it cornered with Tawas Street. Their residence was a spooky looking place that was known as "The Old Kloochie Mansion." Poley Hunault and his crew had moved it to the corner of 8th and Tawas from the downtown area when the city needed space to build a new city hall. It was a two story clapboard house with big windows and a tiny porch that was trimmed with a bit of gingerbread. Arlie bought it for $300 in l932. His first of many additions and alterations was a comfortable two-seater outhouse a few yards from the back door.

If you were looking at this 8th Street slice of real estate from the air you would note that it was situated at the top of an almost perfect triangle. If you cut northwest or diagonally

The old Kloochie Mansion, 401 8th Street

through the 300 block of 8th Street you arrived at St. Anne Parish on 9th and Sable. If you cut southwest through the 400 block you ended up at Joe Couture's store on the corner of 9th and Saginaw. It was in this triangle, anchored by the parish and the store, that the Rock grew up. So let's cut southwest down the alley and through Carr's Field. The Rock always took that route to go to Church and school. That might seem strange, but the Rock always went south to go north. Put your boots on. The alley is usually a little muddy. While we're walking the Rock will tell you why he took that route.

CHAPTER TWO
A CORNER ON LIFE

Joe "Cooch" Couture was a man whom everyone in the neighborhood knew well. His store was the second major focal point in Alpena's west end. The first was the French parish of St. Anne's where Fr. Louis Bouchard reigned supreme and few people ever questioned his decisions. After all, God was clearly on his side and he told the congregation that at least once a week. Joe and his family, like about 80% of the neighborhood, belonged to St. Anne's. Joe never for a moment ever dreamed that his presence and influence was in any way comparable to that of Fr. Bouchard. But it was.

From the time that humans evolved into sapient beings, males have played only bit parts in the continuation of the human family. They added a few chromosomes to the mix here and there and spent small amounts of time tracking down food for their women and children. To stay occupied and out of the way for the serious business of early childhood socialization, they formed men's clubs to play games like hunting, fishing, and war. The beat went on at Joe's Couture's store. Joe provided an environment at the back of his store where men could gather. The place was a major male socialization factor for at least three generations of westend Alpenaites.

Joe was a gracious man who always wore a white apron when he was in the store. He greeted everyone warmly with a Frenchy triple greeting, "ello, ello, ello." All males, regardless of

Joe Couture's store, 1938

age, were welcomed and treated equally. Drinking beer in the back room was reserved for the older inner circle. Joe sold and served the stuff that people needed, everything from groceries to work clothes. In the rear of the store, where the work clothes were displayed, was a large table and a lot of chairs. There was one large rocking chair back there, and most of the time it was occupied by Fred Thornton. He was a dusty looking old man who always wore bib overalls and a broad-rimmed hat. His handlebar mustache was classic. Fred's claim to fame was guiding the grader over the race track when the fair was in town. Males gathered in this rear area of the store to tell stories and play cards, mostly spitzer and cribbage. A big skunk list was posted on the wall to embarrass the guys who never made the first corner in a cribbage game. For those who wanted to purchase food and drink on the premises, there was an honor code. You served yourself and then wrote what you got in a ledger near the cash register, such as a pop and a three inch hunk of pickled bologna. You settled your account at the end of the month.

Most male activity started and ended there, school, church, athletic events, dates, whatever. Every undertaking was prepped and processed into the ground. The character list was like an Ellis Island litany, Romeo Bourdage, Eggie Clearwood, Dobby Keller, Poley Descharme, Rudolph Weezee, Stub Larush, Halver Ritzen, Lorn Dale LeDuc, Clucky Markowski, Poochy Seguin, Boots Boutin, Zeke Zolnierek, and on and on and on.

Catty-cornered from the store was a vacant lot called Carr's field. Here was the neighborhood athletic complex. You name it and they played it over there — even cricket. Everyone got to play regardless of age or size. The lot was bordered on the east by Mr. Livingrock's house and yard. The Rock and his buddies never had much contact with him because he raised large, mean dogs. You know how frequently husbands and wives become more alike the longer they live together, don't you? Well, that happened to Mr. Livingrock and his dogs. Games were always set up so that his fence was the most removed place from activated balls. If anything went over that fence it was gone permanently.

The south boundary, across Saginaw Street, was the Zelinski house. Old Steve was almost as serious as Mr. Livingrock, but he raised kids and a lot of them. They didn't mix much with the store gang. When they weren't working, the old man kept them in the house. The heavy hitters in evening soft ball games frequently assaulted the side of the Zelinski house with flying or bouncing balls. After a repetitious barrage, old Steve would come out and take the ball inside. After some loud protest at his back door by about twenty outspoken rowdies, the ball would finally be tossed back out. From time to time a window got shattered. Then it took a lot longer to get the ball back. One early evening the ball came back covered with gravy. The Rock wondered whether he had made the equivalent of a hole in one, or whether old Steve smeared the ball in spite.

The north boundary to the field was the LaMarre house and yard. Pete and Exilda had an army of six boys and four girls. The guys were really the caretakers of the field. They organized games, officiated when things started to get out of hand, built a basketball court, dragged the field, cut the grass, and did whatever else was necessary. The Rock will always remember the evening that Dotts (Ted) LaMarre picked him to be on his basketball team. Dotts was about eighteen and the Rock was six. To him, this was more of a step toward heaven than his baptism. He even scored a bucket that night. Dotts cleared out a lane and set him up perfectly. The Rock adopted Dotts as his idol for life. He had finally hit the big time with the big guys.

FDR was big enough to acknowledge that behind every important man there was an important woman. Behind all the males who congregated at the Joe Couture Store and the Carr's Field annex, and even many who did not, was Exilda Robinette LaMarre. She was like a Fortune 500 corporate exec who ruled the whole neighborhood. Because she had ten children, every kid in the territory had a LaMarre friend. When guys sought permission from their parents to do anything or go anywhere, such as swimming, a ball game, the movies, the stock response was, "Are the LaMarre kids going?" And that was the final answer.

Exilda Robinette LaMarre was a tall, robust, wonderful lady. When all was said and done she was probably the strongest person in the neighborhood. And you can apply or extend that in any direction. She was one person in the territory with whom you didn't want to get on the wrong side. She got respect from everyone, her husband, her kids, the neighbors and their kids, the pastor, the nuns, and the local government. Big Zil, as we

Big Zil, 1960

affectionately called her in private, always Mrs. LaMarre within a one block perimeter of her home, had clout.

One of the better kept secrets of World War II was that Big Zil played a major role in the battles of the South Pacific. Armand, or AJ , son number four, was a flyboy for the Navy and he labeled his dive bomber "Big Zil." It wasn't until AJ got home and folks noted how his decorated shirt was causing him to walk stoop-shouldered, that they began to understand how Big Zil, per Armando, wiped out three quarters of the Japanese navy. Even Harry Truman saluted Big Zil.

Big Zil must have known from the beginning that she had special power. Just consider how she named her children. Her first was named after a saintly scholar, Albert the Great. Albert was followed by daughter Rena, a word that has regal roots and connotations of rebirth and salvation. Then came Henry, named and slotted by Zil into the long line of holy Roman Emperors. After a saintly scholar and a king and a queen, Zil's imagination really took off on the next two offspring. As in biblical times when names signified roles, such as Jesus = Savior, she shot for the moon and made it.

The Rock has often imagined Zil discussing this issue with her husband Pete. Now we are talking the 1920s in Alpena, Michigan, when only rare individuals got into classical literature, practically no one thought about the liberation of females, and everyone thought of God as being two males and a bird. When a second daughter showed up, Zil reached up and grabbed the name Thea, the Greek word for God, but with the feminine ending. Was she on target! Thea went on to become a Dominican nun and anyone who ever encountered Thea knew at once that the Godhead was a Quaternity and not a Trinity and that Thea shared in it. She was, however, definitely Old Testament in her thinking and acting. She was a fire and brimstone character who left her marks, rheumatic knuckles, bald spots, and erasure burns, running vertically up the back of the neck, on a large number of the population of Michigan where she taught for over fifty years.

The Rock's first of many "holy" encounters with Thea occurred when he was only five years old. He and Thea's brother Dick had decided to sneak out of the daily family rosary that Big Zil hosted for her charges and anyone who was in eyeshot of this happening. Thea spotted them as they went out the back door and the chase was on. The kids scampered north down 9th Street, took a hard right on Tawas, and crawled under the Fleming's porch to hide. In minutes Thea had sniffed them out, dragged them back to the sidewalk by their hair, double-timed them to the house by their ears, and added another decade to the rosary for their conversion.

The Old Testament, as Christians understand it, is a preparation story for the coming of the Messiah. Big Zil knew that a New Testament sequel to Thea had to happen. So when a short while later a son was born, she was ready with a role assigning name. She called him Theodore, gift of God. Ted went on to become a player for Team Vatican, and the thousands of Michiganders who have known him, especially Mexican-Americans and African-Americans, will vouch to the person that he has been an incredible gift of love and service to them and their place and time in history.

The rest of the LaMarre kids were equally singular and distinguished. Big Zil must have foreseen her next son's role in World War II when she named him Armand. As you already know AJ was a one man Armada in the south Pacific. Magdalen and Imogene were feisty but fun loving like their mother. Virgil, better known as "Turtle," was Curly's side kick, and Dick and the Rock, born only hours apart, were like twins.

To this day the Rock is convinced that he was blessed with a special corner on life, anchored by Joe Couture and Big Zil.

Let's take time out now to go to church. That's where the other half of the Rock's socialization took place.

CHAPTER THREE
SEASON TICKETS

Have you ever thought about what it means to belong to a church? The word can refer to both a building and a group of people. But the word doesn't say much. It's not very descriptive. To describe what church is all about, other explanatory terms and symbols have been created. To cite a few, the Christian Church has been compared to a ship, a lighthouse, a bridge, a franchise, a bee hive, and the Body of Christ. These terms add a little bit of clarification and meaning to church membership, but like all analogies they are limp.

To get a better handle on this concept, let's consider what people do when they go to church. The Rock has been in and out of a lot of church buildings and what he has noted is that the vast majority of people there don't do very much . Basically they listen to and observe what the church leaders are saying and doing. The parishioners change positions from time to time, sing an occasional song, recite short prayer formulae, and make offerings. But with all due respect, their external behavior is pretty much like that of an audience at a theater, or fans at an athletic event.

Because the Rock, like a lot of other Americans, has been a sports enthusiast for most of his life, he would like to use athletic jargon to describe the church activity that he was exposed to. The intent is not to ridicule but to amplify and clarify the notion of church in a new language that is familiar to a large number of people.

The Rock's family was Catholic. To be a Catholic means that you are an official fan of Team Vatican. Team players are all priests. The varsity plays its games in Rome. Their roster is stacked with superstars who have made it up through the semi-pros and minor leagues that dot the globe. The JVs play in big towns that have titles like diocese or archdiocese. Each of these places has a player-coach who is called a bishop. Players who are getting old or need experience play in small towns.

There is another group called "religious," and there are a lot of them, such as Jesuits, Franciscans, Dominicans. They generally live in monasteries, abbeys, and priories. They have their own immediate leaders, but they are all subject to the local bishop or coach. Most religious are priests. A few are brothers. Brothers are helpers like ball boys and trainers. Team Vatican is an all-guy outfit and the head coach called the Pope makes no bones about it.

St. Anne Church, school, and rectory

Some women called nuns have their own league, so to speak, but in the eyes of Team Vatican their roles are strictly preliminary or ancillary. They teach, do social work, take care of kids, tend the sick, counsel the confused, sing songs, play musical instruments, and decorate and clean the auditoriums. They do a heaven of a job and the fans really appreciate their efforts. Thousands of folks today wish that the Pope would merge the two leagues and invite some of these women to play on the JVs and someday, even on the Varsity.

Gen and Arlie, the Rock's parents, received their season tickets to Team Vatican performances from their parents at the time of their birth, as had their parents, and their parents, and so on. No one in either of their families had ever questioned their team allegiance or considered rooting for another team. They were fully convinced that Team Vatican was world champ and would always remain so. After all, the head coach, the Pope, was appointed by God and could trace his game plan and play book all the way back to St. Peter himself. So why ask questions? Why not brag and even fight for a winning team that had millions of fans around the world and whose numbers were always on the increase?

New fans got initiated through a ceremony called Baptism. Centuries ago the head coach decided that newborns should be initiated as soon as possible. So when he was eight days old, on July l2, l929, the Rock was taken to St. Anne Church where the local star, The Rev. Louis T. Bouchard, welcomed him into the fan club.

Louis T. was a good guy. Most of the time, like the majority of other Team Vatican members, he wore a black uniform with a white collar. By this unique collar called "Roman," everybody knew whose team he was on, even the Protestants and the Jews. It's interesting today that a lot of non-Catholic ministers are now wearing these "monkey suits" and the Catholic priests are now into shirts and ties with colorful suits and jackets.

Fr. Louis T. Bouchard, 1940

Louis T. was a no-nonsense player. He started on time and with dispatch. So pronto at l:00 p.m. on July l2, Louis T. appeared in the rear, left-hand corner of St. Anne church where the baptistry was located. For this special occasion, over his basic black uniform, he wore a white silk jersey with about twelve inches of lace on the bottom. It was baggy and loose and hung down to his knees. It was called a surplice and most people had no idea what it symbolized. Around his neck he wore a white, embroidered stole that was the official emblem of all Team Vatican players.

Louis T. greeted Arlie and Gen, the Rock, and Grandma and Uncle Frank Keller, who were the Rocks' godparents, in Latin. "Pax vobis." Everybody knows what that means, right? Latin was the official language that all ordained players spoke. It gave everyone a good feeling to know that the game was being played in the same way and in the same language in China, Poland, Italy, Brazil, and Timbuctoo. And that was the case for two thousand years. Now you can't beat that can you? Maybe you could if there was proof that Jesus spoke Latin. And that's possible. He did have a brief chat with a Roman, Pontius Pilate.

After asking Arlie and Gen the obvious question as to why they were there, Louis T. said a few more prayers in Latin and made the sign of the cross on the Rock's head and chest. Then in a raised voice, still in Latin, he told the devil to go to hell and not to bother the Rock anymore. Next, he greased the Rock's chest and back with holy oil which he immediately wiped off. Greasy babies are probably hard to handle. And now the big moment had arrived. Grandma and Uncle Frank held the Rock's head, face up, over the baptistry and Louis poured about three ounces of blessed water on him while he said the heavy words, "Robertus, ego te baptizo in nomine Patris, et Filii, et Spiritus Sancti." It was at that very moment that the Rock had his season ticket stamped on his soul.

The official teaching was that this mark was indelible. It could never be erased. No one ever questioned the indelibility of this stamp, no doubt because it was invisible as was the Rock's soul where the stamp was planted. Louis T. wound things down quickly, greasing the Rock's head with another kind of oil, slapping a white cloth on his chest to remind him that this was now the color of his soul, and holding a lighted candle in front of him to remind him that he was supposed to give good example to others. Finally, he said, *Vade in pace et Dominus sit tecum,* "see you later," and took off for home. There he went immediately to his office where he recorded this event in the baptismal register which was kept in a fireproof safe. Maybe God could see that the Rock had the right punch on his ticket and was officially enrolled in the fan club, but mortals needed visible proof. Future reception of Sacraments would also be recorded in this book.

Arlie and Gen left church with great joy. They had again fulfilled one of their very important obligations. With this new lifelong pass their son, the Rock, was entitled to observe and participate in every event that Team Vatican sponsored. There were five other sacraments like Baptism that were open to him. Added to that there were jillions of sacramentals that he could utilize, like medals, rosaries, crucifixes, palms, ashes, and holy water. Besides that he was offered the guidance and direction of Sisters and Brothers in the spiritual and corporal works of mercy, wonderful education from kindergarten through college, and media screening by the Legion of Decency. And last, but by no means least, there were social and recreational escapades to be enjoyed, such as parochial sports, Vatican roulette, and the most fun of all, bingo.

The Rock, of course, remembers nothing about his Baptism except what he was taught later in catechism class. The blessing that has lived on with him for his entire life, however, is that of his godparents — Grandma Keller and Uncle Frank. They were forever kind and joyful people. They constantly and generously showed the Rock that they loved and accepted him the way he was. They were wonderful models of active charity. Grandma was a neighborhood healer and she knew how to witch water. She taught the Rock a lot about "living water," "giving drink to the thirsty," and "healing the sick."

Uncle Frank delivered milk for several years for the Harris Creamery and later bread for Douville's Bakery. The Rock so enjoyed being with Uncle Frank that during vacations and on Saturdays he frequently worked with him on his delivery routes. He did have somewhat of an ulterior motive when doing the milk runs. The Rock was a basketball freak and he wanted to develop his hands so that he could palm a ball in each one. Stretching to carry three bottles in each hand eventually paid off. By the time he entered high school he had hands like bear claws. Uncle Frank could rightfully be called a "eucharistic" man. Like the Father, he provided hundreds of people with their daily bread and their daily drink. And like the Son, he gave the Rock and others "more abundant life."

When the Rock looks back at all the ticket punching ceremonies he has observed and participated in over the years, thousands, he wonders how so many marvelous and meaningful symbols could become so sadly routinized. When the dust of thinking settles, the same answer keeps peeping through, numbers. It seems that Team Vatican, along with other religious teams, has forgotten the directive that God gave to King David: Don't count. No census. It's quality, not quantity that matters. You've got to do more than run your fans through the turnstiles. People have to know what their tickets are for and what these games are all about, otherwise they become robots.

Later in life the Rock discovered that in years past there were conscientious coaches who thought about these things seriously. One of them — his name is not recorded — cooked up a little jingo that went something like this — "to make the 'ex opere operato' go you've got to see the 'ex opere operantis' flow." What this weird sounding tongue twister means is this: if a Sacrament or ceremony is properly administered, and the recipient knows what's happening and really wants it to happen, then the ceremony is meaningful, and valid. Otherwise it's a magic show. It would be better to send fans to see the magician David Copperfield where they would get their money's worth.

Now when the Rock had his ticket punched for the first time on July 12 he didn't know what in heaven was going on. He couldn't do any "work" like try to understand and respond to what was going on. He was only eight days old, for Pete's sake. But that's what his godparents were there for. In a general sort of way, they knew what Team Vatican was all about and why they played their games. Straight and simple, Team Vatican fans are supposed to be world class lovers. The Coach who made up the jingo knew that the Rock wouldn't be capable of doing any significant altruistic work until he was about 12 years old. That's when the shrinks say a kid becomes "other oriented." Until that time, however, he needed to be oriented toward himself, to learn what a fabulous and unique creature he really was, lovable, acceptable, and deserving of respect in and of himself. But the Rock couldn't do that by himself, could he? No kid can.

You see, rites and rituals, signs and symbols, are for adults, folks who can comprehend their meaning and significance. Baptism means nothing to infants and little children. The ceremonies are for the adults in attendance, and that is why infant baptism, if it is going to accomplish anything, should be a public ceremony.

What really should have happened on that July afternoon is that a whole lot more people than just Louis T., Arlie and Gen, Grandma, and Uncle Frank should have been there for the ceremony. All the people in that community who were oriented toward others and believed that the most important activity in life is to "love your neighbor as yourself," should have been there with bells on to welcome the Rock into their community. The "work" that they should have been doing was that of assuring God and Gen and Arlie by their presence, dialogue, and active participation that they were going to do their best to surround the Rock and all the other little sub-twelvers in town with care and warmth, encouragement and love. That kind of symbolizing would make it easier for the kids to love and accept themselves and thereby become qualified and able to love others. Now that's a lot to think about, isn't it? Remember that old sermon by John Donne, "No Man's An Island"? It's true. "We need one another."

If good old Louis T. had had the kind of orientation that religion needs to be deeply and broadly experienced, he could have done a whole lot more with those powerful and meaningful symbols of water, oil and fire. Everyone could have been involved in the pouring of water, the anointing, the dressing in white, and the lighting of candles. The whole town could have been turned on and empowered. Vatican II has introduced English and upgraded some of the symbolism in the baptismal ceremony, but for the most part the celebration is still a private and isolated event and performed in a mechanical and perfunctory manner.

CHAPTER FOUR
LEARNING
LITTLE LESSONS

In September of 1934, like all five year olds, the Rock had to surrender his freedom and board the educational treadmill. The treadmill, thank God, was in low gear for five year olds. Because St. Anne Parish either could not afford and/or did not have the nuns to operate a kindergarten and grades one and two, the little Catholics went to the public school.

The Rock remembers only two things from his half day kindergarten stints at Franklin School by the tracks. One, he was good at piling large wooden blocks into simulated cars and airplanes. Two, he could fall asleep without a rug as soon as he stretched out. His anatomy seemed to be strung like that of a doll whose eyelids snapped shut as soon as you moved it from a vertical to a horizontal position. The Rock was awakened easily, however, by the reverse procedure, and cheerfully went back to block work. After the first parent-teacher conference, Arlie and Gen were proud and happy to have a potential builder on their hands.

The first and second grades at Franklin were uneventful. The Rock remembers not liking Mrs. Butler who frequently washed out his mouth with liquid soap. His language got sassy and overly colorful from time to time. Mrs. Butler once told him, "You put in your mouth what I wouldn't touch with my hand." He did like Mrs. MacKenzie in the second grade. He's not sure whether she was an amiable teacher or whether Mrs. Butler had so assiduously cleaned up his language that Mrs. MacKenzie didn't need to continue the soap treatment.

The Franklin School

The Catholic kids didn't take the Franklin public school program very seriously. They sensed that they were in a holding pattern at Franklin until they could get into the real school, St. Anne, across the street. Their parents were of the same mind. If the kids raised too much whoopie and didn't study, the common parental refrain was, "Wait till the nuns get them in the third grade."

In September of 1937, the Rock proudly paraded into the third grade classroom at St. Anne. What a change! Somewhere back in the Middle Ages a Vatican superstar developed a theory, it was really only a very shaky hypothesis, that if you could have control over a kid's head until age seven or eight you could make that child a lifelong Catholic. Because these little Catholics had not yet had any formal religious education, the nuns felt that they really had to blitz the kids when they got them in the third grade. So religious education became the number one topic of study.

The first item on Sister Rose Miriam's agenda was church deportment. These kids, of course, had been in church a lot with their families and casually involved in the rituals. They simply imitated what their parents did. There wasn't a whole lot of polish in their execution of the rituals nor was their much understanding of what they were doing. So Sister Rose Miriam set out to clean up their little acts.

Early in that first week of school, the Rock and his new buddies were all lined up on the walk in front of school and processed over to church in silence. When they all had entered the church vestibule, Sister Rose Miriam advised them that they were about to enter the house of God. Firmly and clearly she made it known that silence, eyes down, slow movement, and keeping one's back straight were the best ways of showing respect toward God. Slowly she opened the two large swinging doors that led into the center isle of the church and quietly arranged the girls in a half circle around the holy water font on the left side. The boys were assembled around the font on the right side and Sister stood in the middle of the isle.

There were six holy water fonts in the church, one on each side of the three isles. They were made of white marble and looked like large bird baths. The kids had to stand on tiptoes in order to see the water. Sister then proceeded to tell the children about the nature of holy water. She first pointed to the baptismal font which was about twenty feet away in the left rear corner of the church. It was about three times larger than the holy water fonts and it had a large dome on it. On top of the dome was a two foot statue of a man dressed in raggedy clothes and holding a staff. Sister indicated that the image was that of St. John the Baptizer. She told the children that it was at that very font through the waters of Baptism that they became Christians — children of God and heirs of heaven. That day was and always would be the biggest day of their lives. Nothing, even ordination to the priesthood, would surpass that event. Sister then stated that the best way to recall that great event and to express one's gratitude for such an elevation was to carefully dip one's hand in the holy water and then make the sign of the cross over one's body, forehead to breast, left shoulder to right shoulder.

So first, they had to practice the sign of the cross. Sister quickly pointed out that the wavy, wiggly-fingered motions that most people utilized were not appropriate. The right hand, she said, should be flat, fingers closed, fully extended, and thumb tight against the knuckle of the index finger. Then, with the left hand flat against the bottom of the rib cage, the right hand should move slowly and with dignity to the forehead just below the hair line while one recites the words, "In the name of the Father." Then as the right hand moves slowly down to the center point of the rib cage, just above the left hand, one should say, "and of the Son." The horizontal bar of the cross is made by slowly moving the right hand to the extreme end of the left shoulder and then to the extreme end of the right shoulder. While this bar is being made one should say the words, "and of the Holy Ghost." After demonstrating this several times, Sister Rose Miriam then asked the children to reverently and slowly practice this ritual five times. She watched them closely, kindly corrected a few awkward signers, and complimented the rest. Now why don't you try that five times? It's a good way of centering one's self and it's also good for arthritis and lumbago.

If you think that's a difficult little ritual to remember, you should be grateful you are not being asked to do it á la Hispanics. They make a little cross with their right thumb and index finger and sign themselves on their forehead to the words, "por la senal de la santa cruz." Then they make a cross on their lips and state, "de nuestros enemigos." Next they move to their heart to make a third cross and say, "libranos Senor Nuestro."

That total phrase is translated, " by the sign of the cross, deliver us from our enemies, Our Lord." Then they do the Father, Son, and Holy Ghost routine described above. Finally, they give that little cross, fabricated with the thumb and index finger, a big juicy smackeroo with their lips. Anglos, of course, are always in a hurry and very mechanical. Hispanics, as the saying goes, always have mañana and they tend to be somewhat emotional. Who do you think is having more fun?

Now we are ready for the water. Sister then pointed out that the water in the font was not just ordinary water. It was blessed, set aside, in a special way by the priest to remind us of our dignity and the dignity of others as children of God. She said we needed things like this to keep us focused on what is important in life. "It's easy to forget how much God loves us," she said, "because we often get distracted by work and play and all the things we do just to stay alive." (She was right, wasn't she?)

Sister then moved a little further up the aisle and then invited the first girl and boy in line to dip their hands in the water and make the sign of the cross over themselves. When they did it correctly, they walked up the aisle and joined her. All of the children had their chance and most of them got it right on the first try. They were a little wet and spotted and the floor got a good washing, but they were OK. By the way, the Rock needed three tries and he ended up pretty well splashed. He looked like he had fallen into the font.

Before we move on to the other lessons that Sister Rose Miriam taught that morning, how to genuflect, how to fold one's hands, and proper kneeling, sitting, and standing at the appropriate times – maybe we ought to spend a little more time on the subject of holy water. It might be useful to you.

Now some of you might be wondering how holy water is made. There is more to it than what some comedian stated a few years ago, "Put a pan of water on the stove and boil the hell out of it." The recommended ceremony in the Roman Ritual takes about an half hour. For openers the Ritual requires that "the priest should at least wear a superpeliceo [neat word for surplice] over his cassock and a stole the color of the corresponding season [such as purple for Advent, red for Pentecost]. He should bless the water in a standing position and with head uncovered."

In the Rock's early years most churches had a five gallon, stainless steel dispenser for holy water that was kept near the baptismal font. When the dispenser was dry the priest generally carried the dispenser to the sacristy where he filled it with tap water, performed the blessing, and then lugged it back to the baptistry. The only other ingredient the priest needed was salt, and generally he would remember to bring a handful with him from the rectory. Salt was not an item found in church. The only food served there was offered without condiments, unleavened bread.

Once these minor preparations were in order the priest would vest as recommended by the Ritual and then proceed with the blessing. First he had to exorcize the salt. Part of the exorcism reads like this, "O Salt, I exorcise you so that you may become a means of salvation for believers, that you may bring health of soul and body to all who make use of you, and that you may put to flight and drive away from the places where you are sprinkled every apparition, villainy, and turn of devilish deceit, and every unclean spirit." Next he exorcised the water with a similar prayer. Finally he mixed the salt in the water three times in the form of the cross saying solemnly, "May a mixture of salt and water now be made in the name of the Father and of the Son and of the Holy Spirit". Finally he prayed, "O Lord, shine on this mixture with the light of thy kindness. Sanctify it by the dew of thy love, so that, through the invocation of thy holy name, wherever this water and salt is sprinkled it may turn aside every attack of the unclean spirit and dispel the terror of the poisonous serpent. And wherever we may be, make the Holy Spirit present to us who now implore thy mercy." Then the hard work followed. Getting a five gallon can of sloshing water back down through the church to the baptistry was no easy task.

Blessing holy water was usually left to the younger priests. After going through this initiation a few times, the pastor or one of the older assistants clued the young guys in on some of the fine print in the ritual. There it was casuistically indicated that holy water had the power of multiplying itself. One only had to add water to the batch but must take care not to add more than what was there. Over doubling the water would invalidate the blessing. But no time limit nor number of additions were stipulated. So technically one could start with a drop and make five gallons of holy water. It might take a half hour, but it would at least limit the two way haul of several gallons of water. Also one did not have to vest for the multiplication of the water and that saved another five minutes.

The use of holy water varies with the mix of people in the parishes. Holy water is used to bless homes, religious buildings, pets, crops, cars, airplanes, boats, the sick, the dying, religious articles, and just about anything you can think of. Once the Rock noticed a lady in church washing her money in the holy water font. She was a lady of the evening and thought that this would clean up her act and make her money at least ecclesiastically legal tender.

Some people use a lot of holy water. They use it during morning and night prayers, before and after meals, and sprinkle the kids with it before they go to school. Some drink it with their meals and others take regular baths in holy water. One day in his middle years, frustrated by an exceedingly large number of trips to church either to bless or multiply holy water, the Rock conceived a way to beat this game. On his way home to Alpena to visit his parents, he stopped in the small town of AuGres where the main inlet station for the Saginaw water system was located. Standing on the shore with head uncovered, clothed in surplice and a stole the color of the season, he blessed Lake Huron. On the following Sunday he advised the parishioners that they no longer had to come to church to get holy water. They could draw it from the tap at will.

Another ecclesiastical gesture on Sister Rose Miriam's instructional list that morning was the genuflection. If you know a little Latin you quickly realize that this word means to bend the knee. The practice is that when you reach the pew you are going to occupy, before entering you genuflect. As in all church gestures there are a lot of imitations, but only one right way to do them. The genuflection is made with the right knee. Keeping the back perfectly straight, hands folded over the breast, the right knee is bent until it touches the floor. No thumping sound is desired or required, but many do make such a noise. Now this is not an easy trick to perform. First of all, you have to be in pretty good shape to bend your knee all the way to the floor. Secondly, you need a very good sense of balance to fold your hands and do this knee bend. If you don't believe me, just give it a try. Most people quickly abandon the folded hands and place their left hand on their left knee for balance and their right hand on the end of the pew for leverage to get up from the floor. Very few people over twenty five years of age ever make it to the floor with their knee. The problem is they don't get enough practice. Only the daily church attenders are any good at this gesture. The best genuflecters in the world, however, are the football players who receive kickoffs in their own end zone and decide not to run the ball out of the zone. Just check their excellence the next time you watch a football game.

When the holy water/sign of the cross lesson at the entrance of the church had been completed, Sister Rose Miriam told the children to follow her up to the front of the church leaving a space of two arms lengths between themselves and the person in front of them. When she arrived at the front pew she turned toward the children and slowly demonstrated a proper genuflection. She then invited the children to imitate her performance. Freaky Archambault, the first boy in line, didn't make it and rolled into the center isle. This caused a burst of impious guffawing down the male line and some modest snickers in the female parade. Sister quickly put down this little rebellion by grabbing a hymnal out of the pew and applying it to the head of Pigsfeet Gougeon, the second boy in line and the most impious of the guffawers. She then invited the children to carefully observe her performance as she demonstrated the genuflection for the second time. Then standing next to Freaky to keep him from rolling over again, she urged the children to make five slow and reverent genuflections. They did well.

With that exercise completed she directed the children into the pews, informing them to leave a space the width of another person between them. Boys, especially, of this age are very prone to scuffling and wrestling when another invades their immediate space. When all were seated with their backs straight against the back of the pew, Sister then explained the significance of the genuflection.

She pointed to the center of the main altar where the tabernacle was located. The tabernacle is an elaborate safe. Some are round, some square, and some rectangular. They occupy approximately three cubic feet of space and are covered with a curtain. The Latin word tabernacle means a tent. When the Chosen People wandered in the desert, the Ark of the Covenant, which was a symbol of God's presence and contained the tablets of the Law and some manna, was kept in a tent. In Catholic churches the tabernacle contains the Eucharist, or consecrated bread. That, also, is why a Catholic church is sometimes referred to as another Bethlehem, the Hebrew word that means house of bread.

Catholics believe that the Eucharist is not just a symbol, but really and truly the Body and Blood of Jesus. It is kept in the tent for veneration and for viaticum — holy communion for those in danger of death. So that people will know that the Eucharist is reserved in the church, a large red candle is kept burning near the tabernacle at all times. The Rock was quietly pleased that there was at least one good meaning for a red light. Up until this moment he had picked up only two meanings; one was to stop, and the other he knew better than to mention. Pigsfeet knew and with a knowing wink he reached over and jabbed the Rock in the ribs. Sister didn't know exactly what Pigsfeet was up to, but nonetheless she whacked him on the head a second time with the hymnal.

Sister Rose Miriam explained all of these facts to the children so they would understand the purpose for the genuflection. She indicated that for centuries people of many and varied cultures had used the genuflection as a sign of deference for their rulers. "If human kings and queens and emperors and empresses could be accorded such esteem," she stated, "then certainly Jesus the Son of God and King of heaven and earth merited at least the same amount of deference." The lesson inculcated a serious degree of reverence in the third graders, and they worked hard at being good genuflecters.

While on the subject of reverence, Sister pointed out that in St. Anne's church as in most Catholic churches there were at least three statues of saints, one of the Blessed Mother, one of St. Joseph, her spouse, and one of the patron saint of the church. She pointed out that the statues are like pictures of important family members that most people keep in their homes. Statues, like pictures, remind us of our roots and inspire us to imitate the example of those portrayed. She reminded the third graders that in the Creed Catholics state that they believe in the Communion of Saints, a comforting and broadening doctrine that all people, past and present, are really one family in God and that they can communicate and interact with one another in positive ways.

The final lesson that Sister delved into that long morning in church was to illustrate and explain the proper folding of hands. She first described the beauty of our hands, the wondrous works human beings accomplish with their hands — writing, painting, designing, building, making music — and finally the uncanny ability of hands to almost speak. She made the Rock and his classmates laugh a little when she imitated some of the wildly demonstrative hand gestures of the French people of the parish and the busy and almost uncontrollable hand work of some of the students in the third grade.

Then with quiet grace Sister Rose Miriam demonstrated how the children should fold their hands when they prayed at home, in school or in church. The two hands should be pressed together with the fingers tightly closed and pointed toward heaven. The heels of the hands were to rest on the center point of the rib cage. She concluded by stating that properly folded hands were a certain sign of reverence and respect that God and everybody else could clearly see. It was almost like saying that your hands are like the windows of your soul.

Late in life the Rock saw a movie about the Dahli Lama of Tibet and he was deeply moved by the hand movements of this holy man. In fact, during the movie the Rock almost automatically folded his hands in imitation. He subsequently learned that the folding of hands and bowing slightly to another person was an act of recognition of the Spirit of God in the other person. He wished that Sister Rose Miriam had taught him that meaning of folded hands, but unfortunately, westerners don't always conceive of things the way easterners do. In the west we think that God is out there somewhere, while in the east people think that God is within them. The old Rock is now an easterner at heart.

This, of course, leads to another church gesture that Sister Rose Miriam hinted at when the children first entered the church, the custody of the eyes, keeping the eyes cast down when praying or processing. The purpose of the gesture is to keep out distractions and help the worshipper to center on the deity within. What that behavior brings about sometimes is a false belief that one is in his/her own little telephone booth having a private conversation with God, and as long as that goes well there is nothing else one has to do to be in God's good graces. The truth of the matter is that God is in everyone. That is why

Jesus insisted above all else that we love our neighbor even if he/she is our enemy. Wouldn't it be a better world if we looked other people in the eye and acknowledged there the God who is constantly, and lovingly within all of us? Wouldn't it be better if after the reception of Communion we looked around at all the other people and smiled at them to acknowledge that we are all brothers and sisters? Makes good sense, n'est pas?

When the Rock and his buddies got back to the third grade class room that morning they were ready to rumble. Two hours of concentrated lessons in church were almost beyond their attention span. Because they had missed recess, Sister Rose Miriam decided to let them out early for lunch. Genevieve, the Rock's mother, was a little surprised that her second son was home so early for lunch and wondered what sort of trouble he was in now. She was relieved when the Rock explained the reason for the early dismissal. Her surprise turned to wonderment , however, when the Rock sat at the kitchen table for his usual lunch of tomato soup and a peanut butter and jam sandwich. His silent grace was preceded and concluded with a very slow, reverent, and almost perfect sign of the cross. Poor Genevieve almost lost it, when instead of his usual glass of milk the Rock requested a glass of holy water to wash his food down.

Have a little lunch of your own right now and we'll get back to school in the next chapter. If you live in Michigan near Lake Huron you won't have to look for the holy water bottle to wash down your lunch. Just take it straight out of the tap. You might be able to do the same if you live near Lakes Michigan and Erie which connect to Huron. Remember the mixing rule.

CHAPTER FIVE
SOUL SAVING SACRAMENTS

At St. Anne's, the ultimate goal of the staff was to get the third graders ready for First Confession and First Communion in May. Confession and Communion are like the dual tubes of epoxy glue that bind Catholics to their season tickets. Also, they are Catholics greatest sources of spiritual assistance and the only two Sacraments that they can receive as often as desired.

So it was with good reason that the first lesson of every school day was catechism. For Catholics of the Rock's vintage, the catechism was more important than the Bible. The word catechism comes from the Greek and it means "to resound, to impress by word of mouth, to instruct by question and answer." The Roman catechism contains answers for every question about religion that people can think of. It is resounding and impressive in its logic and often above most peoples' heads. It is chiefly because of this book and its style of teaching that most Catholics are long on reason and wary of experience and feeling in matters religious. To put it succinctly, religion for most Catholics is a head trip. Warm fuzzies are not desired nor required, and if you experience some from time to time maybe they are a bonus, more likely an onus.

The Roman who cooked up the catechism was most likely just out of grad school and an underachiever to boot. You might have run into new teachers who believed they had to teach you what that they had just completed in college, impervious of the fact that it took them 16-20 years to get to that level of knowledge. Third grade catechism was a graduate course in Theology. The Rock and his classmates grappled with questions like Who is God? Why did God make you? What is Sanctifying Grace? They examined material from Scripture, Tradition, and Reason to prove that Mary's conception was immaculate and that the Pope was infallible.

Needless to say, these third graders developed incredible memorization skills but zero comprehension. For the time being it was considered enough for them to rattle off the definitions, such as, "Sanctifying grace is a divine quality inhering in the soul that makes a person pleasing and acceptable to God." The assumption was that comprehension would come later in the higher grades. For millions of Catholics comprehension never came. The same questions were asked year after year and the memorized answers got more complicated and obtuse. The answers were like the cheers the kids chanted for their basketball and football teams — "Who sa sa sa, who sa sa sa! Hit 'em over the head with a big kielbassa!" In essence, the memorized answers were the standardized cheers of the Team Vatican fan club.

In a few short weeks the catechism lessons brought the Rock and his classmates to the topic of Confession. Getting ready for First Confession was like taking an Intro course in Criminology. The Rock and his friends first had to learn about law and where it came from. Then they had to master the ways in which the law could be violated and what the sanctions were for violations. This was really heavy duty stuff for third graders. Basically they were taught that the Law came from God — first through Moses in the Ten Commandments, and next through the Church. Jesus said to his Apostles, "I give you the keys to the Kingdom of Heaven. Whatever you bind upon earth will be bound in heaven, and whatever you loose on earth will be loosed in heaven." Accordingly, over the centuries, Team Vatican cooked up thousands of "binding" laws or canons. They really covered the waterfront in detail.

Sister Rose Miriam explained to the third graders that the first man and woman, Adam and Eve, sinned against God. She didn't indicate what they did, but she stated that God was so angry that he kicked them out of Paradise and told them that all of their offspring, including the present third graders, would be marked with their sin. That is, when they were born their souls would be black and empty of grace. Immediately, however, Sister assured the little children that they didn't have to worry because they had been baptized as infants and their souls were now as white as snow.

Sister Rose Miriam then proceeded to explain another consequence of that original sin. "Baptism" she said, "cleans up the original mess, but all human beings are still left with a leaning or a proneness to sin. It is easy to do if you aren't careful. This proneness starts kicking in when you are about seven years old." That was scary.

Next Sister got into a detailed discussion of actual sin, the ones people over seven get into. There are two varieties: mortal and venial or felonies and misdemeanors. The sanctions or punishments for these offenses are hell, purgatory, and limbo. Hell is a maximum security institution for those who commit mortal sins and die without confessing them. Purgatory is a medium security joint for venial sinners. The punishment is the same as in hell, but you eventually can get out of Purgatory. Limbo is a fuzzy place for those whose Baptism is questionable. For those of you who might be concerned, Limbo has recently been wiped out. There's nobody there anymore. Information as to the whereabouts of the former residents has not been officially released as of this printing.

Because actual sin is a life or death issue for everyone seven or older, Sister Rose Miriam took a considerable amount of time to help these potential sinners differentiate what is mortal from what is venial. For a sin to be mortal three things are necessary: grievous matter, sufficient reflection, and full consent of the will. That means that what you do is serious, you know it is serious, and you decide to do it anyway. If one part is missing the sin is only venial and your soul is still white, but it looks like the snow that is covered with dust from the cement plant. The milky substance of grace is still there, but it doesn't look drinkable. For the Rock and the third graders grievous matter was easy to determine. There was murder, quitting the Team Vatican fan club, and sex. Mostly sex. In their third grade minds that could mean watching another guy urinate, or doing it yourself behind a tree. Some of the girls thought that if they dressed up in their mother's adult clothes they were committing adultery.

With all the Moral Theology in place, the class, supposedly, was now ready for shriving. But first their consciences had to be examined. This meant, in the Rock's case, that he had to look back over his conscious years of life and itemize the various types of badness he had engaged in as well as the number of times. Not really a good way to build up a healthy self-esteem. The Rock had no problem recalling his badness since after all, he was the kid "who would just as soon hit you over the head with a hammer as look at you." Also, he had been asked a thousand times by parents and relatives, "Why can't you be more like your brother Curly?" a nice placid little boy who ate his vegetables, and never said nasty words. The Rock had some problem deciding how bad some of his activities were, but his major worry was how many times.

For weeks prior to the third Friday in May, the day of First Confession, the Rock racked his brain to dredge up all the black ink from his soul. Was it really a sin to smoke the cigarette butts he picked out of the sidewalk grilles alongside of LaBonte's drug store? He couldn't ask Sister Rose Miriam. How would she know? He couldn't ask his dad. He'd get his tail curled twice. And whom could he ask about the black ink liability he might have incurred when he listened and laughed at the gross sexual jokes the big guys told over at Joe Couture's store? And then the numbers. How many times had he disobeyed his parents — 200, 600, 3000 times? How many times had he fought with Curly and bad mouthed the old crones in the neighborhood? How many times did he and Ivan Homant swipe eggs from the Homant's refrigerator and hurl them at Febbie Greenier's barn?

The weekend finally arrived. The Rock had his fourteen pages of black-ink behavior carefully recorded. (Don't be alarmed by the number of pages. His printing was large and in capital letters.) Sister had said that this information should be memorized and not written down, but he knew that he couldn't meet all the requirements, line it all up and keep it in his head for recitation to Father Louis T. Bouchard in the confessional. In his fear he decided to really play it safe and write it all down and then try to slip the pages under the grille or around the curtain to Louis T. and let him read it.

On that Black Friday the boys lined up on the Gospel side of the confessional and the girls on the Epistle side. The Rock thanked God that his last name didn't start with A like Freaky Archambault and G like Pigsfeet Gougeon, the two guys who preceded him in line. He would have a little time to watch what was happening and gain a little confidence. Pigsfeet was a real bad dude. He was already smoking and stealing beer from his old man's liquor store. If he could make it through this ordeal anyone could. Pigsfeet went in looking cocky, but after some loud Louis T. whispers like, "You what"? and "75 times"?, Pigsfeet crawled out looking like he did the previous week when Killer Kenny Sharkey mopped the boys bathroom with his butt.

The Rock was next. He slid by the long curtain and knelt on the leather pad facing the closed grille. Louis was talking to one of the girls on the other side. His knees were shaking but also sliding. It didn't smell good in there. Damn! Either Freaky or Pigsfeet had lost it and he was kneeling in it. When he had just about decided to make a quick exit, the sliding door opened and there was Louis T.'s face two inches away asking, "Did you pee in there?" In terror, the Rock blurted out, "Pigsfeet did it." That calmed Louis T. down a bit, and he then said quietly, "What have you got to confess?" The Rock grabbed his list from under his shirt, reached out around his curtain and inside of Father's curtain and said, "Here. You read it. I can't remember it all." A light went on in the priest's compartment, and after a few minutes he said, "Did you really do all these things"? To a yes reply he then asked, "Did you think that all these things were serious sins"? To another yes reply he responded, " I think someone gave you the wrong informa-

The Rock and Curly, 1937

tion about sin. I don't think you are a bad kid. In fact I think you are a pretty good kid for doing all this work. In the future when you get ready for confession just think of the worst thing that you did and then figure out how you can keep from doing that again. That's all I want to hear. No more written lists. Do you understand what I'm saying?" When the Rock said yes with great relief, Louie asked, "Now what item on this list do you feel the sorriest for and promise that you will try not to do again?" When the Rock replied, "Beating up on my brother, Curly," Louis T. replied, "That's great. You're a good boy. For a penance go home and tell Curly that you really like him and that you're going to try not to fight with him anymore. OK? Now recite your act of contrition while I give you absolution." With great relief the Rock rattled off the prayer and flew out of the box.

When he got back to his pew he had to kneel next to Pigsfeet. When he noted that Pigsfeet's fly was dry and his fist was clenched, he knew that he was in for an alley showdown at recess next Monday. He had born false witness against his neighbor right there in the confessional and now how could he avoid a fight on Monday? Sin was everywhere. Why was Freaky such a pissant? Whoops! There's another one. Well thank God for Fr. Louis' singularity principle. Sure hope it works with God.

First Confession was very serious stuff. But it was only prep work for the most serious Sacrament of all, Communion or Eucharist. For Catholics, Communion is not something symbolic. It's the real thing: the Body and Blood of Christ, the only Son of the Almighty, All-seeing, All-knowing God; the second person in the Blessed Trinity; the Creator and Sustainer of the Universe; the Conqueror of Death; the Omnipotent Judge of Mankind; and so forth. That's pretty awesome, isn't it? So receiving Communion is not something to take lightly. St. Paul, a big time Bible writer, stated that to eat and drink unworthily was to bring down eternal damnation on one's self. What's an eight year old kid to do with information like that?

Saturday was a rather calm day as the Rock and his close buddies tried to keep the white milk in their souls from going sour. He and Burrhead LaMarre almost had a fight in the alley around two o'clock, but Lefty Markowski had a cooler head and kept them at bay. After dinner his mom put him in the tub to try and get his body to match his soul. She laid out his new blue suit with white shirt and tie, tucked him in and reminded him that if he woke up during the night he couldn't eat or drink. Fasting from midnight was required for the reception of Communion. Even the swallowing of an inadvertent drop of water would rule out participation in the event. He slept lightly, wondering what was going to happen the next morning at the 9:30 Mass when Fr. Louis placed that small white wafer on his tongue. Would the floor open up and swallow him because he slandered Pigsfeet in the confessional? Would his tongue catch fire like the bush when Moses talked to God in the desert? Would he hear heavenly music and a voice saying, "Hi Rock. This is Jesus. What's happening?"

No one had given him a clue as to what to expect.

His mother got him up at 8:00 a.m. and helped him suit up in his new attire. He didn't like the fit of the collar and the tightness of the tie, but this was part of the drill. Once at school he gathered with his classmates in their classroom and got last minute instructions from Sister Rose Miriam. At 9:20 they lined up with their prayer books and rosaries and marched over to church to process up to the front pews with Fr. Bouchard leading the way in his golden cope and three pointed hat. The girls in their dresses and veils looked angelic. The boys looked uncomfortable and a little sissified.

The first part of the Mass went by as usual. Louis T., with his back toward everybody, read a lot of Latin prayers at the altar for about ten minutes. Then he climbed into the pulpit to read the Epistle and Gospel in English and say a few thousand words. He was pretty good that day, saying what a nice day it was, how happy he was to see so many children making their First Communion, and what a happy day this must be for the children and their parents. Then after the offertory collection he sang a long song in Latin. This was followed by some bell ringing when he elevated a large, round, thin, white piece of bread and a big chalice. The bells were the sign that Jesus had arrived. The bread and wine had become the Body and Blood of Jesus through the Latin words of consecration spoken by Fr. Bouchard. The kids all bowed their heads and beat their breasts because they weren't supposed to be worthy of this event. After Louis T. sang the Lord's prayer in Latin, Sister Rose Miriam led the first communicants out of the pews and lined them up on their knees at the long communion rail. In short order Louis T., now facing the children, held up a smaller white host and told them in Latin, "This is the lamb of God who takes away the sins of the world." Then he hustled down to the end of the railing and started putting little round white wafers on the first communicants' tongues.

Sister Rose Miriam had given the children specific instructions on how to prepare for this reception. They were to tilt their heads back a little bit, close their eyes, open their mouths wide, and stick out their tongues as far as they could while keeping them flat. After the priest put the host on their tongues they were supposed to close their mouths, straighten their heads, open their eyes, and swallow the host as soon as possible. They were not supposed to chew the host, play with it with their tongues, or let it get stuck to the roofs of their mouths. Never, never, never were they to put their fingers in their mouths in case the host got stuck to their teeth or the roofs of their mouths.

You guessed it. The host got stuck to the top of the Rock's mouth. And why wouldn't it? He hadn't had a drink in over twelve hours and he was scared senseless about this first highly personal encounter with God. But he did remember the emergency rule that Sister had given them. Don't panic. Slowly try to roll the host off the top of your mouth with the tip of your tongue. He waited until he got back to his pew and buried his face in his hands like he was praying. Slowly he worked away with his tongue and after what seemed like half an hour he finally got the host off the roof of his mouth and down his gullet. Then he waited. And he waited. And he waited some more. Nothing happened. The floor was still intact. His tongue was not on fire. There were no voices. The experience wasn't as awesome as confession. In the box he could at least see, and hear, and even smell what was coming down. But Holy Communion? Nothing. Maybe next time something would happen.

After everyone had received communion and Louis T. had locked up the leftovers in the tabernacle, he gave the congregation a blessing and they all filed out singing Holy God We Praise Thy Name, the only English hymn Catholics of that day ever sang at Mass. Parents took a lot of pictures and relatives went gaga over the new communicants and told them how nice they looked in their new clothes. After all the posing the class went over to school and had milk and cookies to keep from fainting. Sister Rose Miriam told them how proud she was of them and what good boys and girls they really were.

A good show. A full house. Still the Rock and his buddies didn't have much of a clue as to what this was all about. They did what they were told to do and obedience has its own reward, or so they say. The fuss that everyone made over them did make them feel wanted and loved in the Team Vatican fan club. Maybe that's all anyone can ask for and expect, or is there more? Should there be more?

Sixty some years later, after almost daily reception of Communion, sometimes even three times a day, the Rock finally had an Eucharistic experience. And it didn't happen in church. He awoke one morning to the smell of fresh bread coming from the kitchen. He shuffled out there, opened the bread machine, and there it was — a beautiful golden loaf of bread. He removed the loaf carefully and cut off a small piece. It was richly textured, warm, and delicious. Then it dawned on him. This was his wife, not just a mere symbol of her. She had taken the time the night before to get out the machine, put in the ingredients, and set the timer. It was she, her energy, the stuff she's made of, that entered into those ingredients, transformed them, and made that bread come alive.

With his Adam's apple in his throat and tears on his cheeks the old Rock ran to the bathroom where his wife was taking a shower. He climbed in, clothes and all, and gave her a crushing hug for her beautiful, life-giving expression of love for him.

Now isn't that what Jesus did at the Last Supper — taking bread and wine, infusing them with His energy, Himself, and asking His friends to consume them so that they would know that He loved them, was in them, and they were in Him as well as in each other?

The knowledge of modern physics regarding energy and its transformation is extremely helpful in understanding what Jesus meant when he offered bread and wine to the Apostles and said, "Take this and eat. Take this and drink. This is my Body. This is my Blood." But knowledge without experience gradually turns cold and rituals become mechanical, don't they? The Creator becomes an object "out there" and we read about the divine activity in books and hear about the divine teachings in sermons. It all becomes so matter of fact. Religion, however, is supposed to be a relationship with God. You might start relating to someone with your head, but the crucial work is with your heart. A true relationship has to be experienced and only then can you make statements and affirmations about it.

The way the old Rock met his wife is a good illustration of how all this works. Friends told him about this lady in glowing terms. They knew, they said, that the two of them were meant for each other. But the Rock had heard that story before and it didn't mean a whole lot to him. Several weeks later he met this lady for the first time. There was an immediate click. As they talked and told their stories with open hearts, shared meals together, played together, touched each other, experienced each other in a valued way, they slowly realized that their relationship was the real thing and they wanted to consummate it in marriage.

Probably one of the major reasons why large numbers of people don't have religious experiences of any type is that a great majority of people who teach about religion don't have a healthy attitude toward the human body. Too many people think that God made a mistake in creating us with a sensing, feeling body, and many of those people have even taken vows to avoid human experiences. Isn't that sad?

So how do we experience what the Apostles experienced at the Last Supper? The disciples on the road to Emmaus felt it. So did the early Christian communities of the Acts. Even today some small communities are both sensing and feeling the experience. A common denominator seems to be the size of the group. One interesting development in this emerging age is a revaluing of the small group for worship and spiritual growth. Why? That is where meaningful and lasting relationships grow and thrive. Above all else Holy Communion is about relationships.

A complement to that development is a new theological explanation of Christ's presence in the Eucharist. He is there because of the community's faith, and not solely because of the minister's actions. Making Eucharist is something that everybody does. You just don't watch it happen. You do it. Also, small group encounters are not restricted by time limitations as are large groups. Dealings are face to face. Symbols are more easily recognized, read, and understood.

Now that's all heavy duty stuff, isn't it. Let's take a time out to reflect on those thoughts: the dignity of our bodies, our wonderful gifts of sensing and feeling, and the possibility of having a personal experience of God.

CHAPTER SIX
ONLY SHOW
IN TOWN

When the Rock was growing up in Alpena's west end, the event of the week for Catholics was Sunday Mass. It was an important social event. On Sunday mornings nothing else was going on. You started preparing for this event the day before. On Saturday mornings the house was cleaned and special foods were prepared for Sunday. In the afternoon or early evening you went to Confession. Before you retired you took a bath. You fasted from all food and drink from midnight on. In the morning you donned your best clothes and got to church on time, since Fr. Bouchard did not like latecomers and early leavers.

When you got to church you knew exactly where to go. Every family rented a pew and your name was written on a card at the end of the bench. In the old days, pews were referred to as slips. In effect, St. Anne's church was like a marina and folks were very firmly tethered to that dock. At that time and place, church was a major source of identity and social activity. There weren't any other significant shows in town.

The Rock's family pew was number fourteen and was situated on what was known as the Epistle side of the church, the right side when you faced the altar. It was called the Epistle side because every day from that side of the altar a segment of one of St. Paul's letters was read to the congregation in Latin. The Rock's family examined the backs of the St. Onge family which occupied pew twelve in front of them, and the Leo and Lemuel Homant families examined the backs of the Rock's family from their number sixteen slip.

Church was a very quiet and serious place. The only people who regularly spoke in church were the priests and little kids who didn't know any better. Sometimes, however, those uninhibited kids said some very insightful things. The Rock recalls one Sunday when Fr. Bouchard got long-winded and profoundly theological in his sermon. A young cousin, four rows back, in a loud voice that everyone could hear, asked the question, "Why is that man talking?" A few kids giggled. Arlie's glare wiped the smile off the Rock's face. Most of the adults agreed with the comment, but they wouldn't let on, the cowards.

One of the Sunday Masses was a High Mass. That meant that the choir sang a few Latin hymns. The other Masses were called Low because there were no hymns. The priests seemed to like the High Masses because they got to croon a little themselves and they got a five dollar stipend. For Low Masses they only received a dollar. The great majority of the people attended the low Masses. The reasons were simple. They appreciated the quiet and usually got out fifteen to twenty minutes earlier.

Once the Mass started there was a good deal of physical movement — standing, sitting, and kneeling. Other than that, rank and file parishioners had the role of looking at and listening to the priest. This was not an easy part to play. For most of the time the priest had his back to the congregation as he talked to God on their behalf. He did that in Latin. So most of the people busied themselves by reading prayer books or reciting the rosary. Kids like the Rock checked out the statuary, the stations of the cross, the stained glass windows, and the funny people. Mass was really a boring event, and the Rock, who had to always sit next to his father for control purposes, frequently caught murderous glances from his parents, grandparents, and neighbors.

When the Rock was in junior high, pew rent was discontinued and open seating was introduced. To maintain income, ushers met folks at the door with coin changers and charged ten cents per customer. It was like going to the movies. The open seating practice gave kids like the Rock new opportunities. You didn't have to go to church with your parents and you could sit wherever you wished. The Rock and his buddies Eggie, Lefty, and Burrhead would meet at Joe Couture's store and go to church together. They developed a little Saturday night routine that still draws a laugh. One would ask, "See you in church tomorrow?" A second would respond, "Yeah. We'll sit by a window." A third would add, "I'll bring the tobacco." The fourth would finish, " And I'll bring the booze." They always aimed for the last pew in the left rear corner. There they were hidden from the pulpit. It was the darkest place and handy for late in and early out. It was also the best place to check out the statuary, not the stuff on the walls, but the "quiffs and quails" moving up and down the aisles.

From the older folks, the kids quickly learned the corner-cutting trick. At first they were shocked by the numbers who came late and left early. But it's what an institution gets when it makes a lot of rules. It was a mortal sin if you missed one of the principal parts of the Mass — Offertory, Consecration, and Communion. So everything before the Offertory, Scripture readings and sermon, were deemed unimportant. So were the final thanksgiving prayers and announcements after Communion. The young guys were also surprised by the large number of folks who were unperturbed about venial sins, poisonous but not deadly, that were incurred by omitting the lesser parts of the Mass, but a little practice soon wore down their guilt feelings.

Another observation that nestled in the Rock's brain had to do with the silence. People were not only silent in church but also silent outside of church with regards to what went on inside. On extremely rare occasions an adult would comment on the sermon or holiday decorations. No one, however, ever talked about what they had experienced in church, what was happening inside of them, or what they were getting out of this weekly event.

Sort of like the child in the fairy tale, "The Emperor's New Clothes," one day the Rock asked Sister Adele in religion class, "Why do I have to go to Mass under pain of mortal sin? It doesn't mean anything to me. There's nothing happening over there in church."

Like the Emperor's old minister who couldn't see the cloth but took great care not to say so, Sister Adele feigned shock and anger and then gave the stock answer. "Well young man, I want you to know that we do not go to Mass to get anything. We go there to give honor and glory to God. By going to Mass we pay on the debt that we owe to God for our sins. It is not necessary for us to understand the Latin, the Scriptures, and the liturgy. On our behalf the priest is offering to God the unbloody sacrifice of Calvary. It is our unique privilege to just be there and we should be everlastingly grateful that we alone have this means of pleasing God. Think of all those people who do not have Mass celebrated for them and are stumbling around in the dark seeking to know God and atone for their sins."

Sufficiently cowed and weighted down with this lengthy and heavy information, the Rock sat. For many years after that on Sundays and frequently during the week, he stoically kept making payments on his "mortgage" to God. Every now and then, however, an inner voice would say, "But the Emperor doesn't have any clothes on." Was this the devil speaking? Maybe, or was it a good angel?

In a sense it was good to be dealing with this ecclesiastical lending institution that wasn't totally heartless and only threatened foreclosure when you went prodigal and came up short on your payments, such as when you skipped Sunday Mass. But then there was Confession or Penance, a Sacrament that made you feel good and bad at the same time. You felt bad because you had to face the fact that you were a creep and you had to tell somebody else about your creepiness. You did feel good, though, when you went into the little confessional booth at the back of the St. Anne Spiritual Bank and told the "teller" that you had defaulted again and he assured you that the owner of the bank was merciful and would give you another chance. You did have to pay interest, however, on the default. It wasn't much; usually three Our Fathers and three Hail Marys.

Unlike Sunday Mass, that Saturday accounting had something in it for you. It was a real experience and you felt it. All the ivories on your keyboard got tickled and touched in the process. The Saturday confession times were much more meaningful than the regimented programs during school days. On Saturdays you usually went voluntarily. Sometimes when your mother thought you were walking on thin ice, she would put a little heat on you to get to confession. On Saturdays you also learned how large the sinner club was. They say that misery loves company. The presence of seniors and middlers did help a lot when you were carrying a heavy load of guilt.

Most of the Rock's young friends sort of enjoyed Confession. In the confessional Fr. Bouchard was a kind and gentle man with the kids. After a few weekly trips to the box they had the routine down cold. "Disobeyed my mother five times. Fought with my brother/sister ten times. Told a white lie twice. Missed my prayers once." Some of the more serious and scrupulous ones, however, got into catechism terms they really didn't understand. They worshipped false gods, took the name of God in vain, committed apostasy and adultery, bore false witness, and lusted and coveted a lot of stuff. They thought they were really bad.

When the Rock got running regularly on the confessional track he tried to keep in mind the advice Fr. Bouchard gave him at his first confession, focus on your big failings and not more than one or two. So one day he noisily bounced his way into the box to sound bigger and older than he was. When Louis T. opened the slide the Rock lowered his voice as deeply as he could and said, "Bless me Father for I have sinned. My last confession was a week ago and I committed pornography once." Louis T. hesitated a moment and said, "Could you explain that a little bit?"

So the Rock, in his bogus bass voice, explained, "Well, the other night I was down at the Boy's Club and one of the older guys asked me if I wanted to check out some of his pornography, and I said sure. Then he laughed and said, 'Kid, you wouldn't know what to do with it'. I told him that I really did know what to do with it, but he just walked off laughing." Puzzled, Louis T. inquired, "Well what was the sin in that"? The Rock replied, "I really wanted to check out his pornography, Father, but I lied. We don't even have a pornograph at our house." Trying to contain himself and sensing a futile and extended explanation of terms, Louis T. simply told the Rock, "For your penance avoid those big boys in the future. Now say your act of contrition and I'll give you absolution."

As later experience confirmed, the Rock's pattern of confessing was standard. Little kids tried hard to pass themselves off as bigger and older, and high school kids and older folks did the opposite. It was easy to pick out the kids. The bigger ones would tiptoe into the box and in a high pitched voice rattle off an innocent recitation: "Bless me, Faaaather. It's been twooooo weeks since my last confeshin. I dishobeyed my mutha four times. I said nasty words eight times. I didn't keep my hands in the right place six times. I missed my morning prayers three times. I'm sorry for all of these sins, Father, but most specially for dishobeying my mutha."

When you look back on it, those weekend rituals that were at the center of Catholic existence had their pros and cons, didn't they? Confession, in particular, was an active Sacrament that demanded your participation. It was an encounter that had potential for spiritual growth. Now here is a very serious question that hardly anyone has addressed for over thirty years. Why has the practice of Confession almost disappeared?

One of the duties that a lot of priests of the Rock's day did not like was that of hearing confessions. There were a lot of reasons: uncomfortable space; whispered conversations; long hours; inadequate psychological training; large numbers that demanded attention; poor understanding of the nature of sin and how to deal with it.

Many of the fathers at the Vatican II Council a few years ago understood that situation rather well. So in article 72 of the *Constitution on the Sacred Liturgy* they declared: "The rite and formulas for the sacrament of penance are to be revised so that they give more luminous expression to both the nature and effect of the sacrament." Practically nothing "luminous" came down from the top. Face to face confession was suggested and small counselling rooms with an optional screen for privacy were set up. But this did nothing about the numbers, the mechanical atmosphere, the understanding of sin, and the clergy's need for modern psychological skills in guidance and counselling. As a matter of fact, this attempt at openness drove away a lot of people who wanted absolute anonymity.

A few priests initiated communal penance ceremonies that tried to indicate that sin and selfishness were offenses against brothers and sisters where God lived and it was with them that one had to be reconciled. These ceremonies also helped to take care of the space, numbers, and mechanical problems. And by means of scripture readings and homilies these creative priests attempted to speak to a more understandable concept of sin and how to deal with it. They offered no immediate counselling in the ceremony but strongly recommended it on a future appointment basis. This approach also drove away those who wanted to remain anonymous. Even though a large number of lay people attended and appreciated these ceremonies, practically all of them got shot down by the hierarchy. The bishops wanted the "old time religion" that seemed to be working just fine.

What most likely caused the biggest and current fall-off in confessional practice was a new, bright, and positive picture of Christian life that was presented to children in catechism classes. Because they didn't have a dark blackboard of hell and damnation to erase, the children quickly took to the goodness and light theme and said so-long to confession. Most adults, on the other hand, had stuff in their heads that was almost indelible and they didn't get from the pulpit the bright and positive stuff that the kids were getting in catechism from some very sensitive instructors, mostly females and mothers. Also, the pulpits were being vacated by thousands of priests whose bright ideas and positive pictures were being forbidden and condemned by the leadership.

Tragically, what was evolving was a lose-lose situation. The baby got thrown out with the bath water, but it should not be forgotten that people are not perfect and they need direction and guidance if they are to be at peace with themselves and one another.

Knowledgeable people who have examined this condition are saying that what happened was that the teaching leadership of the church tried to "put new wine into old wine skins" and the skins exploded. What was needed, according to these scholars, was a new God concept. Now that's an exceedingly large can of worms, isn't it, a new God concept? And the worms are probably big enough to eat your head off if you aren't careful. So let's open the can very, very cautiously, and make sure we've got some weapons handy in case the worms get out of control.

Weapon number one is humility. Meister Eckhart, a brilliant fourteenth century mystic, reminded us that there is a vast difference between the Godhead and God, the Godhead being God as God really is and not the God as we know God. Eckhart says that if God, the one we think we know, met the Godhead, our God wouldn't know him/her/it self because the difference would be so incredibly vast. Carl Jung put it very bluntly. "I am sorry to say that everything that men assert about God is twaddle." So let's face it. We might be pretty smart, but we don't know diddly squat about God as God really is. If you think you do then you probably also believe that you can put the entire Atlantic Ocean in a pail and take it home with you.

The closest view of God ever recorded was a very quick moon shot given to Moses on Mt. Sinai. When Moses pleaded with God, "Show me your glory," God responded, "You cannot see my face for no man can see me and live." When Moses insisted, God replied, "OK. I will put you in a cleft of the rock and shield you with my hand while I pass by. Then I will take my hand away and you shall see the back of me; but my face is not to be seen." Nice polite way to tell a wise guy or a smart ass to kiss off. So be humble. Admit your inadequacy as well as that of all human beings, even our great leaders.

Weapon number two is a firm response. Think about franchising. It's easy because there are a lot of franchisers around, and basically they sell security. They want their product to be recognizable and always the same so that you will come back again and again and again. Over and over they tell you that their product is the best by every measurement concocted by science. They never tell you that a competitor's product is better than theirs or that even you might create a better product at home. You might not have suspected it, but there really are franchisers of religion out there. When you start thinking that it might be possible to formulate a new God concept, you had better watch out. Some big franchising worm is going to climb out of the can and tell you, "How dare you question divine revelation that was closed with the death of John the Evangelist?" Very loudly and firmly speak the one word weapon, "Bullshit."

One of the knowledgeable people referred to above was Carl Jung. Carl was a world class Swiss psychiatrist, son of a minister, and a strongly committed Christian, although not to any of the Christian franchises that you might be familiar with. He also made major contributions to the birth and growth of twelve step groups. This is his concept of God: "God is an apt name given to all overpowering emotions in my own psychic system, subduing my conscious will and usurping control over myself. This is the name by which I designate all things which cross my willful path violently and recklessly, all things which upset my subjective views, plans, and intentions and change the course of my life for better or worse."

Among the many books that Carl wrote is one entitled *The Answer to Job*. At the end of his life, Jung said that the *Answer to Job* was the only book he would not rewrite if he had the chance to do so. It was also the only book that he felt impelled to write. The book is loaded with new God concepts. By the way you can say "Bullshit" to Jung also, and you won't be the first.

At the start of his book Jung emphasizes over and over again that he will not be talking about the Godhead because no human being knows anything about that. He will be talking about the images of God that men have created over the centuries, images that are like their human creators, imperfect. In his essential message, Jung says that Job is the symbol of humankind, and that the God portrayed in the book of Job is not a very nice God at all. He asks that you not take his word for it, but that you read the book yourself. Just to whet your appetite, here is a bit of what you will find. God makes a bet with Satan, his son, that come hell or high water, Job will remain faithful to him. Satan accepts that bet and then proceeds to kill Job's children, destroy his farm, and inflict him with the worst diseases imaginable. Now if your father pulled a stunt like that on you what would you do? Call the cops? Get a lawyer? Job just kept saying, "I didn't do anything wrong. I don't deserve this."

After a whole lot of argumentation and an incredible Fourth of July display of fireworks designed to convince Job that he was a nobody, a sinner, and deserved all this abuse, Job refused to cave in. He continued to insist that he was not a sinner but a just man. Finally, the God depicted in this book got the message or the insight that He, the Lord of the universe, had done Job a terrible wrong. He then came to the conclusion that He had to apologize to Job, give him an answer, and make atonement for the injustice that had been done to this innocent man. God's answer was, "Let's do Christmas. I'll become a man." And He did, and His name was Jesus.

For many people that story makes good sense. Why should poor, dumb, incompetent, ignorant, impotent little old men and women be labeled sinners and blamed for all the suffering in the world, while God, who's got all the marbles and doesn't always behave Himself, goes scott free? Instead of beating their breasts and saying "I'm bad and I'm sorry," people ought to be standing tall and saying, "Thanks for the apology and please, no more crap. We've had enough."

And of course people ought to be imitating as well as celebrating that apology at their level. If God can say He's sorry, then why can't human beings say they're sorry to all fellow creatures who share this universe with them?

Jung put it this way. "Man's suffering does not derive from his sins, but from the maker of his imperfections, the paradoxical God. The righteous man is the instrument into which God enters in order to attain self-reflection and thus consciousness and rebirth as a divine child trusted to the care of adult man . . . The real history of the world seems to be the progressive incarnation of the deity."

The more profound question about this story is frightening. Does the God that has been revealed to us have a dark side? Jesus talked incessantly about His loving Father, but when you

examine the Our Father prayer, even Jesus was a little skepti-
cal. You know how He ended the prayer to his Father. "Lead us
not into temptation and deliver us from evil." That's what His
Father had done to Job, remember, and Jesus was now asking
Him, "Please don't do it again after all the work I've done selling you as a kind and loving parent."

Then there is that curious expression in Genesis, we are
made in the image and likeness of God, and Jesus' comment,
"you are gods." How do we deal with that concept? Any low
level assistant to a prosecutor could easily demonstrate that we
all have a dark side. Where did we get that? Is it a part of our
divine inheritance? Is the balancing of opposites — good and
bad, right and wrong — an essential component of all life, including that of God? Is this evolution of consciousness and
struggle for balance that we are going through also taking place
in God? Interesting questions, aren't they? A lack of consciousness and a dark side in God would explain the catastrophes
and suffering in the world better than blaming them on us and
our sinfulness. We do create problems but nothing on the level
of hurricanes, earthquakes, and plagues that have been taking
place since time immemorial.

So how does all this plug into the Sacrament of confession
or reconciliation? First of all, we aren't as bad and never have
been as bad as some of the religious franchisers would have us
believe. We are imperfect. Period. And God does not take leave
of us when we make a mistake. Robert Louis Stevenson, in *The
Strange Case of Dr. Jekyll and Mr. Hyde*, described quite clearly
what shadow is all about. We have a good side that we exhibit
to the world and a bad side that we try to repress. We live in
the light and in the dark. We are two people. We can be angels
and devils almost simultaneously and our makeup is not going
to change. We need to do more than put on a pretty face or
pile snow on our dung heap.

Do you want to know what's in your dark side or shadow?
What we repress and don't like about ourselves we dump,
blame, project unto others. They have the problem, we don't.
They are wrong, bad, evil , and we are correct, good, and godly.
So make a list of all the things that you reject, hate, and despise
in other people. Now you've got a glimpse of what's in your
dark side, what you don't fully accept and understand about

yourself. It's not an easy activity to engage in, but it's a first and necessary step if we are ever going to be whole people.

Would you like to play a very complicated game? Try to tabulate all the people in your family, your church, your neighborhood, your town, your state, your country, the world who are carrying your shadow around? Then try to imagine what all these people and the world would look like if you decided to recall your shadow and own it?

Do we need help? Is there air? Confession or reconciliation could be one means to help us understand our psychological composition and deal with our dark side.

There is a threefold process in dealing with one's shadow. First we have to recognize it. Then we have to own it, and finally, and very importantly, we have to ventilate it. A wise confessor could be a powerful assistant in this process. Have you ever noticed how your body's shadow shortens as you stand more directly under the sun? A wise confessor could play the role of the sun. Have you ever needed help in making a tough decision? A wise confessor could help you take a good look at yourself so that you could honestly conclude, "Yeah! that's me and I can't deny it any longer." The last step of ventilation requires some ingenuity and a wise confessor could also assist in that regard.

If we don't own our shadow and let it ventilate in safe ways, then it will periodically rise up, surprise us, embarrass us, and wound us. Have words ever come out of your mouth that you didn't really want to say? Have you ever done something and later told people, "I really wasn't myself when I did that?" That's your shadow at work. To keep things in balance your shadow needs regular and specific attention. Suppose a part of your shadow is negative anger or greed. A wise confessor might suggest that you write an angry letter to ventilate that imperfection, but never mail it. Then no one gets hurt by your dark side. With greed, the suggestion of a direct and generous assist to some needy person could keep that trait at bay.

Do you want to know how really important it is to deal with your shadow? Simply stated, your shadow is your ticket to peace, heaven, completeness, wholeness — whatever term you want to use to define your ultimate goal in life. It seems paradoxical like the God who has been revealed to us, but it is our shadow that is going to save us. If you want a classical demonstration of that read Faust.

The points to be made from this somewhat extended sidetrip are these. We are not perfect beings, but we would like to be perfect. At quiet times we notice the chinks and cracks in the image or persona that we exhibit to the outside world. Sometimes we get moved or inspired to do something about it. It would be nice if there was help or guidance available that didn't cost us our face and a fortune. This is not to say that the Sacrament of Penance or Reconciliation is a panacea or the only way to deal with the shadow, but it could at least be a start on a journey.

Maybe someone on Team Vatican could reread article 72 of the Constitution on the Sacred Liturgy that states that the rite and formulas for the sacrament of penance need to be revised and be given more luminous expression. Bet you there are a lot of counsellors and analysts out there who would be honored to help in the revision. Without the benefit of vestments they have been giving very luminous expressions to both the nature and effect of the sacrament for a very long time.

Chapter Seven
ONWARD
CHRISTIAN SOLDIERS

Because babies were baptized as infants and didn't have the foggiest notion as to what was happening to them, early in church history some theologian decided that it was necessary to recharge these little people when they reached "the age of reason", about seven or eight years old. So three ceremonies were designed, Confession and Communion were administered at eight years of age and Confirmation at ten. That's a hard, cold, impersonal word, isn't it, "administer"? It sounds so mechanical. One gets the picture of a ghoulish looking doctor jamming a needle in your arm or a stern old judge dropping a sentence of execution on a prisoner. But that's the word that's used for doing Sacraments, the gestures of Jesus.

At Baptism, parents and godparents make a commitment to help the children to become lovers. They promise to surround them with love, to show them respect, build up their self esteem, and teach them by example to care about others. So the plan evolved that somewhere around the fifth or sixth grade the kids should be given the chance to make a statement on their own, that they were now ready to be not only takers but also givers in this love business. Confirmation is a word that means to make strong or firm. Gradually the emphasis came to rest on strong like in soldiers. The ceremony that was cooked up was long on reason and muscle and premature to boot. Kids, at least in the United States, aren't really ready for this until they are in their late teens.

So Sister Torquemada, the Rock's fifth grade teacher, got the assignment to get these little troopers in line. The new slogan in the fifth grade was, "You've got to be soldiers of Christ." Sister Torque, as the kids referred to her, was the right one to run this boot camp. She was big, gruff, and ubiquitous. She had trouble with one of her eyes. Whether she didn't see well or didn't want kids looking at her, she placed her desk on a raised platform at the rear of the room. She had Febbie Greenier, the janitor, nail the boards of that platform as tight as a drum and cover it with thick carpeting. She didn't want the recruits to be tipped off when she decided to make a quick inspection of their ranks. Like a true drill sergeant she carried a baton, the pointer that was used in geography class, only she carried it backwards with the heavy end up front. The thick end made better and more convincing contact on knuckles and heads. Occasionally, and for variety, she would rouse a playful or dozing trooper with a swift, pencil-eraser burn up the back of his neck The Rock still has scars to prove that what has been said is gospel truth.

Daily, the troops had to stand up and sound off catechism answers that Big Torque fired at them: What is Confirmation? Who is the Holy Ghost? What are the gifts of the Holy Ghost? What are the corporal and spiritual works of mercy? What is a bishop? What is holy chrism? and on and on and on. It was important to know all this stuff, because no less a personage than the Bishop, the local coach of Team Vatican, was going to show up and administer this Sacrament. The first thing the coach would do would be to check the troopers' cheers, their catechism answers. It would be their cheers that would blow down the walls of the new, big, bad Jericho of a world that they had to face. Dogmatic truth, concisely stated, would be their weapon of war.

Well, after many months of training, the day arrived in early May. The Rock got a new white shirt and tie to wear for the occasion. Ernie Burnash, in the little shop behind Joe Coutures' store, trimmed the Rock's hair, and for the second time in his life, he applied shoe polish to his biscuit- toed clodhoppers. Sgt. Torque told the troopers that they each needed a sponsor for this drill. A sponsor is like a weathered buddy who has experienced battle and will help warm cold feet and get one over the jitters. For his sponsor the Rock selected his uncle Lick, short for Aloysius, who lived across the street. He liked his uncle Lick, who was famous for his punctuality and all-around enthusiasm, especially for tackling tough jobs. The Rock thought that these two uncle Lick qualities would stand him in good stead as a soldier in Jesus' army. In fact, he was right on target with the enthusiasm bit.

You see, what the Vatican superstar theologian was trying to simulate in this Confirmation drama was the event of Pentecost. You no doubt have heard about or read about this event in the Acts of the Apostles. Let's review it quickly. One morning the Apostles were all gathered together in an old Jerusalem house and a big noisy wind came up that rattled the windows and curled the drapes. On top of that, some tongues of fire appeared out of the blue and settled on each one of them. Now that's kind of interesting, because a strong wind either blows out fire or spreads it all over the place. The Apostles really got stirred up by this wind and fire. They all started to speak in foreign tongues.

Now Pentecost was a big day for Jews of that time. They came to Jerusalem from all over the world for this big party. On the scene were Parthians, Medes, and Elamites and a whole raft of people from other well known geographical hot spots. When some of these visitors heard the racket, they gathered outside the house. A portion of the crowd thought they heard the Apostles speaking their back home language. Naturally, they were amazed and perplexed, and so they said to each other, "What the heaven does this mean?" Other visitors were not impressed, and they said, "Those guys are really bombed out of their heads."

Now Head Coach Peter didn't like this scurrilous reflection on his companions, so he climbed up on the porch to respond to this effrontery. In a very firm and elevated voice he addressed them: "Listen to me, you Judeans and Jerusalemites. We might be heavy drinking sailors and fishermen from Galilee, but we are not bombed as you suppose. Can't you tell time? It's only nine o'clock in the morning. Besides, we go to church every day at nine for morning prayers, and you know that the rabbis won't let you eat or drink until the prayers are completed.

"Now do you want to know what's going on here? Let me tell you. Old prophet Joel said that in the last days, God would pour his Spirit on your sons and daughters. Your young men would see visions and your seniors would dream dreams. Even your slaves and handmaidens would receive this enlightenment. Well that's happening right now, and I'll give you a further demonstration if you are up to it."

Well these high class visitors to Jerusalem were really surprised that this hick from Galilee had such nerve and forcefulness. They knew he was a hick because his accent was so heavy. Without waiting for an invitation, Peter took off on a two hour sermon that astutely tied the life of Jesus into that of King David. Peter wowed them right out of their headgear and after he gave them his "urbi et orbi" blessing, all they could say was, "Brother, what do we do now?" Peter's answer was succinct, "Have a change of mind and heart and be baptized." Now it was time for Coach Peter and his companions to be surprised. They spent a very long afternoon dipping five thousand people in the river.

Well, after that two minute essay, it must be obvious to you that what Pentecost was all about and what Confirmation tries to simulate is enthusiasm. It's a wonderful Greek word that means "in God." Whether the roaring wind, tongues of fire, and speaking in foreign languages really happened, or whether they were natural or supernatural events, doesn't really matter that much. What this story is simply saying is that these men really got into God or God got into them that morning and they did something about it. They shared it. They did it with gusto. And they didn't need booze or drugs to get it on or off.

OK. Back to the big day in St. Anne's church for the Rock's Confirmation. It was early evening and the place was packed with parents, friends, sponsors, candidates, and clergy. When the coach hits town and you're on the team and want some good playing time, you'd better be there and in your best uniform. So the clergy came out of the woods in droves and filled up the elevated, sacred space on the other side of the communion railing, called the sanctuary.

As the choir chanted "Veni Sancte Spiritus," the candidates filed into the front pews, with girls on the left, boys on the right. They were followed by the smiling clergy dressed in black cassocks and crisp white surplices trimmed with lace. Then came the coach. The Rock had never seen a real coach before and he didn't know what to expect. Coach Murphy was a big, heavyset man and he looked like a winner, but the Rock wasn't sure what he had won. He had never seen a man dressed in red head to floor finery before. Fr. Bouchard's black cassock and black three-cornered hat looked a little weird but it was simple. The Coach's attire raised a lot of questions in the Rock's little head. Why would a guy want to wear an outfit like that? The Rock still wonders. Around his neck the coach wore a gold crucifix on a heavy gold chain. On his right ring finger was a thick gold band with a large precious stone. His hat was like Louis T's, but it was red also, and under it he wore a little red beanie that stuck out slightly in the back.

When The Big Red got to the altar, he took off his hat, adjusted his beanie, and then knelt to pray for a few minutes. Without any fanfare he then made his way back to the communion railing and faced the kids. It was interrogation time. Sister Torque had said that he might ask for volunteers or he might just point to someone. This night he was in a bird dog mood. He first pointed to a couple of girls in the front row and they answered very well.

Then he swung to his left and the Rock immediately decided that his clodhoppers needed re-tying. The coach didn't go for the feint. In a strong voice he said, "You there, with your head between your knees, are you sick?" The Rock knew that he had blown it. When he looked up and saw the coach glaring directly at him he knew it was time to act and speak. So he stood up quickly and said, "Do you mean me, your honor, I mean your Excellency?" That's the proper title for the coach. Sensing that this kid had a little spunk and wasn't going to be totally intimidated, the coach responded, "Yes, I mean you. Are you sick?" Immediately the Rock replied, "No your Excellency. I was just tying my shoe."

"Well that's good," said the coach. "Now tell us what is the Holy Ghost." The Rock was prepared for that one. "The Holy Ghost is the third person in the Blessed Trinity. And that's a mystery."

"And what's a mystery"? fired back the coach. With equal rapidity the Rock replied, "It's something you can't understand or explain. You take it on faith."

"Very good," said the coach, "You may sit down. And by the way, when you get home, have your mother or your father teach you how to tie a non-slip knot for your shoes." When the Rock sat down, he thought to himself, "He might wear weird clothes, but he's no dummy."

After interrogating another dozen confirmandi and receiving some fairly good answers, the Coach congratulated the kids for their efforts and then announced, "We will now proceed to the anointing." He first returned to the altar where a couple of his assistants dressed him with an ornate stole and a golden, floor length cape called a cope. Then they put this jewelled, two foot high, double-tailed, stove pipe hat on top of his beanied head. It was called a miter. Rock's dad had a saw box for cutting angles that was also called a miter. Maybe this was an antique part of a carpenter's uniform. The Coach really looked tall and cut a sharp angle in this get-up. When he turned to face the people, two other players jumped to attention. The one on the right gave the coach a long gold pole with a hook on the top. It must have been seven feet long and was called a crozier. Maybe this was a weapon the coach used when he went soldiering for Christ. The player on the left then opened up a big red book with gold edges, and the coach started singing some prayers in way off key Latin.

When the chanting stopped, the coach, flanked by three visiting players, headed for the far left end of the communion railing. The ushers quickly lined up the candidates with their sponsors behind them along the railing. The player on the coach's right held a golden container of oil called "chrism." The two priests on his left held baskets, one empty, the other filled with balls of cotton. When the coach got to the first person in line, Freaky Archambault, he stuck his thumb in the oil and while he said something in Latin about confirming Freaky in the name of the Trinity, he smeared a big glob on his forehead in the sign of a cross.

When the coach removed his hand, Freaky moved his head slightly to the right in a flinch, and he kept a very careful eye on the coach's hand. At this moment in the ceremony the bishop gave the candidates a blow on the cheek to remind them that they had to be tough as soldiers of Christ. When the class rehearsed this event, Sister Torque played the part of the coach. She claimed that sometimes the bishop would give taps, other times blows. It depended on how well the catechism drill went at the start of the ceremony. Taking no chances, Sister Torque belted everybody at the practice. Those who were not her pets got a windup blow, and Freaky was in that category.

In the catechism drill session, when the coach asked Freaky what the head of the Catholic Church was called, Freaky, who stammered and missed important consonants when he got nervous, responded, "Da-da-da- da Dope." The boisterous laughter that followed, and the bishop's stare, cued Freaky to get ready for the worst. You'd flinch too, wouldn't you, if you were in that situation? The coach surprised him, however, and with a smile, only gave him a love tap on the cheek. Maybe Coach Murphy was even better than a "no dummy." Maybe he had thought this through and decided that the soldier and war bit was out of place for fans who were supposed to be lovers. Why not show the kids a little affection as they officially took on their adult role of loving one another as they loved themselves? That approach could generate a whole lot more enthusiasm, living in God who is love and not a vengeful warmonger.

When the coach moved on to the next customer, the wiper with the cotton balls moved in and vigorously scrubbed the grease off Freaky's head. No grease-heads for Team Vatican. They were into the dry look. These assistants were sanitary, too. One ball per customer. Wiper number two carefully collected the used cotton for disposal. When the coach got down to the Rock he was in a happy mood. After giving the Rock a gentle tap on the cheek, he leaned down and whispered in the Rock's ear, "Be sure to learn the non-slip knot. OK?" The Rock's face lit up and a little tongue of fire was ignited in his head. It might be a lot of fun to play for Coach Murphy some day, he thought.

When all the candidates had been anointed and the episcopal blessing given, three crosses in the air to the right, left, and center, the Bishop and his clergy led the procession out the center aisle and jovially wended their way to the rectory next door. The newly confirmed followed the clergy out and waited on the sidewalk for their parents to find them and take them home. It wasn't a happy ending because there was no outlet for their new gift of enthusiasm.

Provisions had been made for the Coach and his players to celebrate both before and after the ceremony. They enjoyed cocktails and a special dinner before the ceremony and drinks, snacks, and card games after. Shouldn't the confirmed, their sponsors and parents have been included in that party? For some reason it seemed important to keep the two classes apart. Does familiarity really breed contempt or did somebody just make that up?

Recently the old Rock witnessed a young bishop impart a little humanness to the Confirmation ceremony. After the church ritual, the bishop played the piano, sang a few ditties, shared some munchies and even danced with the participants in the parish hall. Even some of his old priests cautiously joined in. Parents, sponsors, clergy, and newly confirmed experienced an enthusiastic oneness that was palpable.

Experience was an almost prohibited ingredient in the Rock's early liturgical life. The ceremonies, not so much in their design as in their execution, were directed at his head, and hardly anything was aimed at his heart. The human, the natural, the instinctual were almost always totally absent. Too bad. The Rock was really getting into being human at that time.

CHAPTER EIGHT
PUBESCENT
POWER PUZZLE

When the Rock entered junior high he became acquainted with the dictionary. It wasn't a completely voluntary encounter. Sister Elizabeth Ann, a tall skinny lady, had a unique way of slowing down overactive sixth graders. If you were caught raising whoopie, she invited you up to the front of the room where there was one of those eighty pound dictionaries sitting on a wheelable metal stand. Well, maybe not eighty pounds, but possibly sixty. Your punishment was to face the wall and hold this tome for about five minutes in the hope that you might develop a serious attachment to tightly packaged wisdom. After fondling leathery old Webster for the assigned time you could then return him to his stand. But you weren't done yet. Next you had to select any five new words that caught your fancy, write down their definitions, commit them to memory, and recite them for Sister and the class the next morning. It was really a great learning device.

Now some, slightly precocious, sixth grade boys, develop a keen interest in "graphic" language. They hear a lot of intriguing stuff from the older guys at recess and in the boys' restroom, and the big guys at Joe Couture's store loved to pique the curiosity of these pubescent knowledge seekers. One never wanted to just plain ask those older characters what their terms and phrases meant. Best way in the world for a burgeoning stud to lose face. You couldn't ask the nuns or your mother. How would they know? If you asked your dad he'd probably wash your mouth out.

So Sister Lizzy's punishment served a marvellous latent function. When you were randomly flipping pages you occasionally came across some very interesting words, and one word led to another, and another, and another, and before you knew it you had important questions partially answered and developed some new knowledge. Not even some of the older studs at Joe's knew this terminology. One day while doing time up front, the Rock decided to just browse through the F's looking for that word that was so frequently used by the older guys. Naturally, it wasn't there. But then he spotted fornicate, and that led to intercourse, adultery, and brothel. On the same page was foreskin which led to penis, and testes. And just above that was foreplay. Wow! Another day he chanced upon menstruate which led to uterus, vagina, menses, menopause, and puberty. Full circle. Pubic hair, breasts, wet dreams. So that's what's going on. Can't you just picture the Rock writing this stuff down, memorizing it, and giving it back to the class the next day? No way, blue jay.

By the end of the school year, the Rock and some of his buddies were really digging virility. One area of major concentration was developing a macho line of talk —especially double entendres and one liners. Lefty Markowski came up with a good one on a Saturday night while they listened to *The Hit Parade*. Lucky Strikes sponsored the parade of best songs and they had an expression "LSMFT," which meant Lucky Strikes mean finer tobacco. Lefty's version was that light sweaters make finer tits. Now please don't get excited about that word. It's even in Webster's 1932 abridged edition.

In the class there was a girl who moved with a swishy, swashy, swagger. Her name was Robin Slatchakowski. She reminded Eggie Clearwood of the healthy bovines he and his friends often observed at the livestock auction near the fairgrounds. So he changed her name to Rotten Snatch-a-cow-ski. One day at recess, Eggie handed Robin an old rusty bolt, and asked her, "Robin, would you like a screw?" Robin was really ticked, and she snapped back at Eggie, "Eggie-head. If you want one dat is, go where are dey."

When the Rock and his mates reached the seventh grade, Willie Wennick, who was a little older than the majority of the kids, proved to be the most irreverent student in the class. For some reason the heavy moral teaching that was coming down on the class didn't seem to register with Willie. As a gift for the pastor or the principal on their feast day, the children were asked to contribute prayers and good works as a spiritual bouquet. The last suggested item on the list was for short prayers or exclamations, like "Jesus, Mary, and Joseph, help me," or "Lord, have mercy on us." They were technically known as ejaculations. You've got the picture. When Sister Lizzy asked students to stand up and spell out their contributions, Willie rose very seriously and with the most unctious voice stated, "Oh Sister! For Father's feast day I am going to offer up 500 ejaculations." Twenty guys almost wet their pants and ducked under their desks but Willie held that straight, serious face through it all.

As previously mentioned, on Saturdays, the Rock and his buddies loved to go to the livestock auction at the fairgrounds, sit on the fence and watch the cattle work out. When they had

Lefty and Dorothy, 1942

enough of that they would pick up samples of Red Man chewing tobacco, head up to the top row of seats in the auction arena, and expectorate all over the place. On Fridays, for fun and games at recess, and just to prove that they were as macho as anyone in junior high, they brought along little miniature bottles of booze that they had "borrowed" from home. Now the Rock understands why some modern scientist says that testosterone should be declared a controlled substance. Would you believe it? This doc says that it's worse than heroin, and it'll make you do weird things. It sure did to the Rock and his buddies.

By the seventh grade the testosterone was boiling and the hormones were oozing. Guys were eyeballing girls to see if all of their bricks were in the right place. Some of the girls, like Delphine McFalda and Dorothy LaBarge (who wasn't really a barge but a compact little cruiser) were getting coy. They would turn a little sideways, roll their wide open eyes, and smile as if to say, "I've got something that you want and you aren't going to get any." A lot of parents were confused, but not the nuns. This was the time to challenge these little devils, keep them busy, and give them some ideals.

For just a few minutes let's consider the actors in this drama. First you've got the kids. They are between twelve and fourteen years of age and really heating up with femininity and masculinity. They aren't sure what is going on. Some of it they like and some of it embarrasses them. But no one in authority talks about it in a positive way. If authority figures say anything it is almost always negative or condemnatory, "Don't you ever let me hear you using those words again."and "Don't do that; you'll go blind. Hair will start growing in the palms of your hands." So the kids talk only to their friends and guys a little bit older. It's the near blind leading those who are about ready to risk a little nearsightedness for an occasional experience. But in this environment, the kids feel guilty for just about everything — for thinking, for asking questions, for testing out their rapidly evolving equipment.

At Rock's house, Arlie, like most fathers, was concerned about appropriate language. Period. So the kid felt guilty about his Webster browsing. The 1932 edition that until now had sat on the shelf next to the encylopedias, had become his constant bathroom companion. His parents thought he had finally become a dedicated student. When Rock decided it was time to go one on one with Del to the show and Aselin's ice cream parlor, Gen thought it was about time that she give her son some sound advice. With a lot of hesitation in her voice she said, "Now be sure to treat Del like she was your sister." He didn't have any sisters. How do you process that kind of information?

Now to the school. Every room the children enter had a crucifix on the wall. The message is direct and simple. Jesus died like that for your sins. Every time people commit a sin they drive another nail into him. And what is a sin? We've been there before haven't we? In the minds of most of the kids at this age sin equaled sex. Some didn't hear that message. Some rose above it. And yes, there were other sins like disobedience, cursing and swearing, fighting, but none of those things put the fear of the Lord in the sinner like sex did, and hardly any of those other things caught the attention of the confessor as sex did. When sex was the issue you sweated a lot and your stomach flipped. Then you tried to disguise the nature of what you had done. You changed your voice. You used circuitous language like "I touched myself irreverently" or "I became overly friendly with this other person." You could never remember the number of times. It was always "about" so many times. The attempt to dissemble, of course, only aroused the curiosity of the confessor. So those were the matters that you got quizzed on. The embarrassment deepened and the guilt worsened.

Not only was there a crucifix in every classroom, there were two other prominent pictures of saints — St. Therese, the Little Flower, and St. Aloysius. They were relatively young as saints go, both in age at their time of death and year of canonization. Therese was a French girl who became a Carmelite nun, and

Aloysius was an Italian Jesuit. Their claim to fame was purity, and the students were urged to pray to them for assistance in their battle with the "flesh." Rock was happy that his confirmation name was Aloysius. He had a special claim to that saint's attention.

The people who were in charge of these classrooms also had a big impact on the kids' struggle. The priests were seen daily at Mass and maybe once every couple of weeks during a short classroom visit. The nuns were present for eight hours a day. Their garb, first off, was otherworldly. They were covered from head to toe. One saw only their hands and their faces. They wore no make-up nor jewelry. The priest's black garb, he said, indicated that he was dead to the world. It meant that he was trying to be out of his body and into spiritual things as fully as possible. He was trying to live out a response to the Gospel question, "What does it profit a man if he gain the whole world and suffer the loss of his soul?" The natural implication that most kids garnered from this symbolism was that the body is evil, an enemy that has to be conquered, an obstacle that has to be overcome if the soul is to be saved. The nuns wore black veils that conveyed the same message, but the basic garb of the Dominicans who served St. Anne was a white habit, the symbol of purity, the color of your soul when it was in the state of grace. The nuns, also, were referred to as "the brides of Christ," and their habits were their wedding garments.

You get the picture, don't you? An environment built with the highest of intentions, but made for confusion, with kids going honestly in the direction of their nature, and adults telling them that they were on the road to perdition, that they must deny themselves and take up their cross. How could things get so badly confused? The real crux of this problem is probably contained in the word "deny." It means to say no, disown, reject, and condemn. Over the centuries well intentioned people have taken that word so far out of context that they have cut off their hands, plucked out their eyes, and even amputated their genitals.

It seems unbelievable that people would do things like that out of love for Jesus. How could people who heard Jesus say, "The kingdom of God is within you," or "I am in the Father, and you are in me, and I am in you," come to think of their bodies as being evil and not a wonderful, beautiful gift from the Creator? The teaching, either by direct statement or strong implication, that the human body is evil, is probably the most severe and harmful blow that has ever been directed at humankind. When people have no respect, esteem, nor love for their total self, body and spirit, then everything and everybody is open to exploitation. And sadly, that has been our existence.

Please don't get the impression that things were all bad for the Rock. He was probably more sensitive to the sin issue than many of his classmates, and probably a bit more idealistic than some of them, and, as many of you readers must suspect, his hindsight has been partially shaped and colored by his adult experiences.

Life in the eighth grade was elevated. First of all the classroom was on the second floor where most of the high school courses were conducted. Everyone felt bigger and more important to be up there with the high school students. They could see the future up close. Then there was Sister Mary Therese. She seemed younger and happier than the teachers in five through seven. She had an easier and more positive way about her. Another big plus for Rock was the basketball team. The eighth grade team played in a league with all the other eighth grades in the city, and there was a ranking and a championship to look forward to at the end of the season.

So right at the beginning of the school year, mostly because of Sister Mary Therese, the Rock decided that he was going to get serious. He knew that at the end of the year an award was given to the best all-around student in the class. Curly had won the award two years before. Cautiously and discretely, Sister Mary Therese let him know that he too was capable of winning the award. He had heard enough of this business of "why can't you be like Curly," so he decided that "he would show them." He would be better. Over the years he had grown out of his hammer bashing approach to life and learned a little diplomacy as well as a little sociological Machiavellianism. That term came much later, of course, but it simply means knowing how to cut corners, work the system, or as the coiner of that expression put it, "Only he who knows the rules can cheat." So the Rock's antennae were always fully extended.

One of the first subtle messages he picked up was that in the eighth grade an astute young man should pray frequently and seriously consider going to the seminary and becoming a priest. It was the studied belief of Team Vatican that young men ascended to the priesthood more easily if they started their climb after the eighth grade. Sr. Mary Therese pointed out early in the year that there would soon be an election for the presidency of the grade school altar boys and that the Rock should think of running. Well he didn't think very long nor run very hard and won hands down. Sr. Mary Therese was in charge of the grade school altar boys.

This office gave the Rock quite a bit of exposure and a modicum of prestige. In the St. Anne altar boy world the heavy hauling was done by the grade school guys. The high school servers took the plums like weddings and funerals, where you frequently got tips, and the late Sunday Masses. The grade school servers did the weekday and early Masses on Sundays. In those days the emphasis was on early all week — especially Saturday when there was no school. One of his presidential "privileges" was to assign servers to various Masses. Assigning guys to early A.M. Masses was a nice way to settle scores with critics and competitors. Another privilege was to get excused from classes in order to train younger boys how to do this routine. As a matter of fact, with all the practice, the Rock got almost as good as Fr. Bouchard at rattling off the Latin prayers. When it came to the Confiteor in the prayers at the foot of the altar, the Rock often ended up in a dead heat with the priest.

There was a subtle proselytizing in this altar boy game that really escaped the Rock . It had to do with the uniform. When it was time to go on stage you dressed like a priest. You wore a black cassock and a white surplice. If the axioms, "you become what you are addressed" and "clothes make the man" are true, then the more frequently you put on one of those little uniforms the more closely you are drawn to putting on the bigger one. It even went further than that. On special occasions the boys wore red cassocks, the color worn by monsignors and bishops, and on Christmas and Easter they wore white, the color worn by the Pope. This was really a pre-seminary ascension. Was the Rock getting caught in his own fancy footwork?

In the old Latin days, active Catholics were urged to arm themselves with a missal. No, this was not a shell, but it did have projectile capability. It was a book that contained the Proper, the unchanging part of the Mass, in Latin and English, as well as the prayers and readings that were assigned for the various days of the year. Because Rock was shooting for the moon, he knew that daily Mass attendance from the opening whistle was a necessity. Also, the eighth graders had front row seats on the Epistle side. They were assigned to this location in the hope that their attentive and participatory presence would give good example to the little people sitting behind them. Out of the blue one day, Sister Mary Therese, in her very gentle way, suggested to the Rock that a daily missal might be a big help for him in understanding and appreciating the meaning and value of the Mass. She also knew how he could acquire a very nice one at a substantial discount. Now what would you have done in a situation like that? Pass up a powerful booster for your moon trip, and at a discounted price? Of course you would seize the opportunity as did the Rock.

Another event and a big counter in the popularity contest that the Rock had entered was the Oratorical Contest. It was an event created by the principals of the three Catholic grade schools in town. The idea was to get the eighth grade students interested in academic as well as athletic competition. The rules and requirements were laid out in November and the competition took place in January. Each school selected its own winner, and the three winners faced off in the auditorium of the school whose turn it was that year. Curly had won this event two years previously at St. Bernard's. The Rock had to attend the event with his parents, but he wasn't impressed. Curly won on his goodness. He was such a clean looking, polite, young man, who could deny him as he spoke so sincerely to the topic "Financial Aid for Parochial Schools." No doubt, the subject matter really helped. It spoke to a question that adults were keenly interested in and they did the voting.

The Rock learned a few things from Curly's triumph. Presence, good manners, and a topic of current interest to the adults, were necessary ingredients, but he knew that he had an asset that Curly had overlooked — his Grandpa Martin. Grandpa was an orator who could talk at the drop of a hat and on any subject. Even his ordinary conversation was animated and juicy. Not only did his tongue pour out well articulated words, his eyes, his hands, and his whole body reinforced the linkage of words. So when Rock dropped by seeking Grandpa's assistance on this project, Robert Martin was ecstatic. No one had ever requested this kind of help before.

Grandpa had two major areas of interest at that time, and they were also closely related. First, there was the Railroad Brotherhood and second was the doctrine of Fr. Charles Coughlin on WJR Detroit every Sunday afternoon. So after a little brainstorming with the Rock, Grandpa suggested that the topic should be Catholics and the Labor Unions. The kid was speechless. Grandpa could have suggested "The Use of the Pluperfect Participle in the Funeral Orations of St. Peter Chrysologus" and the Rock would have been in the same kind of a tailspin. Grandpa assured the boy that the topic was not an easy one, but that he would help him master the basic ideas and provide him with some useful and persuasive data.

The next three weeks were wonderful. Every evening after supper Rock would walk the block and a half down Tawas Street to Grandpa's house and spend an hour with him talking about this subject. Slowly the Rock began to grasp the basic ideas — all people have a right to the good things of the world; it is wrong to exploit workers by not paying them a decent wage, and by working them for long hours in subhuman conditions; it is also wrong not to provide compensation for job related injuries and means of support in old age. Grandpa further pointed out that workers have a right to band together and bargain with their employers over wages, working conditions, and pensions. Next Grandpa loaded the Rock up with names and quotations of distinguished supporters of the labor movement. Among them were American bishops like Ireland and Gibbons, and Popes like Leo XIII and Pius IX. The Rock was convinced that his grandfather was a walking encyclopedia.

After three weeks of these nightly lectures, Grandpa then directed The Rock to write down in his own words what he thought about all of this. It was tough work. After a week and a half he went back to Grandpa with his rough stuff. Grandpa, of course, was thrilled with his budding student. He would have been thrilled even if the kid had come over with crumpled pages printed in first grade capital letters. Slowly, always complimentary, he went over the pages, a correction there, an addition here, a quotation at this point, some examples for better understanding in this paragraph, and so on. By the end of the week they had a pretty good document put together, and even the kid started feeling the excitement. Grandpa gave him four days to commit this text to memory.

After four days Rock had the speech down, but it was as wooden as the Indian out in front of Charley's Cigar Store. After three robot deliveries and the consequent gaining of confidence, Grandpa began to polish the act. First, he got into enunciation. This wasn't easy when you had titles like the encyclical Rerum Novarum of Leo XIII and Quadragesimo Anno of Pius IX. When Grandpa got that in gear he moved on to points of emphasis, volume and modulation, and finally eye and hand gestures. By the end of the Christmas holidays the Rock had become a veritable Patrick Henry and was loving every minute of it. With Grandpa and his parents in attendance, the kid blew the competition away in the St. Anne run-off.

Next came the finals. Fortunately, they took place at St. Anne's this year and that gave the kid a home court advantage. Generally the home crowd was larger than the visitors. That Friday evening the auditorium was full. All the nuns were there and so was Fr. Bouchard. He sat in a large chair in the middle of the center isle right below the podium. Grandpa and the Rock's parents sat in the first row to the right of Fr. Bouchard. When Grandpa saw the setup with Fr. Bouchard, he quickly advised the Rock never to look directly at the priest. He could be very intimidating. The rule was, if you get nervous or confused look at me.

The regulations dictated that the host school candidate spoke last. In some ways, this was a bummer, but in the long run an asset. The first speaker was a cute little gal from St. Mary's named Ruth Bronokowski. She had a bright face and a bubbly voice, but you could hardly see her behind the podium. Her topic was The Importance of Praying the Family Rosary. She did a decent job and Fr. Bouchard and the nuns all applauded warmly when she finished. Most of the parents were lukewarm. In their heads one could hear them saying, "My God! We can hardly get our kids to sit still long enough to say grace at meals, and now this kid wants us to keep them fifteen minutes after the meal to say the Rosary. Is she nuts, or what?" Rock and Grandpa breathed a bit more lightly.

The next speaker was from St. Bernard's, and his name was Johnny O'Callaghan. He was a slightly chubby guy with a full head that was fronted with an almost perfect cherubic face.

The only flaw was a strong, protruding chin that spoke of firmness and determination. You could see Johnny and hear him plainly. He was well prepared. His topic was "The Need for a Catholic Central High School in Alpena." He waxed eloquent, true to his Irish heritage. He carefully ticked off reasons for this project and shook out their numerical order with his fingers. In a thundering conclusion, with his chin fully extended, he pounded on the podium and demanded that pastors and parents come together and get this project underway NOW. Johnny sat down with a heavy sigh of relief. He knew that he had done an excellent job. But why only a warm, polite response?

Poor Johnny. Nobody had told him that this was a rigidly divided community still very much committed to ethnicity. You could read it on the faces of the people in the audience. The Frenchies and the Irish were thinking, "I don't want my kid marrying a Polack." The Poles and the Frenchies were saying to themselves, "Those damn Irishmen. Just because they have a few rich people in their parish they think they own this town and that they are better than we are. And that punk kid up there thinks the same way. After all his old man runs a drug store and he's loaded. How does he think we are going to pay for this? Where are we going to get the nuns to run the school? Somebody ought to straighten that kid out." From the response, Rock knew that if he could calmly get through his pitch, he had this thing in the bag.

Slowly the Rock moved to the podium. Calmly and with a controlled smile he bowed slightly to the left, the center, and then the right. "It is a great honor for me to be able to speak to you this evening. I am a young boy with very little experience. But even a boy, sometimes can see and experience the consequences of selfishness, greed, and injustice. You know better than I do that there are too many families in our little town whose breadwinners work long and tedious hours in unhealthy situations and earn only pennies for an hourly wage. You know that there are many men like my father here who have been injured and maimed at their jobs and who have not received one nickel's worth of compensation. Many of you, also, have elderly parents who have worked all of their lives for merely survival wages, and are now dependent upon you or living out their final days at the county poor house.

"Today in our land and throughout the world there are many brave men speaking out against these injustices and promoting ways of solving the problems." Then the Rock went on to quote Fr. Coughlin, Bishops Ireland and Gibbons, and finally Popes Leo XIII and Pius IX. He followed this with examples of struggles and growth, the railroad brotherhoods, the coal miners in Virginia and Pennsylvania, the stockyard workers in Chicago, and the sit-down strikers in Flint.

"In conclusion," The Rock began, "I would ask of you parents what you are asking of us students, and that is to study and to think. The labor movement has only just started in our town, and many of the organizers have been judged and condemned without a hearing. Our bishops and our holy fathers have told us that the goals of the labor movement are just and honorable, that the worker has a God-given right to a decent wage, a healthy work situation, compensation for injury, and provisions for his old age. And above all he has the right to organize to achieve these goals. But in this organization the spirit that must prevail is that of charity and love. If employers must respect the rights of workers, then workers must respect the rights of employers. Only true charity will generate that respect. Thank you very much for listening."

When the kid returned to his seat, only Grandpa was standing and clapping. His parents and Sister Mary Therese were crying and the rest of the people were stone silent. When he looked at the stunned audience he concluded, "Well, I lived up to Dad's prophecy. I hit them in the head with a hammer and they are out of it. What do I do now?" Slowly the people came to life. Even Fr. Bouchard came forward and shook the kid's hand. Never before had the people of Alpena heard a kid talk about the social teaching of the Church. In fact, never before did they know that the Church had a social message. The kid of course didn't know that either and he wasn't sure that he fully understood what he had just said. Grandpa did, however, and he was so pleased with the kid's presentation that he practically carried him home and tucked him in bed. Needless to say, the Rock won the contest hands down.

As a result of this oratorical success the Rock picked up a life long friend and mentor. Ken Povish was a local hero. When he was a junior in high school he was first runner-up in a national speech contest. His senior year he won the whole bag of marbles. His picture was on the front page of the local paper, and everyone was predicting great things for this marvellous orator. What he decided to do was to go to the seminary and become a priest. Ken and Sister Mary Therese must have been in cahoots, because shortly after his speech making debut, the Rock got a letter from Ken. It was a congratulatory message, but it also had a lot of commentary on his happy life in the seminary.

As you probably remember, the kid was a basketball freak. He started playing at Carr's Field when he was in the third grade. Playing outdoors in the snow and mud does have some advantages. When you get inside you learn that you can run faster, jump higher, dribble more smoothly, and shoot more accurately. Rock's inside game started in the fourth grade. That's when he and his buddies put a team together to play in a new kids league at the Alpena Boys Club. They were dubbed the Rinkydinks. Just to show you how much this meant to the kid, he still has a newspaper clipping of their first game at Memorial Hall, the big gym above the Boys Club. The Dinks beat the Pewees 10-1, and the Rock scored 6 points.

From then on basketball became practically the number one interest in the kid's life. He spent endless hours of his fourth, fifth, and sixth grade years at the Club. He fell in love with Cap and Betty Wixon and their staff. He played other sports, shot pool, collected stamps, worked in the wood shop, but his first love was basketball. St. Anne had a junior high team that started in the seventh grade. Although the team was dominated by eighth graders, Rocky made the team but played sparingly. But when the eighth grade arrived it was bye-bye second string. The Dinks had been playing together for four years and they were bad. Pigsfeet Gougeon played center, Poochy Seguin and Barney Stafford were the guards, and the Rock and Burhead LaMarre were forwards. The junior high league was not just a Catholic collection. The public schools were included, so this was more than ordinary competition. Your faith was on the line. You had to show these pagans that you were more than just dumb Friday fish eaters, statue worshippers, and weirdos who prayed in Latin.

The Dinks were no longer Rinky. They were now the Big Reds, St. Anne's color. Early in the season they lost to Lincoln by one point at Memorial Hall, the Reds home court. They didn't lose another game. McPhee, a mediocre team, bumped off Lincoln late in the season, and so St. Anne and Lincoln ended up tied for first place. By the flip of a coin the playoff game was scheduled for the Lincoln gym. Bad news. The gym was a shoe box and the fans sat only inches from the floor.

Louie Kennedy, who coached both the junior and senior high teams, was a fire-eater in the heat of battle. Otherwise he was a very pleasant and funny man. Before the Reds took the floor, Louie gave them one of his best pep talks. Louie was a believer in vitamin C. So before each game and at half time, he made everyone eat an orange. He also threw them at lockers and people when he got upset. So while the guys were chomping on their oranges, Louie launched into his pitch, "So lemme tell ya. Dis is a big game. And youse guys are gonna win. Do ya hear me?" And they all said, "Yeah."

"St. Anne kids are winnas," Louie went on. "Y've seen da trophies in the case upstairs at school, haven't ya? Well da big one on da top shelf is one I know somein about. Dat's a state champeenship trophy, and we won dat baby in l927 before youse guys was born. I was on dat team with Abie DesChamps, Hank Vanini, Ovila Homant, and all dose utter guys. Everybody was saying we was a bunch of hicks from da sticks and we couldn't do it. Well we showed 'em. We beat the ass off everybody."

Fr. Camille Klos, the assistant pastor, was sitting there, and he said sharply, "Louie!" Louie ignored him and kept on going. "Now no Catlick kids have ever won dis champeenship, but we're gonna do it today. We gonna show dose potlickin Protestant kids dat we's as good as dey are."

Camie Klos tried again. "Louie!" Quick as a whistle Louie threw an orange at him and retorted, "Fadda. Get your ass outa here. Dis is my locker room and quit trien to do my job." Camie got the message and left.

Louie wound it up, "Now boys. Go out dere and give it all ya got. I been watchin dose lunkheads out there warm up and dey tink dey gonna run youse guys inta da ground. Well dey got anutta tink coming cuz youse guys is gonna beat em flat out. Remember where yas come from. Yas got champeen blood in ya. We did it in '27, and youse guys are gonna do it today. Let's get out dere and do 'em in."

Well, with a speech like that what are guys going to do? You guessed it. They played three miles over their heads, and for the glory of St. Anne and their faith, they beat "dose lunkheads" 32-18. The Rock was so tightly wound up that he picked up three fouls by half time. He still sports a chest cavity where Louie hit him with an orange at the break. Mainlined with vitamin C, he lasted till the final two minutes of the game and dumped in a dozen points. Louie was proud. He patted everybody on the back and gave them a parting shot. "Ye're good kids and ya play hard. Now go home and behave ye'rselves. See ya next year in high school and we'll get us another state champeenship."

The champs didn't take Louie's advice, and they proceeded to demonstrate that they weren't good kids in the normally accepted translation of that word. As you probably remember, Pigsfeet Gougeon's dad ran a booze store. As luck or fate would have it — choose whichever is appropriate to your definition of adolescence, Pigsfeet's parents were out of town for the evening. When the cat's away the mice turn into rats. The Gougeon home was only a few blocks from Lincoln, so the subzero weather outside didn't have enough time to chill down their euphoria. First, they had beer. Then they had wine. Finally they tried boiler makers, a shot and a beer. With so much forbidden juice around, naturally they didn't think of food. So just imagine what all that stuff was doing to their stomachs, their livers, their blood, their brains, and not to mention their coordination.

After about an hour of this revelry, Burrhead LaMarre, realizing that he was getting miles beyond Big Zil's inspection limits, hit the road for home. Eggie Clearwood, Lefty Markowski, and the Rock, unable to read the signs of the time, or just to plain read, hung in there for another two hours. When Pigsfeet announced that the well had run dry, the trio grabbed their coats and gym bags and headed for home. The subzero weather was now a blessing. So was the booze, in a sense. It kept them from freezing to death. The cold kept them alert on their long trek across the river to the North end. They joked and pushed each other into snow banks, threw snowballs at passing cars, and for the universe's edification blurted out the foulest obscenities that they could think of.

The Ninth Street bridge was a long and narrow span over the Thunder Bay River. The pedestrian walks were narrow and the safety rails met only minimum standards. When the trio got to about the center of the bridge, Lefty's load was getting to be more than he could carry, and his stomach switched to automatic unload. He leaned heavily on the icy rail and almost slipped through, although his gym bag did. Eggie and the Rock grabbed him and helped him to get his head out over the rail. The ice down there was at least ten inches thick. The lava that came out of Lefty's mouth was so hot that it immediately burned a hole through the ice the size of a manhole cover. Lefty's other emission was not so deleterious. It only solidified the front of his two pantlegs and the tops of his boots.

When Lefty thought he was about ready to navigate again, the trio started to roll on home. They had only gone a few steps when Lefty exclaimed, "I think I've broken both of my knees. They won't bend." Eggie told him to pretend that he walking on stilts. The Rock just kicked him in the knees a couple of times and a degree of mobility was restored as the ice cracked. They made it to 9th and Tawas and helped Lefty in the back door of his house. Eggie headed North to Tuttle, about six blocks away, and the Rock turned West to 8th Street.

The Rock snuck in the back door, dumped his coat and boots on the steps, and moved cautiously to the first floor john and closed the door. He washed his face with cold water, took three aspirins for good measure, emptied his vas, and tiptoed upstairs. Very cautiously he slipped by the open door of Arlie and Gen's bedroom and into the room that he shared with Curly and his two very young brothers. He dropped his clothes on a chair, and without kneeling for his standard night prayers, crawled into bed. He breathed a prayer of thanks for the undetected entrance and a few petitions for forgiveness. His prayers weren't heard.

The first thing he thought was, "Why has Dad got the thermostat cranked up so high?" The next thing that crossed his mind was, "Holy Toledo! Are we having an earthquake? Why is this bed moving around?" And then his stomach went on automatic unload. Hurriedly and very noisily he bolted for the upstairs bathroom . No sooner had the departed spirits started to speak their vile stuff through his mouth, than there was Arlie in his nightshirt to investigate what the kid was hammering on now. He immediately recognized the situation. When he picked the kid up off the floor and was about ready to heave him out the window, Gen appeared in her nightgown. She blurted out, "Arlie! Stop! My God! He's drunk. Let him finish and get back to bed. We'll take care of this in the morning." Never was the Rock more grateful for his mother's wisdom.

The next morning was awful. Arlie had already left for work when the crushed Rock got downstairs. His brothers looked at him like he was a leper from Molokai. Gen was also crushed, but as firm as Rock had ever seen her. "Your father and I are very upset. You are to go to school and come directly home when school is out. Do you hear me clearly? We will talk about this when your father gets home from work. And by the way, hurry and eat your breakfast and get to church. It might not be a bad idea for you to go to confession this morning. This is the worst behavior I have ever seen in a boy your age."

Rock didn't want any breakfast and he hurried off to church. He really felt bad. He was quite certain that the badness came from the booze and not the sin, but who knows, maybe confession would help. The three aspirins didn't work. Camie Klos' confessional was vacant, so he slipped in. When Camie slid open the grill, he said very plainly, "Bless me, Father, for I have sinned. My last confession was about a week ago. I got drunk last night." Almost in anger, Camie said, "You what? How old are you?" After a long harangue, Camie absolved him and told him to make the stations of the Cross three times for his penance. The Rock never had a penance as severe as that before.

When school got underway and he got a look at his buddies, the Rock hoped that he didn't look as washed out as they did. If so, he hoped that Sr. Mary Therese would attribute the look to the hard earned victory at Lincoln. At the recess break not one of the guys acknowledged their real situation. They all lied about the great party they had. Lefty got Eggie and the Rock aside and threatened them with dire consequences if they ever let out that he was the bird who polluted the Thunder Bay River and wet his pants in the process.

When Arlie got home that afternoon, the Rock got the toughest dressing down he ever received in his life. With it came a sentence of three months of hard labor at the kitchen sink and on the linoleum floors in the kitchen, dining room, and baths. And when the snow melted further labor would be required in the yard, the garden, the basement, and the garage. Did the Rock learn a lesson? Yes, for a few months.

The school year wound down rapidly, and very little new happened in the Rock's life. Can a bird fly with no wings? The grounding did produce some positive results. He had a whole lot more time to study and his options for trouble were reduced considerably, so winning the 8th grade best student award became a boat race. Thank God Camie Klos was bound to the seal of confession and couldn't tell the story that would have destroyed the Rock's chances. When the award was given out in June, even Arlie lightened up a little and gave Rock more breathing space When Sister Mary Therese asked him after the ceremony if he had thought seriously enough and prayed fervently enough about going to the seminary, he did not take offense. He finally saw the tipping of a hand that he hadn't noticed all year. Seemed like his con game was really working.

Chapter Nine
CRUNCH TIME

The summer of 1943 was a happy time for the Rock. In July he got his official ticket to manhood, a driver's license. He had been driving for two years with supervision. Arlie decided to kill two birds with one stone when Curly reached fourteen. He taught both of them to drive at the same time, but a license was a big deal. Cars were like little houses on wheels. You could quickly get away from neighborhood supervision and reporting. You acquired new status with the guys and you suddenly became more attractive to the girls. There were rides out in the country, beer and bologna sandwich picnics at the quarry swimming hole, late night sliding spins on the local ice rink, smooth talking in lovers' lane.

There was a war going on, of course, but the Rock and his friends were not too conscious of what was transpiring. The Rock lived near the depot and he saw a lot of sadness and joy there as guys left for the service and came home on furlough. But he didn't know most of these guys very well. None of his immediate kin had yet been drafted. At school, the nuns tried to get the kids' attention with canned food collections, special prayer sessions, and a project called Knittin' for Britain. Even the Rock knitted a pair of mittens.

Gasoline rationing was going on and that presented a few minor problems. Arlie's general rule with the old '37 Ford was if you can get the gas you can use the car. Because there were no high schools in the outlying farm communities, the kids had to come to town for their education. At St. Anne's there were a lot of Brousseaus, Mousseaus, and Rousseaus from Ossineke, and Wachakowskis, Slatchakowskis, and Nowakowskis from Bolton. Their fathers all had tractors and trucks and R stamps. Many stations wouldn't pump gas into cars for R stamps. But the Rock and his buddies had no problems. Poochy Seguin's old man ran the biggest Shell station in the territory. These country boys could even sell you used tires, if you needed some. Another problem was cigarettes, but old Phil Seguin solved that one, too. He found a man who supplied him with bulk tobacco called Hemyard and the appropriate paper. The dudes turned cowboys. They didn't have horses, but they learned how to roll cigarettes riding their bikes.

What thrilled the Rock more than anything that summer was the result of his boiling testosterone. He grew seven inches. By the time school started he reached six feet one and was a

head taller than the rest of his classmates. Because of the promi-
nence of his head, Eggie Clearwood started calling him the
Moose. The name stuck and continues to the present day, even
though the Moose isn't much of a moose anymore, since he
has not grown a vertical inch since that summer, but that's what
he'll be called from now on. Now don't you dare start thinking
horizontally. Frankly, he's now a real moose in that direction. So the name still fits and that's what he'll be called
from now on.

High school was a blast. There was movement from one
room to another, a variety of teachers, and a choice of subjects. But much more importantly there were girls in a wide
variety of shapes, sizes, and attractiveness. Even some of his
classmates got their bricks in line over the summer. And with
these sliding, shifting, smirking, bouncing, buxom beauties there
were parties, dances, and dates. And to top it all off there was
basketball with cheer leaders, a band, fans, sports page commentary, and trips out of town. What more could a young man
want? The Moose was in heaven. Almost.

As fate would have it there were report cards. At the end of
October, Arlie and Gen learned that the kid got an F in conduct, mostly because he had smarted off to old Fr. Joe Simon
who taught religion. In front of the whole high school he asked
him, "Father, why do priests wear dresses?" He got Fs in Religion, Algebra, and History, and a D in English. The D was a gift
of Sister Perpetua who was a close friend of Sister Mary Therese.
She thought she could still detect the small spark of a vocation
to the priesthood in the lad. You know what happened don't
you? The grounding of the Winter/Spring was extended, and
his license was revoked. And worst of all, his eligibility for playing basketball was under serious consideration.

The Moose was flunking Algebra, even with the answer
book that he had "borrowed" from Sister Alphonse Mary's desk.
But he wasn't so dumb that he couldn't add and subtract. At
home, he decided to use the asset that he had in Curly. The
nuns loved Curly and he was on track to be the 1945 valedictorian. Nothing works better than to let people know that you
appreciate their accomplishments and to ask for their advice
and assistance. So he daily complimented Curly on his study
habits and his quickness in setting up assists at basketball practice. Curly was really proud of his speed. He could move like a

deer. At lunch time, when they hustled home for grilled cheese sandwiches and Campbell's tomato soup, they always got in a couple of games of cribbage. The Moose no longer rubbed it in when he won, and frequently let Curly win in close games.

So Curly came around and began to help the Moose figure out the x's and y's and all those other weird algebraic symbols. He also opened up his gold mine of papers and reports that he had under lock and key in a dynamite box under his bed. Now don't get nervous about the dynamite. Curly wasn't a terrorist. Arlie worked at the limestone quarry and they did a lot of blasting out there every day. The empty wooden boxes made good kindling as well as handy storage containers.

Like the guys who had gone off to war, Moose had to fight his little war on two fronts. Now that the tide had turned on the home front, he had to establish a beachhead at school. The line of defense seemed to be the weakest at the library. That's where Sister Perpetua held forth and had her office. So one day the Moose nonchalantly dropped into the library to ask Sister Perpetua how he might bring up his grade in English. After listening to about fifteen minutes of advice, he thanked her and rose to leave. Just as he was going out the door, he cheerfully informed her that he had not totally abandoned the thought of going to the seminary. She smiled warmly. "Wonderful! Wonderful!" was her response. The game was still on. Before religion class that morning he walked up to the front and apologized to Fr. Joe for his rude question about his garb.

Now I know you're worried about the Moose's motivation. Before you write the kid off completely, just ask yourself if you ever do anything with absolutely pure, direct, and selfless planning. The Moose's thought is that everyone's motivation is mixed and complicated, and if at any given moment someone sat you down and asked, "Where are you coming from?" you probably would have trouble giving a direct and simple answer. Maybe you wouldn't even be able to articulate an answer. Another fact to consider is that our culture rewards people who are discreet and don't get caught in their wobble through life, so one can even begin to think that scheming is virtue.

With all of that said, you've no doubt concluded that the Moose got his act back on track. And you're right, his grades came up. Arlie and Gen were pleased with the new fraternal relationship in the house and the improved grades, and Sister

Perpetua got the word out to the other nuns that a warm candidate for the priesthood had been committed to their care and supervision. Louie Kennedy was also pleased that he now had a talented string bean to compensate for a couple of would be seniors that he had just lost to the draft. He wasn't talking about the NBA.

At this time, also, the Moose decided that delivering newspapers was a bit below the dignity of a high school student. He had delivered the *Grit* and the *Alpena News* for four years. He made enough money to take care of fun expenses and some of his clothes. Now he needed a real job and he found it at J.C. Penny. He started as a jack of all trades. Each morning before school he ripped downtown on his bike and swept or shoveled the sidewalk, depending on the weather, and washed the windows and stoked the furnace. After school he unloaded boxes and stacked shelves until the store closed. Next he emptied the waste baskets, swept the wooden floors, and vacuumed the carpets. For this he earned the magnificent sum of 25 cents an hour. Then he ran over to Memorial Hall for basketball practice.

Basketball practice started in early November and after a couple of weeks it became apparent that Curly and Moose were on a collision course for a starting position. Eddie Wheaton and Poochy Seguin were in an identical situation. Thank God that it wasn't Moose's decision, and that Curly was all man when it happened. He could have easily kept his spot on the team by refusing to be the Moose's tutor, mentor, ghost writer, crutch, whatever. But on Nov. 22, there was the Moose, a starting forward when the season opened against Harrisville. He was as nervous as a cat on a hot tin roof at tip-off. His first shot from the left side didn't even hit the backboard and sailed into the fourth row of the balcony. Louie Kennedy groaned and almost threw an orange.

It was a good season. Louie used a lot of players and the Moose was happy that Curly got good minutes and killed many opposing fast breaks with his speed. The Moose averaged eight points that year which wasn't all that bad. Most games ended in the thirties. Twelve and four was a decent season for a team that lost two good seniors to the draft. Because of the war and rationing, state tournaments were not played that year. The Big

Reds complained a little, but offered it up for the guys who were defending the country.

One of the accompanying benefits of rapid growth was body hair. Some was good and some was bad. Armpit stuff had to be washed and deodorized. Stuff on your face was a boon. It made you look older and gave you an excuse to use after-shave lotion along with your underarm spread. Mennen's was the in-brand. Chest hair also looked good sticking out of your jersey. All of these new masculine accouterments wonderfully enhanced the Moose's level of studness. He got so cocky that he decided to test his machismo at the highest level.

Angela Lou Cinapel was the niftiest quiff of the cheerlead-ers. She was also a senior. The Moose was pleased that she accepted his invitation to see a movie at the Maltz theatre, but he was ticked that Curly had the car lined up that night. Yet walking relatively short distances wasn't bad. You had less dis-tractions when you put your arm around a girl, and purred your clever lines into her ear. He picked her up at seven and they made it casually to the theatre for seven thirty. When the house lights went out, Angela Lou reached over, took his hand and held it tightly. The bells started to ring and everything was elevated to a very pleasant level. Moose doesn't remember anything about the show. How could he?

They stopped at Push Em Up Tony's for a burger on the way home, and then settled into a deep and dreamy conversa-tion on the couch in Angela Lou's front room. Time stood still, at least for a while. Then the Moose heard a horn blowing out in the street. He looked out and there was the '37 Ford with Arlie in the driver's seat. He gave Angela Lou a quick peck on the cheek, grabbed his coat and headed for the Ford expecting the worse. Considering the circumstances Arlie behaved rather well. He said simply, "It's two o'clock in the morning. Don't you know enough to come home?" They rode home in silence.

The Moose saw Angela Lou several times after that and thought that he had a steady thing going for himself, but his ego got splattered in the Spring. He was visiting his buddy Eggie Clearwood one evening and Eggie's brother Cliff was home on furlough from Ft. Knox, Kentucky. When the Moose asked him what life was like in Kentucky, he said, "Great! They have a saying down there that the state is blessed with beautiful women and fast horses. Well, it's the other way around. Those gals can teach a guy a lot in a hurry. Look! I've gotta run. Gotta date with a live chick tonight. See ya." When he left, Moose asked Eggie who the date was. Eggie replied, "Angela Lou." End of message and end of relationship.

When summer came around, the Moose and Poochy Seguin thought it would be a great idea to take a trip to Detroit to see the Tigers play and visit some other interesting sights. The Moose knew that the only way to pull this off was to get Curly in on the act. Curly agreed and thought it would be a good idea to include Lou Sowa who had grown up in Detroit and knew his way around there. Well, after checking out train fare, hotel rates, and determining that they had enough money to do it, they presented the plan to Arlie and Gen. After two days of deliberation they consented to a short four day trip.

So early in June on a Monday morning the four dudes boarded the D and M at the depot and headed for "down below," the local idiom for all points south. They were ecstatic. At the first stop in Oscoda, a soldier returning to camp got on board. They recognized him as one of the Kennedy boys who anchored Oscoda's basketball team the previous year. He was going as far as Flint and switching there for Chicago. They talked a lot of basketball and Bill talked freely of his Army escapades. Of course the high school guys believed all the incredible things he described. Before getting off the train in Flint, he confirmed his tales by handing Poochy a box of Trojans. "Take these," he said. "You studs are going to need them when you get to Detroit." At least three of the guys accepted the gift as a real compliment. Curly's mind could not be read.

Like big shots, they took a cab to the Tuller hotel where they had reservations — two double beds in one room on the l0th floor. Rather tired, they got a bite to eat and hit the sack early. The next day was going to be their first visit to Briggs Stadium — probably the biggest shrine in Michigan. A Detroit cousin had secured seats directly behind the Tiger dugout to watch Michigan's team take on the Yankees. The Tiger lineup was loaded with stars like Hank Greenberg, Rudy York, Charlie Gehringer, Pinky Higgins, Birdie Tebbets, Hal Newhouser, and Dizzy Trout. The boys got what they came for. They saw all of these guys up close, and Hal Newhouser threw a two hitter by the Yanks for a four to nothing win. What a day! They walked back down Vernor Avenue to their hotel. On the way they picked up a bag of sliders and some RC Cola at a White Castle to eat in their room. Catholic kids liked RC Cola. They thought RC stood for Roman Catholic. The boys celebrated the Tiger victory and the wonderful day by filling up three of the Trojans with water and dropping them on pedestrians ten stories down.

The next day they took an early bus out to Greenfield Village to visit the Ford Museum. It was interesting, but not completely captivating. To liven up their last evening in town they decided to take in the first performance at the Broadway Burlesque. They were uncertain about being allowed in, but nothing ventured nothing gained, as Sister Perpetua was fond of saying. "God! If she only knew she'd flip her wimple," they clowned. So, with stubble, it was really only peach fuzz, on their chins, hair disheveled, and wrinkled jackets with turned up collars, they walked up to the ticket window. Not a question asked. "Are we studs or what?" they thought in their macho heads. They were really early and got seats in the front row. The music was raucous when the show began and the MC comedian was grosser than anyone they had ever heard. Willie Wennick couldn't carry this guy's jock strap.

When the comedian bowed out, the music cranked up and the curtain flew open. There were at least fifty women standing there wrapped only in G strings. The Moose's body experienced a blast of heat that was a hundred times more intense than the fire that greeted him at birth. The fireworks that went off inside and outside of his gangly frame exceeded the candlepower of the Fourth of July stuff Beezo Couture shot on Arlie and Gen's roof in 1929 by at least a zillion times. What an incredible sight! Remember the Moose had no sisters. This was the first time he had witnessed a full frontal view of a female. And there were fifty of them. The bumping and grinding that followed further enhanced the heat and the fireworks. After an hour of this stuff, the Moose knew that he now had enough fantasy material to last him a lifetime.

The guys walked back to the Tuller and all they could say, with the exception of Curly, was "Holy Shit." But it wasn't holy. The Moose suspects that at least three of them, Poochy was doubtful, were praying fervently for a safe trip home and the chance to get to confession. Their prayers were answered. Old Fr. Joe Simon wasn't shocked and gave them only the regular three Our Fathers and three Hail Marys for a penance. For once God sure was good to some pubescent adolescents.

Late in the summer the Moose fell into a wonderful part-time job. Willie Wennick was an irreverent sort of guy, but he was also a very versatile musician. He played piano, violin, trumpet, drums, and accordion, and he played them well. In July he was asked to provide some music for a dance at Fireside Inn out at Grand Lake, so he asked the Moose and Gerry Seguin if they would like to start a trio. Gerry and the Moose got introduced to music the previous year when Sister Elizabeth Ann started a school band. Gerry loved the drums and talked his dad into buying him a second hand set. For a couple of weeks it looked like his parents were going to split and his brothers and sisters were going to leave home, but Gerry quickly became another Gene Krupa and he started beating out rythmns in a pleasing way.

Sister Lizzy talked the Moose into trying the clarinet. He took a couple of lessons from Bert Shepherd, a full-time, local jazz man. Then he squeaked and squawked at home for several weeks, where Arlie came close to converting his pea shooter into kindling. But by summer time the Moose had the hang of the liquorice stick and decided it was time to compete with Benny Goodman and Woody Herman. So Gerry and Moose met at Willie's house every night for two weeks and worked up a repetoire for Fireside Inn. The debut went well and the Star Dusters were on their way.

In August the Moose was in Howe's Music Store getting some new sheet music and noticed a used sax for sale. It was only twenty five dollars. After minimal discussion, his folks let him invest. The Moose soon learned that this Elkhart horn already had twenty five years on its antique record. It was a C melody that leaked badly. Arlie, who had

Moose and his "pea shooter"

104

to do regular maintenance on his wooden leg, had become a first-rate mechanic at fixing faulty hinges and rebuilding worn out pads. He helped the Moose to get this worn out horn reborn. By September, the Dusters had a new sound and two vocalists. The Moose's voice had finished cracking so he and Gerry started harmonizing. No trio on this, though. Willie's voice was much worse than Louie Armstrong's; in fact it was below zero on every scale.

It was a busy year. School dances on Fridays and frequent wedding gigs on Saturdays. Thank God basketball games were played in midweek, so the Moose did not have to play both ends against the middle. The flipside of this exciting five bucks an hour job was an empty love account, and by the January semester break, rapidly cascading grades. Would this qualify as one of Carl Jung's synchronicitous events?

As far as Arlie and Gen were concerned grades came first. Curly was still available for consultation and assistance, but the Moose wasn't. He still worked before and after school at Penny's, either practiced or played basketball after work, and rehearsed with Willie and Gerry after that. So it boiled down to getting some work done during study hall, and getting Sister Perpetua into the equation. When he told her that he thought the music was helping him "get over girls", and that he was thinking more seriously about the seminary, she quickly assured him that she understood his time bind, and she promised that if he worked hard and consistently in the time available, even his meagre efforts would be generously rewarded. And they were. Soon the other nuns, and even Sister Eugenia, who was super strict, were asking, "Why didn't you tell us that you were going to the seminary?"

Things were grim in 1945. The State Basketball tournament was cancelled again. Louie Kennedy, with a stable full of talent and an undefeated season, ran out of dreams and retired. The war had really heated up and so did the costs. There were a lot of gold stars hanging in neighborhood windows. Frank O'Donnell's plane crashed in the Pacific. Hank LaMarre got killed in the Normandy invasion. Earnie LaCross was lost in the Battle of the Bulge, and Ray Putcummer and Cousin Blackie were captured and sent to a German prison camp. Curly graduated in June as Valedictorian, but left for Fort Hood, Texas the following week. Seminarians Ted LaMarre and Ken Povish, with whom the Moose had been corresponding off and on for two years, were not going to get home for the summer. They had been classified 4 D, one step below morons, and for appearance sake were confined to their seminary cells for the duration.

So what do you do when the world is crashing in on all sides? Can you help make it a better place? Should you make love and not war? Should you offer your life, like Jesus, for the sins of the world? Do you look for a safe place to hide until things settle down? Do you give your relatives and friends a different dream and maybe a positive impetus to hope? With all of those difficult and unanswered questions and more in his head, the Moose went over to the rectory and filled out an application for the seminary. Maybe things would clear up in the future.

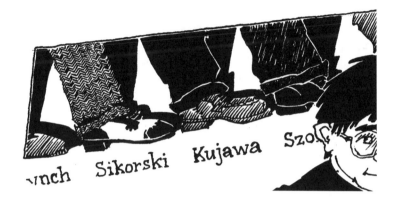

vnch   Sikorski   Kujawa   Szo

CHAPTER TEN
TO SOW OR
NOT TO SOW

One day while browsing with his old tutor Webster, the Moose decided to check out the word "seminary." His two friends and mentors, Ted LaMarre and Ken Povish, were there, so he thought he would investigate what the dictionary had to say about the place. What he learned was a mixture of surprise and confusion. Webster said the word came from the Latin *semen* which means "the fluid produced in the male reproduction organ." It also stated that the word was "related to *serere*, to sow." Immediately the Moose's mind came up with a new concept. Most of the terms that his friends used to refer to what makes males males were gross and unrefined. Why not call it a "sowing machine?" and he did.

That was the only plus information that he picked up. The rest was puzzling. What would you think if the place where your two heroes were in school was called a seedbed or a nursery? What little ideas would pop off in your head when you noted that succeeding words on Webster's pages were seminate and one subtitled artificial insemination. The Moose knew that going to the seminary meant no more girls, that you put your "sowing machine" in cold storage for the duration. So why all this sexual inference?

All the Moose could conclude was that the name was woefully ambiguous.

To go along with the chosen symbolism, it should be pointed out that Alpena was a very fertile spot for growing priests. St. Anne's and St. Bernard's produced one about every six years and St. Mary's was not far behind. When the Moose decided to go to the seminary in 1945, there were about a dozen guys from the territory already in attendance. As he met them he was awed by their smarts, their friendliness, and their masculinity. There wasn't a clunker in the bunch. Ted LaMarre had been invited to play on Catholic U's basketball team when they went to the NIT in the early forties. Chet Pilarksi and Art Mulka were major league calibre baseball players. Jerry Skiba was the best tennis player in town and held several speed skating records in Michigan. When the Moose decided to put his sowing machine in deep freeze, he knew that joining this group of guys was not a totally negative trade-off.

Before getting into seminary life, maybe it might be interesting to take a look at the reasons why the Moose and thousands of other guys took their "sowing machines" out of circulation in the 1940s and 1950s. The Moose does not want to rule out the possibility that God can intervene in life and point a finger at someone as Uncle Sam did and say "I want you in my army." The odds are, however, that God believes in Billy Occam's razor — "Beings are not multiplied without necessity." Vocations are not miracles.

For years Team Vatican has pushed a concept called vocation. The team has its own unique interpretation. In the traditional view, everyone is called by God to do something with his or her life. Basically, you find out what that is by praying, checking out your mental and physical equipment, and by seeking counsel. In the Catholic hierarchy of values there are three primary vocations. Number one, and most important of all, is the priesthood. Number two is the religious life (brothers and nuns). Number three is marriage. Butcher, baker, candlestick maker, and all those trades are secondary vocations.

When Team Vatican requests prayers for vocations and does vocational recruiting it is talking about numbers one and two. Folks don't need any encouragement to do what comes naturally. Number three, marriage, is really a residual category. There is no insistence that people get married nor any heavy recruiting for the married state, but if you don't get married on Vatican terms you're not married, you're shacking. Team Vatican controls all of Boardwalk.

Consider the cards that the Moose had in his deck. For him, the fundamental option in life was heaven or hell. To get to heaven you had to be in the state of sanctifying grace when you died. There were seven aids or sacraments for accomplishing that. Chief among them were Confession and Communion. To go to hell was simple; one unrepented mortal sin was enough. During the Moose's formative years, as you've already read, the only possible mortal sin was an abuse of sex. In terms of serious matter, confessors said consistently that sex was "semper mortale," always mortal. That was the basic emotional environment the kid lived in.

The physical environment was a bit more subtle. The Rev. Louis T. Bouchard was a powerful figure in Alpena. His presence dominated most of the activity in the neighborhood. Everyone stood up when he entered a room. Hats were removed or tipped when he was outside. He was always addressed as Father with a capital "F." His word, even his nod, was law. His brick residence was the nicest in the area. His shiny, ever new, Packard was conspicuous. Even his low-howling, sausage shaped Bassett hound ruled the playground. "Don't mess with Father's dog. He'll eat you."

It did not escape the Moose's attention that when Ted LaMarre and Ken Povish were home on vacation, they sat up next to the altar for Mass dressed like priests. And when the Moose served Mass as an altar boy on those days, he frequently heard Father invite Ted and Ken to join him for breakfast at his house. Giving up better halves for better quarters earned a lot of respect and deference.

Then there was the attention and vested interests of relatives and friends when a guy threw his hat in the seminary ring. Just as the Moose, in his mind, was getting a tighter grip on eternal security and picking up a good measure of social esteem, so were the people who were surrounding him. He was, in some respects, their ticket to upward mobility both spiritually and temporally. TeamVatican was well aware of this social force and carefully nurtured it. They sponsored little groups like the Mothers of Seminarians and Parents of Priests that bumped families up the status ladder in their communities and dioceses.

It is no big secret that in the 1940s and 1950s, Catholics in the U.S. were working class folks. The G.I. Bill put a lot of young Catholic veterans on the mobility escalator of education, but the tough teaching on birth control caused the escalator to creep for them. It wasn't until the late 1950s that Catholics in large numbers started to rise into the middle class. When the Moose went to the seminary in the 1940s there were very, very few middle class kids there. So what is being said here is that in the heyday of vocations the real impetus to join Team Vatican was mixed — most likely social first, and spiritual second.

During that summer of 1945 the Moose didn't play as hard as he wanted to. He had to go to school. Early every morning he stopped at the rectory for a lesson in Latin from Fr. Joe Simon. That summer investment saved him a little pride and a year of work at St. Joe's Seminary in Grand Rapids.

St. Joe's was called a prep seminary. It included four years of high school and two of college. Almost all of the students started in the 9th grade. There were few in-between students

at St. Joe's, 1945

like the Moose and few tutorial or special programs for the in-betweeners. They let you start the year where you thought you belonged, but as soon as they saw that you couldn't cut the mustard, they bumped you down to the level where you could.

Fr. Joe Simon had a good reputation. He had been a recognized Scripture professor at the Josephenum Seminary in Columbus, Ohio, before he retired to Alpena to live with his brother Bill who became pastor of St. Anne in 1944. They had another brother, Fr. Henry, who had been a professor at St. Joe's before he died. So on Fr. Joe's reputation, Msgr. Tommy Noa, the rector, decided that it would be best for the Moose to start at the l0th grade level. The Moose was a little bit irked by this down-scaling of his life. But it only took him about a week to learn that he was lucky that he wasn't bumped down to the 9th grade level. He had all he could do to stay where Tommy put him.

St. Joe's was a German institution and the emphasis was on languages. You did six years of Latin and English, five years of Greek, and two of French or German. There were the regular courses in History, Chemistry, Math, Speech, etc., but the languages got the lion's share of a person's time. Remember that the Moose was a jock, a musician, and a small time con artist at St. Anne's. Latin and Greek were formidable obstacles for a guy who didn't know how to parse an English sentence. Because almost everybody was so super serious at this place, the only people you had a slim chance of conning were a few fellow classmates.

For the first semester, the Moose "consulted" some of these guys on an hourly basis. Larry Kujawa, who sat next to him in study hall, really saved his seminary life. And that's a very euphemistic way of putting it. Larry was a very shrewd dude. Maybe that's why he left at the end of that year.

If you've ever been in the military, a mental institution, or a prison, then you have some idea what a seminary is like. These outfits are called total institutions. That means that when you are in one of them your life is totally, completely, regulated. The bell that rang out instructions from get up to go down was called "vox Dei," the voice of God. If that's what heaven is going to sound like, you can have it.

Life was perpetually observed by authority. The professors, who were priests, did the general surveillance. Their main areas of patrol were the chapel, class rooms, and study hall. To extend the surveillance to every nook and cranny, some fifth and sixth year students were invited to be prefects, a term borrowed from the jargon of the Roman army. Only the better students got these invitations and they generally considered the invitation to be an honor. Rank and file guys often regarded them as stoolies. There were prefects for everything — dorms, refectory, recreation, walks, etc. Sometimes it is truly amazing what a human being will put up with when he or she is on a vision quest.

One interesting and effective means of social control was silence. First there was grand silence. It lasted from communal night prayers at 9:30 p.m. until breakfast at 8:00 a.m. Prefects were there to enforce it. The message was that grand silence was a time for communing with God. Because most of that time was spent in sleep, it is too bad that the authorities didn't fill the students in on Carl Jung's belief that the closest we'll ever get to hearing the voice of God is in our dreams. Petite silence was observed in study hall, the library, and at lunch and dinner. Listening to older students reading hagiography during meals was, at least, boring. Their not reading to us at breakfast was a treat.

The authorities believed that participation in the maintenance of the institution would be beneficial for these young students. Faculty member Wild Bill Hoogterp was in charge of this program. He had students shoveling snow and coal in the winter, working in the yard in the spring, raking leaves in the fall, and building compost piles all year long. The students often referred to Bill's outdoor projects as "digging holes to bury dirt."

There was also a lot of interior work, like scrubbing and waxing floors, cleaning windows and working in the refectory, a fancy name for the dining hall. Ten students would get assigned to a three day hitch. Five did the clean up with carts that they wheeled into the dishwashing room. There another five scraped, sorted, and stacked dishes into trays for the washer that Sister Karen operated. Guys would compete to get close to Sister Karen. She was young and from Saskatoon, Canada. She had a delightful coquettish way about her. When the dishes came out of the washer, the five cleanup guys then redistributed them on the tables. The Moose thinks his senior year record of carrying and distributing a pile of 23 plates without dropping any still stands.

The cleanup, redistribute job was a cherished one. It represented a chance at better food. The oval faculty table was situated at the front of the refectory. They didn't eat the same food as the students and often remnants were left on the platters and in the bowls. After lunch and dinner, the faculty always exited first and led the students to the chapel for a short visit to the Blessed Sacrament. As soon as the last faculty member left, the race was on. The race was between the two nuns who served the faculty and the cleanup crew. The crew had an edge because the nuns were forbidden to come out of their swinging doors on each side of the oval table until all of the students had left, but it wasn't much of an edge because the crew had to fight the traffic flow of students who were anxious to get out of the refectory and into other activities. Of course you never wanted to be seen by the nuns who would report you for thievery, but let it be known that many a growing boy risked and won a spicy chop, a small fillet, or a piece of pie.

Because the institution was deep into Latin, the boss of the place was called the rector. The root of the word means to rule or straighten. It should not come as a surprise to you that even the youngest of the Latin scholars made the logical connection between the words rector and rectum. Sometimes it was true and sometimes it wasn't. As was previously indicated, Tommy Noa, a short, stocky man with penetrating black eyes and a rich baritone voice, was the rector when the Moose arrived at St. Joe's. He was distinguished by his snorting — he must have had a bad sinus condition — and his attention to shoes.

Tommy was a Monsignor, and that office entitled him to wear a red sash around his waist, and red buttons and red piping on his cassock and cape. Every evening when night prayers were completed, Tommy was the first to leave the chapel. As the students exited in two lines and hooked left to ascend the stairs to the third floor where the dorms were, Tommy stood off to the side with his eyes cast down. His principal function at that time was to listen to the apologies of guys who had committed rule misdemeanors that day. Felonies were reserved for the confessional. Generally he just nodded and that was it. Occasionally he would schedule a clarifying hearing. Before he left for a coaching job in the Upper Peninsula at the end of the year, Tommy told the students that while he stood there every night he examined their shoes. He indicated that he could identify every student in the school by the condition of his shoes, and that shoes make men just like clothes do. When the Moose heard that he thought Tommy had missed his true vocation. With such keen observation power, he should have joined the FBI or the CIA.

The faculty represented a pretty good bunch of guys. Jim Moran was the best teacher the Moose ever had in his 26 years of education. Moran taught history and was full of his subject. Class was like being there when it happened. Charlie Salatka was a kid on his first assignment when the Moose was at St. Joe's. He was a maniac on the football field, but got quickly domesticated two years later when he was shipped to Rome to study Canon Law. That stint led to a coaching job in Oklahoma City when he got a little older. Spike McGee was a jubilant literateur, and he even got jocks like the Moose interested in poetry and mythology. John Thome was the choir director and a very good one. The students really needed him. The world said, "wine, women, and song," and seminarians were only allowed the singing.

The school was jammed with a lot of talented and idealistic young men. In all of Moose's life, he's never encountered a group that worked and played so hard. Work included 30 hours of classes over six days, 28 hours of rigidly supervised study and at least another 10-12 hours of private brain bending. Weekly there were 16 hours of scheduled recreational activity and an option for about another 10 hours if you had your studies in line. Chapel exercises consumed about 24 hours a week.

The name of the seminary game was "keep 'em busy." Only on rare occasions did a student leave the grounds with permission. To do so otherwise meant immediate expulsion, as did smoking and drinking. Breaks came at Christmas, Easter, and the summer. When you factor in the necessary eating and sleeping it adds up to total control.

In a class a couple of years ahead of the Moose were two superstars. They alternated at one and two in just about everything they engaged in. They also ended up at the opposite ends of the spectrum. Jimmy Kavanaugh became one of the first priests in the U.S. to resign and go public with his story. He has subsequently written a long list of popular novels and poetry. Eddie Szoka resides in Rome and is Cardinal Archbishop in charge of Team Vatican finances.

Jim and the Moose were both jocks and they banged heads in just about every sport. Ed was not much of a jock, so he and the Moose put their heads together. When the Moose first sat down to eat at St. Joe's he sat directly across from Ed, who was the junior table prefect. Ten guys sat at a two by six foot table. At one end sat a sixth year student prefect whose job it was to slice and fetch Sister Anita's homemade bread. It was the only item that made the food palatable. When apple sauce was served, bread spread with sauce disappeared like there was no tomorrow. Evening study hall was also a noisy place, as you can well imagine if you've ever been into apple sauce in a big way. Ed's job, as a fifth year man, was to carry and pour water. Table prefects had to eat in a hurry because they were on the move three or four times a meal.

Ed recognized immediately that the Moose was a jock, but he did discern a spark of intellect in him. He started recommending biographies and classical literature for the Moose to read in his spare time. He helped him jazz up his writing with apt quotations and sophisticated phrases, urged him to write and memorize poetry, and introduced him to the music of the masters. Ed, by the way, was a very good musician. When he played his accordion people's feet wanted to polka. Trouble was there were no eligible partners.

At that same table there sat another very interesting freshman. He was a shy, slight, redhead from Munger potato country. His name was Leo Lynch. At first Leo never said much. When he did talk, however, you knew that some serious machinery was running underneath that red hair. He quickly became the academic star of the freshman class. He was a star in just about every activity he engaged in — choir, theatre, athletics, charity.

As soon as baseball games got organized it quickly became evident that Leo had special talent. At shortstop he moved with the agility of a cat. His sure hands gobbled up ground balls like a powerful vacuum cleaner and fired them to first at about 95 m.p.h.. His powerful wrists, quick, clear eyes, and quiet confidence made it impossible for a pitcher to throw anything by him. He was always a base runner.

In the summer, Leo played in a Saginaw Valley League for the Munger Spuds. When he returned to the seminary for his junior year he carried a card from a Yankee scout that stated, "If you ever decide to leave the seminary, please give me a call." The Lynch boys knew how to play the game. Brother Jerry made it big with the Pittsburg Pirates. His pinch-hit home-run record is probably still standing. Leo never did baseball in a major way, but he did get to Rome's North American College to try out for a spot on Team Vatican.

The person who really helped the Moose get through the St. Joe program was his best friend, Harry, "the Hat" Sikorski. He was another kid who got turned on to the seminary by Dotts LaMarre. He came as a special student the year after the Moose arrived. The administration didn't mess with him like they did with the Moose. The Hat was an extremely talented individual in every area. In his first year he worked a miracle that will expedite his canonization when he dies. He made a student out of the Moose. The Hat would get so excited about lectures that he had heard and books that he had read, and run such a stimulating commentary on their subject matter, that his friend couldn't help getting excited about the stuff himself. Can you imagine the Moose using his spare time to pour over volumes like *The Thirteenth, the Greatest of Centuries* by Henry Adams, and *The Idea of a University* by John Henry Newman? He did read them and enjoyed them. Gospel truth.

At St. Joe's there was a stimulating ritual that negatively helped move the Moose through the seminary . At the end of the first semester, all 300 students were gathered into the main study hall immediately after lunch. In short order the entire faculty marched in and in their wake came the Bishop in episcopal regalia. The rector came forward and carefully announced the

TO SOW OR NOT TO SOW

procedure for the distribution of report cards. When a student's name was called, he was to stand and listen while the rector read out the grades that he had made that term. Then the student was to come forward, kneel before the Bishop, kiss his ring, and accept his card. This was the day the Moose came the closest to bolting out the front door and hitchhiking home to Alpena.

There he was, a BMOC from St. Anne's high school in Alpena, listening to a threatening rector announce to this throng of competitors that the Moose was the dumbest guy in the sophomore class. And to make matters worse, the throng already knew that it was his second trip through the tenth grade. He managed to stumble up to the front to kneel and kiss the Bishop's ring and get his card. When the Bishop told the Moose that unless he shaped up in the very near future he would be sent home, the Moose almost told the Bishop that it was his turn to do some kissing.

The Moose did manage to get his act together with the help of guys like Larry Kujawa, Harry "the Hat," and Eddie Szoka. When the last report card was read in June of l950, the Moose was in the solid middle. It's been said that that's where real virtue stands.

CHAPTER ELEVEN
THE MEXICAN WAR

In the summer of 1950 the Moose launched into a program that would keep him occupied for the next twenty years. Those who participated in the program affectionately called it the Mexican War.

The Saginaw Valley of Michigan is one of the most fertile farm areas in the United States. Five rivers flow into the Valley. In the late 1930s it became increasingly more difficult to recruit local people to do field work of picking potatoes, tomatoes, fruit, pickles, hoeing, and harvesting sugar beets. Recruiters found willing workers in the Rio Grande Valley of Texas. Little by little, a steady stream of "Tex-Mexs" made their way to Michigan and worked in the Saginaw area during the summer and early fall. Temporary camps sprung up all over the place and soon there were thousands of Mexican-Americans scattered throughout the nineteen counties that made up the Diocese of Saginaw.

In 1945, a newly ordained priest, Fr. James Hickey, gifted with both vision and concern, initiated a diocesan wide program to serve the religious needs of these migrants. Encouraged and aided by his pastor, Msgr. Harold Bolton, and his fellow assistant at St. Joe's parish, Ted LaMarre, Jim sought out Spanish-speaking priests teaching or studying at American universities to come and assist in the program. He also recruited major seminarians to be the sidekicks of the priests so they could do the "two by two" thing that Jesus had recommended. One of the first seminarians recruited was Ken Povish.

The Moose had no business getting into Spanish. He was barely making it in Latin and Greek, and they were highly regarded requirements. But it goes to show you what a young man will do when he has heroes out in front of him. After lunch and dinner at St. Joe's Seminary there was time for about a twenty minute walk around "the path." So twice a day, the Moose and the Hat, who was also a LaMarre fan, walked and quizzed each other on Spanish vocabulary and tried out basic sentences on each other. At first, their accents were guess work and approximation, but things picked up the following year.

Every fall more and more migrant families jumped out of the stream and sought work in Michigan's expanding automobile industry. In the city of Saginaw there emerged a rather large Mexican-American community that settled in the east end near the GM plants and St. Joe's parish. A young lad by the name of Jose Sanchez got the LaMarre bug and entered St. Joe's seminary in 1947. Pedro Chantaca came in 1948, so the Hispanic education of the Hat and the Moose took off both linquistically and culturally. The following year both of them were invited by Fr. Hickey to participate in the summer program. Thanks to Joe and Pete, they became perhaps the best assimilated gringos in the State.

As soon as school was out for the summer, with a bit of trepidation, the Hat and the Moose made their first appearance at the seat of diocesan power. They had heard that the floor around the bishop's throne was very slippery, but Fr. Hickey welcomed them warmly. He gave them basic instructions as to where they were to live, what priests they would be working with, when and where general meetings would take place, and what would be expected of them. Then he took them out to the parking lot and gave them the keys to their vehicles. The Hat got a 1934 Chevy and the Moose a 1936 supercharged Cord. When you've never had a set of wheels to call your own, this was arrival time.

After a little coaxing, they managed to get these antiques in gear, said good bye to their new boss and headed west. It didn't take them long to traverse the thirteen miles between Saginaw and Hemlock. The Hat was assigned to St. Mary's and his host was Fr. Martin I. Kalahar. Ken Povish had spent two summers with Martin I. and told wonderful stories about this delightful Irishman. The Moose had fallen in love with this man before he ever met him. His open, warm welcome convinced the Moose that he had a new friend for life.

With a bit of sadness and anxiety in his heart the Moose headed out M32 for Merrill, another small farm community six miles down the road. When he got to Merrill he found the situation lonelier than the road. His knock on the rectory door awakened Fr. Freddie Ryan from his nap. He lumbered out on the veranda and pointed to a house about a block away. Mrs. Jacobs had a room for him over there. He also indicated that there was a restaurant on the main drag where the Moose could eat. All he had to do was sign the checks and the diocese would take care of them. Then he said, "Good bye." A nice introduction to the Team Vatican locker room.

A couple of days later the Moose learned that clouds do have silver linings. After morning Mass he encountered Lucio

Silva who was Fr. Ryan's "gato" or jack of all trades. From that moment on the Moose had a Mexican "papa" and he became Lucio's and Maria's baby and seventeenth child. They named him "el hijo grandote," the tall son. Lucio and Maria were at most five foot three and their tallest child was five seven. And at this time they were well into their 60s.

The Silva home was a cozy, immaculate place, and the peace was tangible. Louie, Lucio's nickname, had a garden in the back of the house that was a half block long and filled with a great variety of flowers, fruits, and vegetables. He had more than two green thumbs, he had green hands and feet. Maria told the Moose that he could never go to the restaurant again and that he was to come there for all of his meals. Very emphatically both Louie and Maria told him, "aqui esta su casa" — this is your house, and they meant it. They even wanted him to sleep there, but the Moose did not want to offend Mrs. Jacobs, another wonderful person.

Slowly, the Silvas rounded out the Moose's Spanish indoctrination. Soon his speech was peppered with colorful idioms and expressions. His palate also was peppered with exotic and spicy flavors. Louie grew some peppers that he called "cenisas del infierno," ashes from hell, that would "pica y repica," bite coming and going. The Silvas had lived in the area since the early 1930s and were the "patrones" of many other Mexican families who had settled in the area. Louie also knew where all the migrant camps were and regularly visited these places to welcome people and provide for their immediate needs. Needless to say, Louie was the real "pastor" of the area and the Moose was only his "pistolero."

Nicanor Gonzalez was a Mexican Jesuit who came to help fight "The War" that summer. During the school year he taught at the seminary in Montezuma, New Mexico. He lived at St. Mike's in Maple Grove, and celebrated Masses on Sundays for the migrants in Maple Grove, Hemlock, and Merrill. He also came at other times when his services were needed for baptisms, confessions, and marriages. Nicanor was a gentle and cheerful priest. He got even better when Louie was around, which was the case with everybody. Louie had a beautiful way of telling everyone how great they were and how great everybody else was. Even Freddie Ryan was a saint in Louie's eyes; actually, he was just old and tired. It was really Nicanor's and

Moose's job to do what Louie was doing, but unfortunately they believed that their job concentration was in other areas.

The first task of all workers in the Mexican Apostolate was to take a census of the migrants in the area. This was the way to line up the work that had to be done. It should be pointed out that at that time piety was part legalistic and part numerical. One got to heaven by keeping the rules and frequenting the Sacraments. With Louie riding shotgun for him in the old Cord, the Moose was welcomed at all of the camps and given reverence and respect that he had never dreamed of. With Louie's warm and jovial translations, the census work was duck soup.

Within a week Louie and the Moose covered thirty camps and completed the census. They discovered only a few infants that had not yet been baptized, a large number of youngsters who had not made their first Confession and Communion, larger numbers who had not been confirmed, and about fifteen couples who had not been married "in church." Just about all of them did not keep their Sunday Mass obligation. The battle was engaged. For legalistic counters this was a major front that had to be energetically attacked. The growing season allowed only an eight week campaign.

At the time of the census, Louie passed out flyers indicating the place and time for Confessions and Sunday Mass. That was the first salvation salvo and it was an effective one. Over twenty families showed up for Mass the following Sunday and Nicanor was pleased. That was twice as many as showed up in Maple Grove and Hemlock. When Louie opened up a hall closet with food and clothing for needy people after Mass, Nicanor, also, began to understand who the real "pastor" of this place was.

Two other opportunities were laid out for the migrant families at the census taking visit. One was the Guadalupe Clinic at St. Joe's in Saginaw. Because none of the migrants and a large portion of the Mexican-American residents had health insurance, Monsignor Bolton and his assistants organized a clinic to meet these problems. A group of nuns with medical training were enlisted to staff the clinic. Interns and residents from the three local hospitals volunteered their time four days a week. Hundreds of migrants poured through the clinic every summer.

A second need of both residents and migrants addressed at St. Joe's was that of finances. Next to the clinic a credit union was set up where people could deposit their meagre savings and earn a little interest. At the same time their savings could become the cash that brothers and sisters needed to meet immediate financial needs . Interest costs were manageable and rebates were often paid at the end of the year. Hundreds of families were able to fend off poverty through this union of like-minded and caring people. Several young Hispanics from this institution went on to spread the credit union movement to Latin America. That St. Joe credit union has grown and merged a half dozen times over the years, and today is the largest and most efficiently run community federal credit union in the United States.

Prior to that first Sunday Mass in Merrill, the Moose had spent several days planning his strategy and drawing his maps. His goal was to try and hit all of the camps where there were children in need of Sacraments at least twice a week. He wanted to lay out this scheme to the families that came to Mass. This would not be easy. Child labor laws were rarely enforced in agriculture and even little children could pull weeds from among the sugar beets. Older children could easily wield a hoe. Survival for migrants was a family endeavor. To convince parents to leave children at a camp for catechism lessons and an older child to supervise them, was not an easy order, yet with Louie's encouragement, many of them did.

By picking up a few children at smaller camps and transporting them to a central location, the Moose was able to arrange a catechism session a day at ten camps on a bi-weekly schedule. He used his evenings to prepare older children for Confirmation and did paper work for those couples who were able and willing to get their marriage validated.

Teaching catechism, at first, was very taxing. The Moose's fluency in Spanish still left a lot to be desired, especially in this area of catechism. He neither knew if catechisms were available in Spanish nor where to get one if they were. So he started writing simple stories about God, creation, and Jesus that he could read to the children, and basic questions that he could utilize to see if the children were getting the points. Because his Spanish was like that of a little child, the technique worked wonderfully. He also learned that gestures and symbols were very effective means of communicating with children. A smile still comes to his face and life flows into his right arm and fingers when he thinks of the answer to the question, where is God? (A finger to the sky) Esta en el cielo; (A finger to the ground) Esta en la tierra; (A big wide circle) Y esta en todo logar. The kids loved these active kinds of responses, and the Moose started thinking seriously about new ways to teach religion.

The most effective part of the Moose's teaching had nothing per se to do with religion. He carried a bat and ball in his car all the time. After a catechism lesson, he played ball with the kids for at least an hour. In the evenings he brought along a 16 mm projector and old Laurel and Hardy movies. The slapstick of Gordo y Flaco was a source of great relaxation for people who had worked ten to twelve hours in the hot fields.

Those evening visits were delightful and educational times. Slowly, the Moose's Spanish ears got tuned in. The migrants didn't speak Spanish like the books indicated. It was spiced and blended with a lot of beautifully inflected English. The seminarians called it "ensalada chopiada," chopped salad. For instance, one evening a man was describing the unfortunate behavior of his son, "Mi hijo backio mi carro y lo wreckio." The only Spanish word in that sentence is *hijo*, son. Another lady described their planned evening recreation, "Vamos a watchear TV."

On another very hot evening the Moose heard a charming "ensalada chopiada" conversation between two old señores. They were seated under a tree with their knees pulled up and their sombreros pulled down over their foreheads. One of them lifted his sombrero a little and said, "Ya know, Pedro, when I'm a leeve in Mehico, I'm a raise bools. Beeg toros fuertes (strong bulls). An von day I'm a sheep cinco (five) torros a la toreo (bullring) in Guadalajara. An da bool fighters, da toreadores, dey lika mi bools, cus dey go so derechito (straight) por la moleta." When Pedro just nodded, Enrique kept on going with his story, "sheeping bools" to Cuernavaca, Morelia, and Guanajuato. Finally, Pedro lifted his sombrero and replied, "Ya know vat, Enrique? I'm a tink youse a da beegest bool shipper en todo el universo."

Before the migrants departed at the end of July, the Moose had prepared 24 kids for their First Confession and

Communion, 26 for Confirmation, and helped get five marriages validated. In terms of numbers, if that's of any import, it wasn't a bad campaign. In terms of cross-cultural growth, broad human experience and friendship, it was a super colossal summer.

One of the highlights of each week was dinner with the Hat and Fr. Kalahar on Sundays. Martin I. was always amiable and had a million stories to tell. One interesting fact that the Moose learned was that St. Mary's Hemlock was probably the only Catholic parish in the country that ever gave money back to the parishioners. In Martin's early years as pastor some parishioners urged him to build a new church. He didn't think the people could do it, so he made a deal with them. He suggested a total they should reach at the end of the year and if they made it they would go ahead with plans. If they didn't he would give them their money back. As he had predicted they didn't meet the goal and he mailed them back their money as he had promised. People, including the Bishop, were stunned.

Martin I. was often in hot water with the red and purple people at the chancery office. One big reason was his refusal to accept the Church's negative stance on birth control. He didn't contradict the Head Coach in the pulpit, but he did preach about the primacy of the individual conscience, and urged people to make up their own minds. Martin I. was no dummy. He had been educated at Innsbruck in Austria and was not one who caved in to authoritarian statements. His warm relationships with people, his down to earth, story filled sermons, and his intellectual honesty were traits that deeply impressed the Moose.

Another memorable experience that the Moose had that summer was getting to know the Emiliano Guerrero family. Some years earlier the family had jumped out of the migrant stream and settled in Saginaw. But every summer, Mrs. Guerrero and a large number of the children moved out to Merrill to supplement Emiliano's income by hoeing sugar beets. The Moose met the family at Siete Casitas, seven little houses. The kids were all bilingual so they helped the Moose with his Spanish when he came for catechism lessons, fed him lunch, listened patiently to his heavy stories, and made him feel important. Today all of those kids are married and have their own grandchildren in abundance.

Fr. Bob and (directly to his left) his Mexican "papa," Lucio Silva, 1963

Forty five years later, the Moose's Adam's apple plugs his throat when he visits these folks— the Guerreros, the Silvas, the Arciniegas, the Ramirezes, and many, many more. He wants to shout and cheer when he observes how they have climbed the long and hard road of poverty and prejudice and become such generous contributors to the American way. The Moose just wishes that more gringos either had or would search for the opportunity to know Chicanos like them. They have been lacing our society with glory for untold years and someone should be telling their story in capital letters.

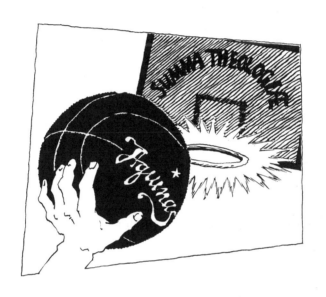

Chapter Twelve
MAKING A
MAJOR MOVE

Moving on to the major seminary was a big deal. It was called major, no doubt, because this was the time, junior year, when most college students selected a particular concentration of study, like biology or psychology. For seminarians it was philosophy, the love of wisdom. The big deal was that now the seminarian became a semiofficial member of Team Vatican. He was put on the payroll to the extent that the Coach of his diocese picked up the tab for his education. In reality it was just a long term loan. There were two other items that completed the big deal package — a private room and clerical garb.

In the 1950s there were a lot of major seminaries around and they were full. Lower peninsula Michigan guys were sent to places like Baltimore, Cincinnati, Washington D.C., Montreal, and Detroit. A few of the brainy ones who were deemed good coaching material were sent to Rome. Others with a particular scholarly bent were sent to places like Innsbruck and Louvain.

A fascinating amount of lore has arisen around this seminary appointment business. The official teaching was that a good deal of praying went into the process so that the Holy Spirit would select the right people for the right places. That's a nice thought. When one looks at reality, however, it's quite evident that the Holy Spirit gets a short and well-edited list of eligibles for selection to the top spots. In other words, the Spirit is not given a whole lot of freedom.

There was, and probably still is, a fatherly and affectionate relationship between pastors, Bishops and "their boys," the ones they foster, promote, and push through the seminary. Now the Moose doesn't intend to insinuate what might be going through your mind when you see that phrase, "their boys." You're on your own in that judgment. Because of the law of celibacy priests are not supposed to have children, but it's not easy to put down parental sentiments, nor the urge to replicate yourself in one way or another. A lot of that has gone on in the American church, and quite likely in the universal church.

The first Catholics to arrive in the U.S. in large numbers were the Irish. They brought their own clergy with them as did the Italians, the Poles, and the Germans who followed in short order. But the Irish, who primarily settled in cities, had the advantages of numbers, the English language as their native tongue, and a closer familiarity with the dominant culture. So they quickly came to dominate the politics of the American church and maintained that dominance into recent decades; they did that by controlling episcopal appointments.

The first stage in that process was to start grooming candidates for the episcopacy in their final seminary years. Early Americans priests got their training in Europe. Quickly, however, seminaries were started in Baltimore, Bardstown, New York and Boston. But with headquarters in Rome, the Church soon decided that students who showed signs of being "episcopal timber" should be socialized — catch the spirit, learn the culture, make the ties at the Vatican. So in the mid l800s the North American College, a seminary for future bishops, was built in Rome.

As the American church grew, so did competition for slots at the North American. The bishops made the rules and it was only natural that the dioceses which contributed the most dollars to the institution got the most slots. The great majority of bishops were Irish, so the great majority of students were? One guess. And later the great majority of American bishops were? Same answer will do.

Now this isn't sour grapes. Students like the Moose who knew early on that they were not episcopal timber and had no desire to cross the pond and grapple with another culture, things were tough enough at home, voiced a little witticism about their peers who were selected for Rome. They referred to the role or mission of these students as "going to Rome to piss in the Tiber." The origin and the meaning of the expression is uncertain. Most of those destined to be homebodies smiled and laughed at the expression because it sounded a little vulgar and risque. A few caught the underlying symbolism. These guys were going to Rome to mark their territory.

After World War II, the non-Irish bishops, a very small group from very small dioceses, began to flex their muscles and insisted that they get slots in Rome for "their boys." When Stephen Woznicki got promoted from auxiliary bishop of Detroit to the ordinary of Saginaw, he didn't wait very long to start promoting "his boys." So in the 1950s and 1960s a significant number of outstandingly well qualified "skis" and "aks" got shipped across the pond.

Sadly, for Steve's sake, only one of his boys eventually won a ring and a crozier. Maybe the rest forgot to do their thing in the Tiber. Or maybe they got shut out in the second round.

Regularly the Apostolic Delegate in Washington requests brief slates of "episcopabile" from the Bishops of the U.S. so that when a vacancy occurs or there is a need to increase the ranks of the hierarchy suitable candidates will be on deck. The screening process is serious business. Letters are sent to associates and neighbors of the priests recommended. Absolute confidentiality is demanded before, during, and after the investigation. A strong insinuation of eternal consequences for any violation of the secrecy goes with the letter.

The Delegate then forwards his recommendations to Rome where the Pope, supposedly, is the final decision maker. The amount of filtering that takes place between the investigating letters and the Pope's decision is unknown. Certainly the Delegate has friends both in the U.S. hierarchy and in Rome, as well as close connections with powerful lay folks, and you couldn't blame these individuals for throwing their weight around, could you? That's how the game is played.

Certainly with the advent of John Paul II, the ethnicity of the American hierarchy has changed. Stephen Woznicki must be smiling contentedly wherever he is. Diversification is a wonderful thing, but ethnicity, it should be pointed out, has a lot to do with political and philosophical stance. It's no big secret that there are a lot of folks in the world who aren't happy with John Paul's "boys," including a lot of clerics who have written negative recommendations to their Apostolic Delegate. "Whatever happened to that talk about collegiality?" is a frequently and universally asked question today.

Now back to the Moose's first official assignment. He wasn't envious of classmates Gradowski and Michalski who got early appointments to Rome. They were first class people and top flight students. The Moose's secret hope was that he would get sent to Detroit. His two heroes, LaMarre and Povish, had gone there. Also, the Detroit school had a college basketball team and played outside competition. Despite the heroic efforts of Eddie Szoka and Harry the Hat, the jock genes in the Moose remained dominant. A July letter from the Saginaw Coach, Stephen Woznicki, confirmed his hope. Sacred Heart Seminary in Detroit would be his new home for two years.

When the Moose walked into his assigned, second floor room in early September he thought he was in heaven. He was 21 years old and this little 10 x 8 cell was his first bit of private

Sacred Heart Seminary

space ever. There was a single bed, a desk with a double book shelf, a chair on wheels, a closet, and a small Gothic window that looked out on Chicago Boulevard. Even the common bathroom was right next door.

The first item on the agenda that day was orientation in the chapel at 3:00. Philosophers, as they were officially dubbed, were to attend in their appropriate attire. That meant cassock and Roman collar. The Moose was both proud and excited when he put on his new white, collarless, shirt with French cuffs. He carefully slid a little gold stud into the front and back of the shirt and then snapped on the Roman collar. And finally, the official uniform, the cassock. The recommended procedure for garbing oneself was to first kiss the back of the neck of this garment. Its sacred purpose was to both identify a man as one of God's chosen ministers and remind him that he was supposed to be "dead to the world." Not bombed out of his head as that phrase sometimes indicates, but thoroughly separated from wine, women, song, and all those other attractive things.

Anyway, the Moose kissed his neatly pressed cassock, slipped in both of his arms, and then fastened six feet of buttons that ran from his collar to the floor. From now on this was to be his attire at all times except for sleep and recreation. What an incredible arrival time for a working class kid from Alpena!

During the orientation ceremony, the Moose noticed that he was perspiring quite freely and that his neck was becoming seriously irritated. When he later went to the recreation room of St. Thomas hall where the philosophers lived, he noted that the second year guys immediately pulled off their cassocks and collars. Underneath they wore only raunchy T shirts and shorts. He also observed that their cassocks were made of cotton. His was a woolen, hand-me-down from an ex-seminarian in Alpena. Needless to say, he quickly learned where to purchase a light weight cassock, and never again wore a monkey shirt.

Along with the garb and the private room, there was another exception that differentiated the major from the prep seminary. That was study. The academic time table remained pretty much the same, but philosophers were freed from rigid study supervision. They were en-

wearing a cassock, 1950

couraged to do more than before, but now in their room or in the library.

Like in the minor seminary, philosophers took courses in English, history, homiletics, and other basic subjects, but now the concentration was on philosophy and now was the time to utilize the six years of Latin studies they had endured in the minor seminary. Text books, lectures, questions, responses, papers, and exams all were in Latin. With all deliberate speed a quick history of philosophy was reviewed. All old and young philosophers, with the exception of Aristotle, were resurrected and reinterred with only brief obituaries, "Nice try but no thanks." In about a week, Bubbles Link, the main professor, got to Thomas Aquinas, a disciple of Aristotle, and remained Thomistic in his presentations for the next two years.

Bubbles was always a pleasant and jovial person, but not a very good teacher. He read the text to the students word for word. He would take questions and would respond to them, but the fundamental task of the students was to memorize the book. To make things lighter for himself, and probably to create the illusion that he was not just reading the book, Bubbles tore the binding from his text, and came to class with only one folio at a time in a manila folder.

One mental faculty that was highly developed in students at St. Joe's in Grand Rapids, was memory. Conjugating Latin and Greek verbs was a daily class exercise. The memorization of classical authors like Homer and Virgil were weekly assignments. The students didn't always know the whys and wherefores of their recitations, but they were pros at getting it down cold. So Bubbles' style of teaching fit their mode of learning. When first semester grades came out, five of the seven A's that were given out to the class of 60 were collected by St. Joe grads, and guess who was one of them? It was probably one of the worst things that ever happened to the Moose's academic career. He can still rattle off a lot of philosophical definitions, but he knows very little about philosophy.

Because class was not very challenging, for a little variety, Harry the Hat cooked up a little table game with a few of his friends. It was a sing for your supper deal. In order to eat at dinner time, the participants had to recite twelve new lines of poetry. It was a blast and no one ever went hungry. Memorization continued to get easier with practice and guys could pick up twelve new lines at a glance. In short order, the Hat and his crew could rattle off complete versions of the "Hound of Heaven," "The Highwayman," "The Cremation of Sam McGee," "Gungha Din," and many others.

At Sacred Heart, the Moose encountered a whole warehouse full of new buddies. Three of them have become lifelong friends. Dan Walsh was without question the best-liked person in the institution. He was a class AAA nice guy, and he didn't come in last. His motto was "be more concerned about other people than you are about yourself." Dan, also, was probably the brightest guy in the school. Life for him was an exhilarating game. He endlessly created and organized fun activities — studying, singing songs, shooting pool, or playing football in deep snow. He learned everybody's needs and quietly met them whenever he could.

In the same league, but in a different mode, was Tom Gumbleton. His great love was ice hockey, and he has skated through life like it was a hockey game. His style was and is shrewd offense. At Sacred Heart, he attacked whatever was on

The old quartet: Dick, Rock, Dan, and Tom, 1991

the agenda whether it was study, prayer, play, or food. Even walking down the hall with him demanded careful attention. In a careless moment you could become a part of the wall. Body checking was one of his multiple skills.

In the 1960s Tom became the youngest bishop in the United States. Today he is probably the best known bishop in the world next to the Pope. Theologically and philosophically, however, he really isn't next to the Pope. He's at the other extreme. The people who know of Tom are on both sides of the key religious issues of the day. Half hate him and half love him. Those who really know him and not of him, will quickly tell you that he walks like Mother Theresa did, only a little bit to the left.

As of late, the hockey game of life is getting more difficult for Tom. He's just about the only offensive player on the Vatican hockey team. The rest are all goalies. As a result Tom gets beat up a lot. Almost all games end up in shutouts. Playing alone, Tom hardly ever gets the puck beyond the blue line. His own net is so tightly packed with goalies that it's almost impossible for opponents to slide a puck by them. Shutouts, however, don't draw crowds. Ties are like kissing your sister, and even that is sometimes suspect in their league.

The third angle in the Moose's new triangle of friends was an enigma to most people. It was difficult to get a handle on the contrasts in Dick Lauinger's life. He was not a brilliant phi-

Basketball team at Sacred Heart,1951: The Moose, #7; The Hat, #3; and Dan Walsh, #15

losopher. At least not in Latin. His questions in class often seemed off the wall, like diversion or sabotage. He was a dedicated weight-lifter and his physique was impressive. When he just stood up he inspired caution in people. They knew that in an instant he could pin you to the floor or the ceiling. On the other hand he spoke with a marked gentleness and wore a perpetual smile. His mischievous blue eyes were always dancing. He knew more about art and music than anyone else in the school, and he practically read the library dry. He was the best orator in the class. Classmates called him the Geek because he was so delightfully different. He's still at it. Guess what he's doing in his retirement? Just for the heaven of it, he's driving a school bus every day, trying to make life cheerful for the little guys. What a treasure!

The gym at Sacred Heart was more than regulation. The one at St. Joe's Seminary was in the basement with only a fifteen foot ceiling. Three of the walls were in-bounds half way up. The light bricks seven feet up from the floor marked the out-of-bounds area. Four guys on a team were too many. But Sacred Heart? Wow! Three intramural games could be played simultaneously. The Moose prayed in there more than he did in the chapel and he definitely spent more time in the gym.

At Sacred Heart, all the philosophers were prefects. Some did study halls, some did dorms, some did the refectory, and some did recreation. You know where the Moose did his prefecting. Perfecting his game in the gym. There was an hour rec period every evening after dinner. Some of the high school kids would go into the gym to shoot around. The Moose's job was to turn the lights on, get out a few balls, and keep heated-up kids from slaying each other. When the bell rang, he shooed everyone out except the Hat. While the kids were present the Moose and the Hat usually got a side basket for themselves to practice their shots. When the kids left, Moose and Hat remained and did full court run-outs and new moves, like in flight 360s to the basket from the free throw line.

Joe Schmo, short for Szymaszek, a faculty member, was assigned to coach both the high school and college teams. He was a super guy, but he didn't have a real love for the game. He was pleased when the Moose and the Hat showed up for try-outs. When the season opened they were both on the college starting five. Soon after the high school season started, Joe asked the Moose if he would be his assistant coach. What a deal! Midway through the season Joe stopped coming. "Call me if you need me," was his only directive. So for the rest of that year and the next the Moose was practically full time into basketball. He and the Hat even wrote a book on basketball for Father Joe. It was made up of conditioning and warm-up exercises, various types of defenses and offenses, and motivational theories. It was illustrated with diagrams and plugged with sage quotations from the old war horses of the game.

What more could a young man want? A private room. Elevated status and upward mobility. Outstanding buddies. An unintrusive academic program, and a chance to get submerged in his favorite recreational activity. The two year stay at Sacred Heart was pure, wonderful, breeze time. The Moose can still smell that healthy aroma of the locker room, or is it the odor that emanated from his closet in St. Thomas hall? He sure wore a lot of raunchy stuff under his cassock while he was there.

CHAPTER THIRTEEN
THE REAL
PRIEST FACTORY

In the late 1940s, Detroit's Cardinal Mooney convinced the other bishops of the Michigan province that they needed their own school of Theology. The number of Catholics in the city of Detroit alone had reached a million. New parishes were springing up all over the place. Vocations to the religious life and the priesthood were on an increase. Lay Catholics were starting to move into the middle class. To all indications Team Vatican was moving into the Golden Age.

Ground was secured in Plymouth and a new institution of Umbrian design was constructed in short order. It was a posh place by seminary standards. Each student not only had his own spacious room but also his own private bath. There was a small lake on the property and a lot of rolling acreage, so a nine hole golf course was put in to convert duffers into pros. To make this a break-even enterprise, students had to contribute 35 hours of labor annually in order to play. The Moose never got to be much of a golfer, but he rapidly became a scratch weed-eater.

In September of 1952 the Moose and his classmates moved out to Plymouth on the last leg of their journey to the priesthood. Theirs was the largest class in history, and they filled St. John's to capacity. The mood was serious. The classical studies at St. Joe's and the philosophy at Sacred Heart were simply prep courses for the study of Sacred Theology. They provided the students with mental tools to deal with the "real issues" of life.

The priests in charge at St. John's were called Sulpicians. They had their origins in France and were big contributors to the spread of the Catholic Church in the U.S. Basically, they were diocesan priests who believed they had a vocation to train young men for the priesthood. All of them were scholarly men who had done further graduate work in some area of theology. The rector was a smiling, feisty Irishman from California named Lyman Fenn. The Moose thought that he was a good double for the movie star Barry Fitzgerald. Lymie was a no-nonsense professor and administrator. When you dealt with him you did it straight up with not the slightest whiff of gaminess.

John McManus was one of the Moose's favorite professors. He ran the library and taught Liturgy. His long suit was warmth and understanding. He guided the Moose through all kinds of doubts and worries and did something that no one had ever done before. Mac convinced the Moose that he was a likeable person in and of himself, and that he didn't have to become someone else in order to be accepted. For years he had heard the message, why can't you be more like Curly, the kid next door, or down the street? Mac's counsel was very liberating.

Another major gift that Mac gave the Moose was the advice to not endlessly replay events in his life and to forgive himself for mistakes. After a basketball game, for example, most guys would shower, go their room to study a bit, and then go to bed. Not the Moose. He would shower, try to study, and then when the lights went out, sneak back to the gym to walk through the entire game and scold himself for all the mistakes he had made. Naturally enough, the Moose developed a severe case of colitis that dogged him for four years. His weight went from l85 to 120 and he looked like a character from an El Greco painting.

In gratitude the Moose has passed on Mac's advice to just about everyone he meets. Please help yourself to as much as you want if you need some. It's really wonderful to know that you are unique and that you don't have to be in competition with anyone. As a matter of fact, it's downright impossible for you to be anyone else. Just for the heaven of it, why don't you read those last couple of sentences again, and if you don't need that bit of Mac wisdom for yourself, pass it on to everyone you meet.

Mac also used to needle the Moose about his lack of scholarship. As head librarian he used to check the library cards to see where his books were navigating. Remember that bit of verse, "There is no frigate like a book to take us lands away?" When Moose was in his final year at St. John's, Mac discovered that the Moose was the only guy in the whole institution whose card remained blank for four years. The Latin text books were just about all the Moose could handle. His theory was that if he needed further amplification of a topic at the present time, he would probably need it again in the future. So he bought the book and forgot about the library.

Another professor whom everyone loved at St. John's was Jack Castellot. He was a blonde, handsome priest who taught Scripture. He was always impeccably dressed and heavily starched French cuffs always extended two inches out of his cassock sleeves. As he lectured, he frequently wiggled his hands and adjusted the cuffs. Guys often imitated him and joked that his wrist joints came loose and he had to screw his hands back into his arms.

Students looked forward to Jack's afternoon lectures. Most of them had read the entire Bible on their own at least five or six times. If you had approached any of them in private, and they were in an honest frame of mind, the great majority of students would have told you that there was much about the Bible that they did not understand. To be truthful about it, because they had read the Bible seriously and frequently, they had more questions, suspicions, and doubts than other people.

Four days a week and for four years Jack cheerfully and enthusiastically helped students put the Bible into the contexts of literature, history, linguistics, and culture. He quickly pointed out that the Bible was not a book but a small library. It was put together over a long period of time, written by a great variety of people from different places and backgrounds and in different languages. Some sections were added and others subtracted over the centuries.

Jack answered a lot of thorny questions when he pointed out that the library was never intended to teach science, and that the best scholars in the world are still divided on what is meant by inspiration and how it happened. Those scholars are still arguing about which books belong in the library, and they dance very cautiously around the question of how we know that only these books were inspired by God.

Probably the best advice that Jack gave to the Moose and his colleagues was that the library is a collection of short stories that record the history of God's interaction with a particular people. Each story stresses certain aspects of this salvation history. These points are what readers should be looking for. The terse phrases that preachers tend to beat people over the head with are generally not the intended points of the authors. Jack encouraged the students to browse freely in this library and enjoy the beauty of imagination and language that it contained. The Moose would like to pass that encouragement on to you. He would also urge you to be open and inquisitive about what current scholars are discovering. God did not stop talking when the last book in the library was printed.

Class time at St. John's was scheduled with the same ferocious intensity as it was at St. Joe's and Sacred Heart. The students didn't know anything else, so no one complained. The texts and lectures were in Latin, as were papers and exams. What made all of this palatable was the fact that students were getting into what they thought they had to know in order to be priests. Most of them studied eagerly and earnestly. This was crunch time. Dogmatic and moral theology along with Scripture and Canon Law were mainline courses. Biblical Greek and Hebrew, Church History, Patristics, Liturgy and Homiletics all got lesser but, nonetheless, serious attention. Years later the Moose learned that he had accumulated 175 hours of graduate credit in his years at St. John's, enough for two and a half Ph.D's.

An idealistic kid like the Moose often got overwhelmed with what he was expected to know. His understanding of religion was accumulated by a series of questions and answers proven and established by Scripture, Tradition, and Reason. A priest, in his mind, had to be a walking answer machine. He imagined that there were hordes of people out there who were just dying to ask him questions and listen to his answers. He had developed a pretty good memory, but when he looked at all the articles of faith in Dogma, the hair splitting arguments in Moral, the refined distinctions of Canon Law, and the intricacies of Scripture, he knew that he would never master it all. He realized that there were two kinds of knowledge, knowing it yourself and knowing where to find it. So he underlined just about everything in his books and kept copious notes of lectures and group study sessions.

The Moose also realized that he would not be able to carry all of this recorded and catalogued knowledge with him all the time, like on airplanes and trains, walking down the street, and visiting in peoples' homes. So he did commit to memory some basic stuff that he knew for certain people would inquire about. Other stuff, like the five proofs for the existence of God, he wrote down on paper in very small print and carried in his billfold.

To this day, over forty years later, no one has ever asked him for answers to those questions. The moral to that story is don't do today what you can put off until tomorrow. Life rarely evolves the way you think it will, or as Fr. Mac used to tell the Moose, "Live your life in little chunks. Living in the past or in the future is like trying to go downtown in a rocking chair. Lots of action but no mobility." Now just in case you don't trust the logic in those statements and you need some proof from Scripture and tradition, try these on for size. "Sufficient for the day is the evil thereof." (Jesus) and "Don't be like a dog that goes back to its vomit." (Peter).

There were a lot of fun times at St. John's. There were the usual rec times for intramural football, baseball, and basketball. With no gym it was like back to Carr's field in Alpena for the Moose. His early training there equipped him for the mud and the slush encounters. Hockey was played on the lake in the winter time and in the spring and fall there was golf. Alums would return frequently for visits and golf. On sunny days, when a lot of shiny alum cars circled the front drive, old Lymie would look out from his second floor screened in porch and remark, "These boys were sent out into the world to do good, and they did well."

Every year in May, Lymie would read the student body a papal bull entitled *Quam Ingens*. It means "How Powerful." This definitely was not a bull in the colloquial sense. It was a Team Vatican statement on the importance and seriousness of celibacy. It treated the subject in every imaginable way. The reading was primarily directed at the third year guys who were getting ready "to take the sub." This was not a scary underwater boat ride, but it was close. Sub stood for the subdeaconate, the first of the major orders.

Holy Orders is one of the either/or Sacraments. Since the twelfth century, when celibacy was fully mandated by Team Vatican, a person could only receive six Sacraments. Orders and Matrimony precluded each other. Statistically but not officially, things have changed today. Well over half of the priests under 60 in the U.S. are married. A large number have received both Sacraments, but with the stipulation that they not exercise their priesthood except in emergencies.

The meaning of Holy Orders is under intense discussion today. For many centuries it was thought that orders referred to the ascending line of offices or positions that the clergy occupied from acolyte to bishop. A more recent interpretation that makes good sense to the Moose, at least, is that orders are the directives or commands of service that some individuals are given by the people. That's the way things seemed to have worked in the early Christian community described in the Acts. The distinction might seem inconsequential, but the behavioral results are monumental. If an order is a position that you occupy, then you are the boss. But if an order is something you are asked to do, then you are a servant. And that's what Jesus "ordered" his followers to be, holy servants.

When the Moose was at St. John's, holy orders were given by a coach or bishop. Before any orders were given, however, a man had to become an official member of Team Vatican. Initiations have taken many forms over the years. Some Native Americans had to run the gauntlet. The Hebrews cropped "sowing machines," and Team Vatican cropped hair. The rite was called "tonsure." When one completed this ceremony he became a cleric, or a member of a different social class called the clergy. Now whether this new class was a part of the original revelation or not, or whether it was a bonus or an onus for Jesus' message, only history can tell.

Somewhere near the end of his second year at St. John's the Moose had his hair clipped in five places — front, back, each side, and the middle. In the old days, guys had their whole heads shaved with the exception of a thin ring around their head. You've no doubt seen pictures of monks with these cool hair-does. Of course they've been well upstaged by modern hair designers. With the clipping by Bishop Donnelly and the signing of a contract the Moose became incardinated to the diocese of Saginaw. The word meant that the Moose was "hinged" to the bishop of Saginaw and his successors. Canon Law said "There must be no headless clerics floating around." All of them had to be hinged somewhere before they could swing. To function outside of one's diocese a cleric had to show his incardination ID. It was a means of control and accountability.

On the following day, the Moose and his classmates, now under full contract to Team Vatican, got their first orders. They were called minor and that made good sense because the orders were meaningless. An acolyte is an altar boy. A lector is a reader. A porter is a doorman. (Three activities that the Moose had been engaged in for years.) An exorcist drives out devils, although the coach forbade the use of this power except with his very special permission. The ceremony was brief. The newly clipped cleric knelt before the coach who presented him with a candle, a book, and some holy oil and water. He then put his hand on his head and said a few Latin prayers. When that was done, the Moose was led to a door in the sacristy that he opened and closed. This was the symbol of the porter.

The Moose and his classmates started to get antsy in their third year of theology. The bull *Quam Ingens* was read for them in particular this time. They were no longer on the sidelines cheering the toreadores or teasing the bull like the picadores. They were in the ring alone with the bull. When the final days of the school year arrived, the Moose and his buddy Dan Walsh did something that only a few people did. They called time-out. Independently of each other they decided they needed more time to decide whether they wanted to wear tin pants for the rest of their lives. That's the way seminarians referred to celibacy.

The Moose went up to Saginaw to work with migrant workers that June and July. In August he went home to Alpena to sort out this critical issue. Believe it or not, it was Big Zil's niece who pushed him back into the ring. Florence Kowalski's son Fuzzy was in the seminary at the time, and one morning after Mass he invited the Moose home for breakfast. Like Zil, Florence was a strong individual. She had a wonderful sense of humor and a directness in her approach to life. While discussing the Moose's quandary, she stopped him in mid-sentence and said, "After Chet and I decided to get married, we fought like cats and dogs for six months. After we took the step the problems all went away. I think you just ought to go ahead and do it." And he did.

When he got back to St. John's in Sept. Dan had also returned and was resolved to put on "the tin pants." School started with a retreat, and at the end of it their classmates would receive the second major order, the deaconate. Dan and the Moose would get a double dose, the sub-deaconate and the deaconate. On Friday evening after dinner they went through the rehearsal with their classmates and retired to their rooms. When Dan got to his room, he said "bull" like it was meant to be said and left for home.

The next morning, quite upset by the absence of his friend Dan, the Moose cranked up some nerve, entered the ring, and took the bull by the horns. By this gesture he sentenced his Keller-Martin genes to solitary confinement for life.

THE REAL PRIEST FACTORY

The fourth year of theology was filled with highs and lows. With the deaconate came some new privileges. Deacons got to wear an over-the-shoulder stole. They were allowed to preach. Also, it was permissible for them to baptize and distribute communion when there was a need. Finally, they could be the left or right hand man for a priest at a solemn high Mass. They were simply glorified altar boys.

Preaching is what they did the most. First of all, they practiced on their fellow students. For summer homework, all third and fourth year students were assigned a sermon topic. When they got back to school in the Fall, four students a day, two at lunch and two at dinner, gave their summer creations to faculty and fellow students. The Moose had a couple of very interesting topics. In his third year his topic was, "Why do Catholics Reverence the Sacred Heart of Jesus." His fourth year topic was even more exhilarating, "The Circumincession in the Holy Trinity." It would be interesting to do a study to see how many seminarians developed stomach disorders while they were incarcerated.

The Moose gave one real sermon while at St. John's. Across the road from the seminary was Dehoco, an abbreviation for a woman's prison, the Detroit Home of Corrections. Every Sunday one of the professors celebrated Mass there for any of the women who wanted to attend. There were some real tough ladies locked up at Dehoco. To get the students accustomed to front line work, the priest took along one of the deacons to preach. The Moose got a red hot topic for his first extramural endeavor — The Fifth Commandment, Thou Shalt Not Kill. He got several icy stares. One of the guards told him later that there were several ladies present who were charged with violating his topic.

On Saturday evenings four deacons got a night on the town. Sort of. They would bus into Detroit to Sacred Heart Seminary and sleep there. On Sunday mornings two would do their subdeacon and deacon thing for a solemn high Mass at the Seminary, and two would travel down Chicago Blvd. to Woodward Ave. and do the same thing at the Cathedral. On the weekend the Moose was let out, he had an experience that almost stopped him in his tracks. When he got off the bus in Detroit, a blond vision passed by. He only got a side view of her face, but the rest of the package was very neatly wrapped.

It took him four months to erase that vision from his memory. In the meantime his tin pants became very irritating.

There was a remedy for this irritation that all clerics received at their ordination to the subdeaconate, The Breviary. Celibacy was appropriately called an onus. The Brev was called a bonus. It was one's constant companion, like a wife. The Breviary, or the Office as it was sometimes called, was a four volume set of books that contained daily readings from the Psalms, Old and New Testaments, Scripture commentaries, and the lives of the saints. There were also a variety of prayers and hymns interspersed among the readings. It was all in Latin.

The prayers were supposed to be said at the various hours of the day, Prime, Sext, None, Vespers, and so forth. The thought was that the guys on the firing line should pray in sync with the monks in the monasteries who chanted this same stuff in choir. It took about an hour every day to recite these prayers. The verb recite is used advisedly. Because the priests in "the world" were supposed to be in tune with the chanting monks, their obligation was to pronounce every word with their lips. But no hissing was required or desired, especially if there were people around. To this day the Moose is a very slow reader. Out of habit he pronounces everything he sees.

Why the Brev was called a bonus is at best uncertain. The four volumes were heavy and the routine for recitation was complicated. The language was not always easily translated and understood. Some of the commentaries were unbelievable. You may have heard the expression that someone "lies like a second nocturn." That's right out of the Brev. One of the classics was about St. Jerome or some other anchorite. It is stated that he was so pious, that even as an infant he abstained from his mother's breasts on Wednesdays and Fridays. How about that?

On the other hand, the recitation kept you occupied and focused on holy things for about an hour. In the seminary one did pick up some status points with lower classmen. Everyone was into "playing priest." Being able to parade around the halls reciting the Brev like the professors did, gave deacons some elation and esteem. Also, walking around while reciting the Brev provided some good and necessary exercise.

But here's the hooker in the bonus, onus debate. The penalty for not reciting the Breviary in the allotted time, only near-death experiences created valid excuses, was hell fire. It was a mortal sin. If that's a bonus so is cancer.

Before the Moose made Team Vatican, some smart old guys created a group called the Near East Society. If you paid your annual dues, about fifty dollars, you could substitute the Rosary for the Breviary if you had to travel a few miles. A lot of old guys killed two birds with one stone everyday. They'd take a little ride after lunch or dinner and recite the Rosary while they drove. Wouldn't you know it? That group got shut down a couple of years before the Moose was ordained a priest, and that's the next subject on the agenda. Ordination to the priesthood.

QUANDO UNO NO PUEDE LEER, HAY QUE PENSAR.

CHAPTER FOURTEEN
PRIESTHOOD OR SACERDOTAL START

On the first Friday evening in June of 1956, eight nervous young men assembled at Queen of Angels retreat house in Saginaw. They were the Michigan trained segment of Bishop Stephen Woznicki's "twelve apostles." The other four had studied their Theology in Europe and were to be ordained there in the immediate future. Previous ordination classes got no larger than six. This class was the answer to the Bishop's prayers. Now he would have the priests to adequately staff the parishes of his far flung diocese.

It was a long night for most of the eight. It was still possible to get out of this celibacy commitment. It would take a long time to get the dispensation from Rome, but it was possible. At that time it was believed that after ordination to the priesthood, the door was permanently closed. That has changed, of course. Since the late 1960s thousands have been dispensed. Anyway, the Moose was nervous and he noted that others in the group who had blood in their veins and not a mixture of ice water and vinegar were also a bit jumpy. Before trying to get some sleep, the Moose made the Stations of the Cross to the biblical refrain that had sustained him during his final year at St. John's. "Once you have put your hand to the plow let there be no looking back." The Moose has often wondered how many other people have viewed their choice of vocation in life as the start of a march toward death. What were you thinking when you took your biggest step in life?

The next two days were a blur. The fuzzy eight were driven to the cathedral about 8 A.M. They had been fasting from food and drink since midnight as was the custom in those days. The cathedral was already full with families and friends. Just about all of the priests of the diocese had come for this big event. There was a long procession from the rectory to the cathedral. The eight ordinands, dressed in long white albs with vestments folded on their arm, preceded the bishop to the altar. There they prostrated themselves on the floor while the choir and clergy chanted the litany of the saints. The litany was comforting to the Moose. He felt like he was joining a tough team that had chosen the "narrow way" and made it to the top. He also appreciated the chance to stretch out and catch his breath.

When the litany was completed, Bishop Steve, standing at his throne with mitre on his head and crozier in his hand, read some admonitions to the candidates and followed that with

First Mass,1956 (l.to r.): Dan Walsh, Ken Povish, Ted LaMarre, Pastor Wm. Simon, and The Rock

prayers for courage and strength. Then he moved to the center of the altar and sat on his faldstool facing the candidates. In alphabetical order each of the candidates came and knelt before the bishop. He imposed his hands on their heads and recited a formal prayer of empowerment. Next he anointed their hands with Holy Chrism, and bound them with a white cloth called a manutergium. Finally they were presented with a chalice and paten which they touched with their anointed index fingers and thumbs. Now they were priests forever according to the order of Melchizedech.

When this ritual was completed, priest friends helped the newly ordained to prepare for reciting the remainder of the Mass with the bishop. They put on all of the priestly vestments and then knelt at a stool that supported a large Latin missal. Their assistants, LaMarre and Povish in Moose's case, helped them find the right places and turned pages for them. The Moose remembers being awed by the recitation of the words of consecration. He had read them thousands of times in his missal, but he had never said them out loud. Drinking from the chalice at Communion was also a new experience. It was his first time for Communion under both species, bread and wine.

At the end of the Mass, the newly ordained knelt in a line at the foot of the altar. Then all of the priests in attendance came and imposed their hands on the heads of the new priests.

It was a meaningful symbol of unity and empowerment. The Moose easily recognized the pressing hands of his mentors, Ted LaMarre and Ken Povish. As they processed out of the cathedral to a thunderous *Te Deum* the newly ordained were greeted by a churchful of wet and smiling faces. Back in the rectory reception room the Moose got to greet his parents and three brothers. They were so proud and happy. The Moose was stunned when his own parents greeted him in unison,

"Congratulations, Father Bob." That would be his name from now on.

The following day, Father Bob celebrated his first Mass at St. Anne's in Alpena. The church was filled to overflowing with relatives and friends. More than a few eyes opened wide and many mouths emitted a slight gasp as the procession wended its way to the altar. At the front carrying the cross was Father Bob's good friend from Detroit, Jim Hopewell. Jim was six feet five and an African-American. There were no African-Americans in Alpena.

Dotts LaMarre and Ken Povish served as deacon and sub-deacon at the Mass and Ken preached the homily. His old buddy Dan Walsh was Master of Ceremonies. Father Bob made it through his first celebration without a hitch. With so many assistants standing around it was impossible to make a mistake of any consequence. At that time the blessing of a newly ordained priest was thought to be extremely beneficial for the spiritual well-being of the recipient. So at the end of Mass for about forty five minutes, Father Bob moved up and down the communion railing blessing and imposing his hands on the heads of everyone in the congregation. At the end of the blessing each recipient kissed his newly anointed hands.

The ceremonies were concluded in the hall with a banquet for immediate family and close friends. At the end of the meal there were a few speeches by visiting clergy and by Grandpa Martin. Grandpa was bursting with pride and eloquent in his praise. Finally, Fr. Bob got his chance to speak. Filled with emotion and confused with his new status and the deference afforded him, he could do little more than thank his parents and grandparents, Ted and Ken, Big Zil, and all the other people who had made this day possible. By the time he had greeted all of his relatives and friends and administered more first blessings, the afternoon was just about over. Exhausted, Fr. Bob went home to his old room and crashed. Never before or since has he experienced such a moving and awesome transition.

After a two week vacation for unwinding, sending out thank you notes, tabulating his loot, and paying his bills, Fr. Bob packed his new black Ford Fairlane, and headed down to Saginaw. He was thrilled with his first assignment, assistant to his old mentor Ted LaMarre at St. Joe's, Saginaw. This was a dream come true. Fr. Bob was a working class kid and St. Joe's was a working class place. This is where, in his set of values, he belonged. No one else envied him his assignment. For most of the clergy this was a place to avoid.

St. Joe's was in Saginaw's first ward, the oldest part of town. By 1956, the majority of the Irish and Poles who had lived in this area had migrated to the west side of the river. Houses were small and old and most were now occupied by blacks and Hispanics. The area was dominated by a huge Chevrolet foundry where most of the residents found employment. The ever present dust and smell of the cupolas made its dominance physical. The Chesapeake and Ohio tracks ran through the ward, and the railroad yard ran along the edge of St. Joe's property.

The parish plant occupied about a block and a half. The nondescript church was on the corner of 6th and Sears. Next to the church on 6th Street was a large frame building that served as the rectory. Three priests were in residence, Ted, Bob, and Aristodemo Rodriguez. Further down 6th Street and on the next corner was the credit union, a new, nicely appointed brick building. Behind the church on 7th and Sears was a large frame building that housed 16 Dominican nuns. Across Sears and practically on the tracks was an old dilapidated building that had been the original school. It was now converted into a small second floor gym, three first floor classrooms and a cafeteria. Next door to the convent was the newer school, but still very old and creaky. Grades four through eight were on the first floor and the high school was on the second. On the other side of the school was the Guadalupe Clinic and the convent of the Missionary Sisters of the Holy Ghost. With the exception of a few square yards of grass around the rectory everything else was paved with blacktop. Like the rest of the neighbors, St. Joe's was firmly planted in the asphalt jungle.

Fr. Bob's papers indicated that he was supposed to report at St. Joe's on Friday in time for dinner. When he pulled up to the back door at 5:l5 P.M. he found the house empty and a note on the door. "On a sick call. Back by six." About 6:15, Fr. Ted returned and the two of them drove over to One Arm Frank's for a fish dinner. Once back at the rectory, Fr. Bob unloaded a portion of his belongings and toted them upstairs to his new quarters. Then he sat with Ted for a couple of hours and got filled in on his new responsibilities. About ten he went to his room, finished his Breviary and retired. In the morning he went out to unload the rest of his stuff, but found the car cleanly stripped. Welcome to St. Joe's. For the next six years he never got ripped off again. Of course he never left anything in the car again, and always left the doors unlocked. It made it easier for the needy to discover that there was nothing to take and they didn't have to jimmy locks or smash windows to find that out.

The first thing that Fr. Bob learned about life at St. Joe's was that sleep was not a high priority item, although it had always been high on his list. Early in his seminary career he had vowed that nothing would stand in the way of his sleep and recreation. He kept that vow religiously for eleven years. Dotts LaMarre was a man with golden ears. It seemed like everybody in the territory wanted to talk with him. They rang the doorbell early in the morning and rarely was the house empty before midnight.

As the low man on the totem pole, Fr. Bob had to "feed the nuns" at 6 A.M. six days a week. That's clerical parlance for celebrating Mass in the convent chapel. Lymie Fenn had regularly assured the seminarians at St. John's that if they were going to be faithful to their clerical promises, a minimum half hour of meditation before Mass every day was an absolute necessity. You can tell time, so you know what that meant for Fr. Bob.

It wasn't only the schedule and the interior activity of the rectory, however, that was an obstacle to sleep. Trains clanged and banged through the C &O yards twenty four hours a day. Well over half the workers who ended the second and started the third shift at Chevrolet traveled on 6th Street. When freight trains were switching in and out of the yard the traffic on 6th backed up for blocks in both directions. Anxious workers got their message to engineers by sitting on their horns. Slowly Fr. Bob got used to the noise and conditioned to less sleep. The conditioning helped when his ears began to pick up a little gold tint and people wanted to talk to him when Fr. LaMarre wasn't available.

Fr. Bob's first of many fascinating encounters occurred on his second Sunday in the parish. The 8 A.M. Mass was going on and he was alone in the rectory with Bousha Kessler, a delightful lady who came in six days a week to cook. Answering the front door bell he saw a lady in what the Hispanics call "un estado interesante," pregnant. He invited her into the front office and quickly learned that she was mute. So he took out a pencil and a piece of paper and wrote, "What can I do for you?" She immediately wrote back, "I'm going to have a baby." He could see that and smiling approvingly he wrote the word, "When?" Again she scribbled quickly, "Right now."

He blurted out something like "Holy Shit!" and thought, "They never taught us anything about this in the seminary." Then he went flying out to the kitchen to get Bousha. She quickly evaluated the situation and ordered Fr. Bob to immediately pull his car up to the back door. Bousha carefully loaded the lady in the back seat and then climbed in the front seat. Fr. Bob quietly wondered why Bousha got in the front seat and whether this was a violation of the Bishop's order about never riding "solus cum sola" in the front seat. A single male with a single female. But things were too far along to worry about that. He roared out the driveway and took a left on 6th heading for St. Mary's Hospital. And wouldn't you know it? There was a freight train creeping through the yards. After what seemed like a half hour, the tracks cleared and the trio, no, quartet, rocketed off to the hospital. At the hospital, two attendants wheeled a gurney to the car, put the lady on it and there was the baby. Fr. Bob was in shock. This was something he wasn't supposed to observe. Bousha calmed him down and made him feel better when she indicated that it was a good thing the baby wasn't born in the car. He would have needed a new rear seat.

When Fr. Bob got back to the rectory, for the next two weeks he was sort of proud of his escapade. How many priests had ever done that? He even went to the hospital to visit the mother and child. Then the fan got hit. The hospital sent him the bill. When the staff asked the lady who brought her to the hospital, she wrote, "El padre," the father. And when they asked her what the father's name was, she wrote "Roberto Keller."

He was a father, but not that kind. He hadn't even had time to get his sowing machine out of the box.

It was only a few months later that Fr. Bob learned that his machine was not that well packed. After the first snow fall, the high school seniors wanted to go tobogganing up North. Dotts LaMarre was enthusiastic and offered to provide the transportation and drivers, himself, Fr. Bob and Fr. Morales, a new assistant from Mexico. After the last Mass on Sunday, eighteen students packed into the three cars and headed north. The day went beautifully, and in a sense so did the ride home.

Seated tightly next to Fr. Bob was a dark eyed, olive skinned, incredibly equipped piece of God's handiwork. Her eyes flashed, her voice was like soft classical music, and her skin, when her arm brushed accidentally against his, was like electricity. His horn blew immediately. Please be assured that nothing physical followed. But the popular song "96 Tears" by the local Question Mark and the Mysterians really got to him. He shed more tears than that inside and outside for the next several weeks.

Dotts LaMarre picked up on this immediately. He saw Fr. Bob as a returning astronaut who was radio active and needed to be quarantined. He suggested that Fr. Bob take a week off and go visit some pious people or places. Fr. Bob decided to get in touch with his old buddy Dan Walsh who was going to law school and selling insurance. His hope was to see if Dan had any assuring ideas on how he could repack his sowing machine and insure it against further rattling. Dan was marvellous. His new, though somewhat limited, experience with the opposite sex was enlightening and comforting. Their short trip to the shrine of the North American Martyrs was sufficient, at least, to reset Fr. Bob's blown fuses.

When Fr. Bob got to St. Joe's a significant number of black families had joined the parish. Their interest in Catholicism had been generated by the welcome and care that many had received at St. Mary's Hospital and by the work of Msgr. Harold Bolton, Fr. LaMarre's predecessor, who was a social activist with broad and insightful vision. He helped engineer the construction of a low cost housing complex, developed the Guadalupe Clinic and the Credit Union, welcomed all comers to the school, and recruited a black priest from Illinois to serve on his parish staff.

Twice a year, a weekly information class that lasted for 16 weeks took place at the large meeting room of the credit union. From 20 to 25 people came on a regular basis. In Jan. Fr. LaMarre put Fr. Bob in charge of the program. It was a very stressful job for the first several weeks. He worked very hard at the lectures he presented and quickly his lofty syllogisms put everybody to sleep. But the people kept coming back and slowly educated him. Finally he simply let them ask questions about what they wanted to know, and he soon discovered that this procedure created a much better learning experience. Why the Latin liturgy and the dull emotionless music? Why so few blacks in the church? Where do Catholics stand on the race issue? What makes these nuns tick? How come Father LaMarre is always smiling and laughing? Where does Father Horton find all the time to visit the hospitals every day? Why don't priests get married and have kids?

When Fr. Bob gave the group the stock answer on celibacy they all laughed out loud. One man piped up, "Man, you gotta be gettin your jollies somewhere." The sessions got better every week. Sitting in front of that black mirror Fr. Bob learned that he wasn't a giant with a lot of answers, but a midget with a lot to learn. It slowly dawned on him that it's extremely important for everyone to have an abundance of cross-cultural experiences. They cut people down to size, the human size, the only size that matters.

Fr. Bob was doubly fortunate. He had two cultural mirrors at his fingertips. There were also a lot of Mexican-Americans in the parish. Trying to speak another language is a revelation in norms, values, beliefs, and symbols. He never realized how narrow-minded and arrogant he was. The way he thought, expressed himself, saw the world were elements of only one perspective on life. There were many more valid ones, and considering them opened up a whole new world. Fr. Bob was beginning to understand what the book The Ugly American was all about.

Conrado and Cornelio Velasquez taught Fr. Bob several wonderful cultural lessons. They were a father and son team that Fr. LaMarre hired to do janitorial work in the parish. Conrado, the father, spoke no English. Cornelio, about fourteen, had never been to school. He was considered a retarded child, but he was bilingual. He learned English spontaneously from his brothers and sisters and the kids in the neighborhood. When the nuns, for instance, wanted to communicate with Mr. Velasquez, they had to go through Cornelio. It took a couple of years for the lesson to sink in with Fr. Bob. He thought that he was some kind of a hot dog because he could rattle off a few hundred Spanish words. Cornelio was really good for his ego.

One summer day when the lawn mower died, Fr. Ted asked Fr. Bob if he would run down to Sears and get a new mower. To his surprise it came in a box. When he got home he opened the box and found the instructions and the parts, wheels, guards, handles, cables, nuts, and bolts. After about a half hour he had put on one wheel. Then he got summoned into the house by a phone call that proved to be lengthy. Before he went in he asked Conrado to see what he could do with the assembling of the mower. In a very short time, he was still on the phone, he heard the roar of the engine and then saw a smiling Conrado go whizzing by the window cutting the grass.

When Fr. Bob got back outside he looked at the box and the instructions sitting to the side, and he said to Conrado, "Conrado, you didn't even look at the instructions. How did you do that so fast?" He smiled and said, "Aw, Padre! Quando uno no puede leer, hay que pensar." When you can't read you have to think. Fr. Bob will never forget that remark and its significance. Throughout his life he has encountered thousands of people who read and are considered to be highly educated. But a large number of them don't know how to think as well as Conrado.

Fr. Bob was a busy kid at St. Joe's. There were the regular things a priest does, celebrate Mass and Sacraments, recite the Breviary, prepare and deliver sermons, visit the sick, give private instructions and counsel, and respond to the needs of people on the phone and at the door. Along with these duties, Fr. Bob taught daily in the high school and visited grade school classes on a weekly basis, directed a boy's choir, coached the varsity basketball team, wrote a weekly column for the diocesan paper, gave Spanish homilies on a Saturday morning radio program, and ran three diocesan programs for the Bishop — The Mexican Apostolate, The Cursillo Movement, and the Rural Life Conference.

Everyone but the Bishop thought that assigning the Rural Life job to Fr. Bob was a mistake. If there was any place in the diocese that was urbanized it was St. Joe's. Every bishop in the U.S. was assigned to some committee by his fellow bishops. So Steve Woznicki, who had earned his spurs in Ham Town, Detroit's Hamtramck, got assigned to the chairmanship of the National Catholic Rural Life Conference. He, also probably thought his assignment was a mistake. Wanting to look good with his peers, however, he decided to make his diocese a model program. Believing in the philosophy that if you want to get a job done, ask the busiest person, Steve told Bob that he was going to be the diocesan director. So Fr. Bob became an asphalt farmer.

What asphalt farmers do is talk and write a lot. Fr. Bob started a weekly column for rural life in the diocesan paper. He wrote about co-ops, credit unions, the ideal of the family farm, the danger of strontium 90 in milk, outfitting your tractor with a flexible pole and a red flag, and many other heavy duty topics. He wrote a monthly newsletter to all pastors with suggested readings, sermon topics, liturgical celebrations, diocesan meetings, and bulletin fillers. In the spring and fall, he would take the Bishop out to rural parishes to bless the crops and the harvests. Fr. Bob asked his boy's choir if they wanted to go on these trips. The answer was simple; if it meant getting out of school, of course they did. "The Spics and the Spooks," as they called themselves, were a real plus on these trips. As the Bishop processed into the fields with full regalia to bless crops and animals, the choir in red cassocks, white surplices, and Buster Brown collars, chanted the litany in Latin and appropriate hymns in three part harmony. The press was there to take pictures and report on the activity. The Bishop and the people loved it.

After several years of this full court pressing, Fr. Bob was getting a little frazzled around the edges. He started to needle Steve about his hunger for Munger. St. Norbert's in Munger was a neat little place not far from Saginaw where Bob's mentor Ken Povish had been pastor for several years. It was also the potato capital of Michigan. He kept telling Steve that if he was going to do a good job with the Conference he ought to be out of the asphalt jungle and have a little place of his own with three acres, a cow, and a few Rhode Island reds. Steve laughed but promised nothing. Not many months later, he moved Fr. Bob eight blocks down 6th Street to Sacred Heart parish where the asphalt was in serious need of repair.

Chapter Fifteen
BROTHER MARTIN

While he lived in Saginaw, Fr. Bob met a large number of wonderful people. One of the most fascinating was a man named Brother Martin. Brother Martin was not a religiously professed brother. Somewhere along the line, he acquired the custom of addressing everyone as brother and almost everyone reciprocated. If a person had an official title, Martin just added brother to it. For example, Fr. Bob became brother-father. The nuns were brother-sister, and the two young men he eventually moved in with were brother-brother.

One Spring evening when Fr. Bob was at St. Joe's, he answered the front door and met Brother Martin for the first time. He was attired in an oversized suit that someone must have given him. The coat was snugged together by several large safety pins. The pants bagged and dragged badly. He sported a well worn white shirt with a screaming red tie. A beat up, black, felt hat rested on his ears. For a boutonniere, a dead bird perched in the kerchief pocket of his coat. On each arm he was escorted by an appropriately attired lady of the evening.

Martin doffed his hat, and in a speech pattern that was very difficult to understand, he announced that he was Brother Martin. Fr. Bob shook hands with him and said, "Pleased to meet you. I'm Fr. Bob. Won't you come in?" The escorts peeled off Martin's arms and the happy trio filed into the front office. The ladies were overly atomized with colliding colognes and the room smelled like a dime store perfume counter, maybe worse. After everyone got seated, Brother Martin in his high pitched, staccato voice stated his problem, "Brotha-Fatha Bob, Iz a gotta litta probem. Iz a needa cuppa dolla." Fr. Bob assured him that he could help with that and excused himself to go into the other office to get the key to the poor box.

Fr. LaMarre had a practice of dealing with the poor that most people, including Fr. Bob at first, thought was off the wall. When folks came for a handout, he simply gave them the key to the poor box in church. He told them to go and take what they needed and then bring the key back. The lock was to keep the kids out of the change. When Fr. Bob first saw Dotts doing this he quickly informed him that he was nuts. Dotts calmly informed his young sidekick that people put money in the box for the poor. Many of the people who came to the door were poor, so it was their money. Why was Fr. Bob so judgmental? Fr. Bob recalls today that that box was very much like the vessel of oil that Elisha utilized to redeem the widow and her children. It's a good story if you haven't read it. First Book of Kings, in case you are interested.

So Brother-Father Bob gave the key to Brother Martin and he and his two escorts went over to church to get what they needed. When Brother Martin returned with the key, the two ladies who had not said a word at the door or in the office, were not with him. At first, Brother-Father Bob thought that Brother Martin had paid what he owed the two ladies, and that was that. As he got to know Brother Martin better he became convinced that the ladies were simply using Martin to make a few bucks on a slow evening. Brother Martin was the simplest, most unsophisticated human being that Fr. Bob had ever met. He didn't know how old he was, what his surname was, where he came from, or where he plugged in. Fr. Bob would have bet heavy money that Brother Martin's "sowing machine" registered "tilt" from day one.

Fr. Bob's guess was that Martin was in his mid thirties when they first met. As for residence, the only answer Martin ever gave was that he lived "in the country." Didn't we all? For a while Martin had a job. He daily cleaned and mopped the back end of a neighboring butcher shop. He probably lived on salvageable scraps.

Brother Martin found his way back to St. Joe's rectory with ever increasing frequency. He never wanted much, never more than fifty cents. On a couple of occasions when Martin returned the key to an empty box, he reported that he had split what he had in his pocket and put it in the box so that the next guy would get a little. If Martin requested a little assistance from an individual, and the person responded that he was broke, Martin would insist on sharing what he had in his pocket with that individual.

One evening when Fr. Bob was on his way to his information class at the credit union, be bumped into Brother Martin and invited him to come along. Martin was thrilled and soon started coming every week. He was ever polite to his new brother-sisters, and brother-brothers, and always sat in the back. He appeared to be listening attentively, but Fr. Bob often worried that he was talking way above Martin's head. At the end of each session, Fr. Bob asked if anyone had anything they wanted to say before they left. Brother Martin would then stand up and give a couple of minutes of testimony that no one could hear clearly nor understand. Soon the group came to realize that Martin and his testimony were beautiful in a reverse sort of way. So every week the group clapped when he finished and thanked him for sharing his life with them.

At the end of that winter session anyone who wanted to be initiated into the church was invited to attend the Easter Vigil. Brother Martin wanted in. He came to the Vigil looking super sharp in a new suit that Fr. LaMarre bought for him. The verbal parts of the ceremony seemed to just blow over Martin's head, but the symbols and gestures of love enveloped him. He beamed more broadly than ever before during the Baptism and the Eucharist. Even his rotted out teeth took on a new lustre.

When Fr. Bob moved down 6th Street to pastor Sacred Heart he lost touch with Brother Martin for a couple of years. But when "Brotha-Fatha LeeMa" got transferred to another city, Brother Martin found Brother-Father Bob. It was a happy reunion.

One day, a very sad Brother Martin punched the door bell. He was sick, had lost his job, and couldn't live "in the country" anymore. The parish owned a nearby house where volunteer workers resided. Two young college grads, Dick and Enos, were living there at the time. They cheerfully made room for Brother Martin. Moving in for Martin was easy. What he owned he wore. It was absolutely inspiring to watch Dick and Enos teach Brother Martin how to use a knife and fork, brush his teeth, shave, and comb his hair. Brushing his teeth was his favorite activity. He frequently would use up a half a tube of paste a day.

Living in the rectory and doing part-time maintenance work was another prince of a volunteer named Mike. He hired Brother Martin to help keep the school neat and clean. For a couple of days he walked Martin through his job, showed him where the supplies were, and where to dump the trash. Brother Martin was walking on air.

One day shortly after Martin was on his own, an overtime meeting in the school delayed Martin's cleanup work. About 5:30 P.M. Fr. Bob was in church celebrating evening Mass for a small group of people. He had just finished his little homily when the front door of the church opened and there was a smiling Brother Martin. He started walking up the center isle carrying a large galvanized garbage can. Fr. Bob thought, "What's Brother Martin up to today? Is he bringing this can up to the altar as a symbol of his work for the Offertory of the Mass? Wonderful insight!"

When Martin got to the communion railing, he took off his hat and said, "Excuse me, Brotha Fatha." He then put his hat back on and proceeded across the sanctuary into the sacristy dragging his noisy can across the marble floor. When Fr. Bob got back to the rectory and narrated this little story, Mike laughed and explained what had happened. When he was walking Martin through his job, he had used the church route to show Martin where the incinerator was in the church basement. Brother Martin always did what he was told. The existence of a large side door at ground level that led directly to the incinerator had escaped his attention. After Mike demonstrated the new route everything was OK. No more symbolic gifts for the Offertory procession.

Somewhere along the line, nobody knew how or why, Brother Martin developed a concern about his bowel movements. He came to the conclusion that if he had three movements in one day then that would be the end of things. So every day at the end of his cleaning and incinerating, he would either ring the doorbell or walk past Fr. Bob's office window to let him know what the score was. Most of the time it was a finger sign, one or two.

Shortly before Bob left to go to graduate school, a disturbed Martin had to talk to him. The score that day was two and a half. Now Fr. Bob really wasn't an expert on these matters, nor did he understand how halves were calculated in this game of nature, so he simply told Brother Martin that he had nothing to worry about. As supporting evidence in his counseling, he told Brother Martin about his own seminary bouts with colitis when the numbers on his scoreboard went into double digits. A grateful Martin was in awe and thought that Fr. Bob was some sort of superstar.

A few months after Fr. Bob left for grad school, he was told that Martin had disappeared. Fr. Bob wondered then whether Brother Martin had maxed out at three. Today, however, he firmly believes that Brother Martin was a Jesus/Joshua type who came to teach the people in that part of Saginaw that "unless

you become like little children you cannot enter into the kingdom of heaven."

You know, there must be at least two or three Brother
Martins in every neighborhood in the country. The trouble is,
most of us brother-brothers and brother-sisters are not looking
for that kind of brotherhood. Why is it that so many of us have
trouble seeing our local Brother Martins and finding the key
that fits the poor box? It would probably do all of us a lot of
good if we would get our inner vision checked every now and
then. It could also be fun to look around in that junk drawer
where we throw things that we don't use much anymore. Bet
you that you might find the key to the poor box buried down
there somewhere. Why don't you just take a look. Just for the
heaven of it.

cada chango por su mecate

Chapter Sixteen
IT HAS TO BE YOU

On a Monday afternoon in early August of 1961, Fr. Bob was seated in the lobby of a downtown hotel in Chicago with his twelve "pistoleros," colleagues who had just finished the summer campaign of the Mexican War. There were six priests and six seminarians who had served as aides-de-camp for the priests. This trip to Chicago was a reward for their three months of hard work attending to the religious needs of the migrants in the Saginaw Valley.

After checking the group into the hotel, connecting them to a neighboring church where they could celebrate daily Mass, and distributing to them some extra cash to cover their food and recreational needs, Fr. Bob, in his anglicized Spanish, announced to them that they were on their own until departure time for the return trip to Saginaw on Thursday. Some of the priests appeared to be a little puzzled by the directive. Then Padre Alberto, better known as "Abuelito," grandpa perked up enthusiastically and stated, " Oh! Padre, what you are trying to say is, "Cada chango por su mecate," every monkey on his own rope.

The priests all laughed understandingly and were pleased with the permission to cut loose. Most of the seminarians got the gist of the "dicho" and smiled politely. Fr. Bob liked the sound and imagery of the expression and wrote it down for future usage. Over the years he has used the expression so frequently that it has become, for all practical purposes, a principle of living.

So you ask, why should this axiom, that every chango or human being should be left alone to climb its own rope, be used as a principle for living? That's serious business. Well, there isn't a simple answer. In one of his encounters with friends, Winnie the Pooh suggests that if we want to know what is seriously going on about anything, we have to answer three questions: The What, The Who, and The Which To Do.

Number one. What is this chango? The mother of one of Fr. Bob's students put it perfectly. She claimed that her daughter was "an unrepeatable miracle." When you stop and think about it, the human machine is truly a miraculous invention. Consider the five senses, the respiratory and digestive systems, the communicating and self-healing faculties, bipedal locomotion, super flexible arms with shoulders, elbows, wrists, and wonderfully agile fingers with opposable thumbs, and crowning it all, a portable, wireless computer whose potential has never been fully tapped. Is there anything more wonderful in the world than a human being? To quote an old song, "Every time I hear a new born baby cry I know why I believe."

Examining the physical part of the human machine answers the What question. Equally wonderful and awesome are the inner, invisible, spiritual attributes of the psyche that answer the Who question. In each of us there is the I or the Ego, that core, that voice that tells us who we are and assures us that we are distinct and unique. The Ego, the center of our consciousness, is by nature shy and fragile and does not like to be overexposed. So it always wears a mask called a persona. Most people wear a lot of masks — one at home, another at work, a third at play, a special one for church. The Ego, however, is not alone in the psyche. It has a counterpart called the Self. The Ego's function is to be the eyes and ears of the Self.

Depth psychologists, like Carl Jung, tell us that the Self is the center and circumference of the psyche. It is the indwelling of the Spirit, the Divine Guest, the Source of Life itself. What more could be said about the dignity and the distinctiveness of the chango?

And now the final question, "Which to do?" If the Creator actively and creatively dwells within the creature, then the obvious response to the question is to listen to the Self and to respond to the information that it communicates to the Ego. The Self speaks to the Ego in dreams, a universal and symbolic language. The purpose of dreams is to provide information that is not known to the Ego, to balance, regulate, clarify the awareness and the activity of the Ego.

The principle, every monkey on his own rope, is not easy to accept and abide by considering the socialization we receive from our groups as soon as we exit our mother's womb. How many times have you ever heard a parent, a teacher, a clergy person, a spouse, or even a friend, say to you, "All I ask of you is that you be yourself as fully as possible," or "I will make zero impositions on you"?

Some people occasionally think and talk about giving others all the rope they need, but few practice the principle totally. Most of us are afraid of what might happen, especially with children, if we were to leave them to their own devices. But there are all too few people who seriously believe that there is an indwelling spirit or force in every person which or who exhibits an active and creative interest in that individual. And even among those few who believe this, there are hardly any who trust that spirit completely. Why?

Most creation stories tell us that somewhere in their development human beings were told that they were "damaged goods." The story that most Western people are familiar with, Genesis, labeled the damage as sin. The story indicates that the first pair of people, Adam and Eve, were given a test which they quickly flunked. They ate a forbidden fruit, maybe a lemon or an orange, and as a result their hard wiring got screwed up and they became instantly prone to evil. With all myths, it's a tragic mistake to take it literally, but that's what most people do with Genesis.

Symbolically, what the Genesis story is saying is this. When human beings moved from an automatic, non-reflecting, non-differentiating existence to conscious, differentiating existence they experienced in themselves the power to choose one thing, one behavior, over another. They found themselves free to label some things, some behaviors, as appropriate or good and others as inappropriate or bad. With emerging insight and power like that you can readily imagine what an horrendous conflict began to take place in their lives.

The process, of course, is still going on in your head. When you were a little kid you didn't know and didn't care about reflecting and differentiating, being right or wrong. But minute by minute, day by day, you were carefully taught by your relatives and friends what they thought was right and proper and what was wrong and inappropriate. Like our predecessors, we are all in constant turmoil trying to put differentiating labels on what passes in front of our consciousness. Think of the long list of topics that separate and divide us — religion, war, gun control, capital punishment, drugs, homosexuality, abortion, Aids, and racism, among others. Because there are as many opinions on a topic as there are heads, total agreement on anything is very hard to come by, and life gets tedious and complicated.

There is a growing number of people who are beginning to support this "cada chango" principle or theory. Most of them are advocates of the MBTI — the Meyers-Briggs Typology Index. Jung was the psychologist who established and defined the basic psychological types. It was his research and also that

of Isabel Myers that indicated that every human being operates out of an unique blending of preferences relative to four
areas of human concern. 1. Where do we focus our attention.
2. How do we take in information. 3. How do we make decisions. 4. How do we orient ourselves to the outer world. The
Index is an excellent means for individuals to learn about and
appreciate their uniqueness and their special gifts. It also helps
them to more clearly know and actualize the Creator's plan for
them.

But there are too many people moving in the opposite direction, laying down the law, giving orders and ultimatums,
punishing violators, blocking and denying creativity, jamming
people into categories, making odious comparisons, and stress-
ing aggressive competition. At the time of birth, mothers are
urged to push their child from the womb. But after the child is
born, a lot of mothers wrap their arms around their child and
forget to continue pushing it to independence and the fulfill-
ment of the Creator's call. In this regard one of the biggest
offenders is Mother Church. It has a lot of wonderful initiation
rituals for the various stages of life, but no graduation ceremony.
It never tells people that it has only so much to offer for the
journey into wholeness, and that sooner or later people have
to leave and get on with their own personal quest.

Without doubt, the biggest reason why so few people believe in and trust the creative work of the Spirit in each individual
is the human fear of being alone. A young neonatologist once
told Fr. Bob that the most traumatic journey in the world is that
short trip through the birth canal. The psychological trauma of
being cut off from the mother is probably more severe than the
physical pain. The experience seems to leave an almost indelible mark of fear on every person. From that moment on all
human beings start looking for another person to fill the void,
someone who will be there for them, someone who will relieve
them of full responsibility for their life. The message that we
least want to hear is that we are alone and that our life journey
in most respects must be made alone. No other human being
can do it for us. Jung called the journey "individuation," becoming our true self. Distance-wise this journey is even shorter
than the trip down the birth canal. It takes place in the psyche
when the Ego says to the Self, "I am your servant. I am here to

do your will." Jesus explained it as taking up the Cross and following Him.

When the Ego makes that alignment then the enlightenment begins. The creature is not alone at all. There is only unity with God and all creation. In the old days people believed in many gods. Then they said there was only one God. Now, the holy people are saying there is only God, and this is mysticism.

In summary, then, what the axiom, *cada chango por su mecate,* is saying is that every creature has within itself direct and easy access to an understanding of its own individual purpose or goal in life as well as the necessary means or energy to fully accomplish that end. The axiom, finally, raises another very important question: if the Spirit of God, the Higher Power, is a permanent resident in every creature, why would any human being want to mess around with, or try to direct or control another person's existence?

It would seem, then, that the posture that we should assume, the role that we should play, toward another person, especially if we are parents, seniors, counsellors of whatever class, is a mixed one. We should be part travel agent and part cheer leader, pointing out as well as we can the many avenues of life that are open to travel and then supporting the choices that others make.

In a magnificent poem titled "The Hound of Heaven," Francis Thompson gives voice to God, the Self, relentlessly pursuing the Ego. In a gentle way the Self assures the Ego that the pain of being alone and the bending of its will to the divine will can produce positive results. Also, in a subtle way Thompson offers convincing support for the axiom, *Cada chango por su mecate.*

> Strange, piteous, futile thing . . .
> Alack, thou knowest not
> How little worthy of any love thou art!
> Whom wilt thou find to love ignoble thee
> Save me, save only me?
> All which I took from thee I did but take,
> Not for thy harms,
> But just that thou might'st seek it in my arms.
> All which thy child's mistake

Fancies as lost, I have stored for thee at home:
Rise, clasp my hand and come!"...
Ah, fondest, blindest, weakest,
I am He Whom thou seekest.

Chapter Seventeen
THE SHORT COURSE

One noon in mid fall of 1959 a young man by the name of Ruben Alfaro joined Fr. LaMarre and Fr. Bob for lunch. Ruben was on a mission. You could see it in his eyes and entire demeanor. A couple of weeks previously, Ruben had attended the first Cursillo in Michigan at the Cristo Rey center in Lansing. Like so many other people, Ruben's hero was Fr. LaMarre. He had come to share this new found treasure with him. Even though he had practiced what he wanted to say, he couldn't contain himself. His enthusiasm in explaining the Cursillo was all over the place. That didn't bother Fr. Bob. The enthusiasm was enough and he wanted to try the experience as soon as possible. In his mind the Cursillo had to be something extraordinary to create so much religious enthusiasm in a young man like Ruben.

Under the tutelage of LaMarre and Povish, Fr. Bob had examined and experimented with every program that he thought could generate insight and enthusiasm in fellow Catholics. He was a part of the Liturgical Conference, The Vernacular Society, Biblical Studies, Young Christian Workers, the Christian Family Movement, and Cana Conference, to name a few. They all produced good results, but none of them generated the enthusiasm that he noted in Ruben. So it was decided that afternoon that Fr. Bob and four candidates that he and Fr. Ted would recruit, would make the next Cursillo in Lansing in late November.

With little descriptive information other than that a Cursillo was like a retreat, Fr. Ted and Fr. Bob set out to twist arms. With a lot of pressure and an offer to pay the freight they convinced Frank Chavez, Victor Cortez, Jose Ramirez, and Roberto Uribe to give it a whirl. On the last weekend of November they went to Lansing and the whirl turned into a tornado. When the quintet returned to St. Joe's rectory late Sunday evening, they were five unstoppable talking machines. All Fr. LaMarre could say was that he was finally getting a glimpse of what the first Pentecost must have been like.

To state it briefly, the Cursillo is a three and a half day, semi-sensitivity training program in Christian leadership. Now that doesn't generate any enthusiasm, does it? It didn't generate a whole lot of new candidates either. What did generate thousands of candidates across the U.S. was the testimony and the joyful living of those who had experienced the Cursillo. It was quickly learned that the more one tried to explain the Cursillo to a potential candidate the more resistant that person became. So the stock recruiting line adopted was, "I can't explain it to you. It's an experience you have to have yourself."

Candidates could have been told that the cursillo was a mystery, which it really was, but that would have further alienated them. For centuries, the experience of getting baptized and confirmed was referred to as an introduction to the Sacred Mysteries. When most people hear the word mystery they think it refers to something you can't understand. It can also refer to an experience, or learning by living, and that's what the Cursillo is really like. It's not just a head trip like studying the catechism or attending an information class.

The title is interesting, *Cursillo de Cristiandad*. It means a short course in walking with Christ. The walking is important. Finally someone started talking about religion as a personal relationship and not a legal, rational system of dogma and morality.

In the late 1940s, a doctor by the name of Eduardo Bonin and a priest named Suarez got the movement off the ground on the Island of Majorca. From there it spread rapidly throughout Spain. In the 1950s, several young Spaniards who had made the Cursillo came to Waco, Texas, to train with the U.S. Air Force. With the assistance of Spanish-speaking priests in Texas the movement took off slowly in the Southwest.

When a young Puerto Rican priest in Lorain, Ohio, heard of the movement, he took a group of men to Texas for the experience. In short order the spirit became contagious and moved north to Mexican-Americans in Michigan. Then with the drive of bilingual laypersons and gringo priests the course got translated into English and spread like wild fire throughout the Midwest and the East for both men and women It's still going and now is found in other churches that are not Catholic.

The guts of the course is made up of 15 lectures that last from one to two hours. Ten are given by lay people and five by a priest. The lay people talk about having an ideal, the nature of real piety, the need for study, knowing your environment, and things like that. The priest talks about God's gift of Life, the Sacraments, and obstacles to godliness. These

Fr.Bob (far right) at first English cursillo in Saginaw

talks are illustrated and experienced by para-liturgical ceremonies like Confirmation renewal. During the lectures the men sit at round tables and are encouraged to take notes. After the lectures they discuss the subject matter with a leader for about an hour, collectively put together a written summary, and draw a colored poster that expresses their core ideas. In the evening, each table group presents their summaries and posters to the whole group. That activity does generate some excitement. There are prayers and Mass each morning and night prayers each evening. Meals are in common and spiced with jokes and songs. So are the breaks between lectures, creating more excitement. The closing ceremony on the last evening is really exhilarating. Those who have taken the course previously, sometimes hundreds of people, come to serenade the new cursillistas and encourage them to live "the fifth day" — the rest of their lives — with joy and enthusiasm. You know what? Forty some years later a lot of them are still doing just that.

Shortly after Fr. Bob and the quartet got back to Saginaw and reality, they started planning how they might share this experience with others. With the encouragement of Fr. LaMarre and the support of Fr. Luke at nearby St. Rita's who had an empty school building, the five got in touch with Fr. Antonio

Hernandez in Lorain to see if he could bring a team to Saginaw to get the show on the road. They were willing to come and a date was set for the middle of January. Then the work started. It wasn't easy to convince a group of men to take a day and a half off work to make a retreat. The priests did, however, convince thirty five men to come. The course went without a hitch, and about a hundred men from Lorain and Lansing came for the closing. Even Bishop Woznicki came and he was overwhelmed with the enthusiasm of the group. He gave his blessing to the movement.

Fr. LaMarre's Spanish wasn't super sophisticated, so when he heard that some folks in San Angelo, Texas were going to put on a February Cursillo in English, he signed up with the same results. What impressed him was the intellectual content of the Cursillo. Because of the enthusiasm of those who had participated, most clergymen, long on logic and reason by training, were wary of the program. In things religious, the in-Catholics were and still are very dubious about any display of feeling and emotion. They thought that the Cursillo was nothing but a short-lived Jesus jag.

In March, Franciscan Fidelis Albrecht, planned to bring his San Angelo team to Cincinnati. Because hardly anyone had heard of the Cursillo there they had trouble getting recruits. So Frs. Ted and Bob went to work. It was their belief that if the Cursillo was going to take root in the diocese and get support from the clergy, it was very important that there be some heavy hitters on the team, like doctors, lawyers and business executives. They succeeded in recruiting fifteen well educated laymen from the Tri-city area of Saginaw, Bay City, and Midland. The results were the same — informed enthusiasm.

Cincinnati had little trouble recruiting candidates for their second effort in April. They accepted only five candidates from Saginaw. This was a very important Cursillo, however. The official church acceptance of the movement was on the line. In March, at a conference in Chicago, Fr. Bob managed to convince Cardinal Carberry of St. Louis that he should attend a Cursillo. Fr. Bob sat at his elbow for three and a half days to answer his questions and record his evaluations. The movement got the Cardinal's written and pictorial endorsement. Who would dare contradict a prince of the Church?

When Cincinnati scheduled a third Cursillo for May, they had no room for candidates from Saginaw. So Fr. LaMarre called a meeting of the men who had gone to Cincinnati earlier and the bilingual Hispanics who had attended at St. Rita's. He asked, "What do we do now?" Everyone was dubious and fearful. Only Fr. Bob had attended more than one Cursillo. The only literature available was a manual that he had secured from Majorca. Fr. LaMarre finally resolved the long discussion, "We will put on our own Cursillo here at St. Joe's in June." Everyone assumed that he would be the spiritual director, but he quickly kicked that assumption in the head when he added, "Fr. Bob will be the spiritual director." Fr. Bob heard the thunder. He was a mouthy, cocky kid, but he also knew his limitations and fears. Few people realized that by personality type he was an introvert. Preaching sermons, giving formal presentations tore up his stomach as well as his sleep. He fully believed that he had neither the knowledge nor the experience to undertake this task. When Fr. LaMarre saw his look of shock, he simply said, "You can do it. So do it." And he did it.

Within two weeks Fr. Bob had translated the core of the Spanish manual. That included the rector's guide, the day to day, minute to minute ordering of activities, the fifteen "rollos" or lectures with accompanying rationale and motivation, and appropriate prayers and songs. At the same time he and Fr. Ted were selecting and convincing men to direct the program and give the lectures. Several long group meetings followed as talks were assigned, reviewed, and rehearsed. By mid June the team was ready to deliver, nervous, anxious, and scared, but ready.

Those who were not part of the team were also busy. Cots and bedding for the thirty five men they had recruited had to be secured. Volunteer cooks, food, and cleanup people had to be found. But by the third Thursday in June the place was ready and Saginaw's first homegrown Cursillo got off the ground. Some recruits came from Detroit, Lansing, and Chicago. For the most part they were professionals — politicians, doctors, chemists, lawyers. Even five members of the local clergy were in attendance. The results were the same — informed enthusiasm.

The Catholic press began to pick up on this new phenomenon and soon requests for space in Saginaw Cursillos came in. Then there were requests for teams to conduct courses in

The first women's cursillo in Saginaw.

other areas. Before the year was out, Saginaw teams were conducting one Cursillo a month in town and one on the road. When the first women's Cursillo in English was conducted in California, four Saginaw women flew out to bring the experience back home with the same results. The same development process for women developed on the local level.

Over the next four years, Saginaw teams introduced both men and women Cursillos to most of the major cities in the Midwest and East. They even went international to Canada, the Middle East, and Italy. Their peak experience was a Cursillo in Jesus' hometown of Nazareth with Patriarch George Hakim in attendance.

In January of 1959, the new rotund and jolly Pope John XXIII announced that he was going to convoke an Ecumenical Council. His intent was "to open a window in the Vatican" and let in some fresh air. The Catholic bishops of the world and many non-Catholic participant observers convened in Rome in October of 1962. Four lengthy sessions followed before the Council was closed on December 8, 1965. This Council received worldwide attention and approval. It was probably the most momentous event in the history of the Catholic Church. The roar of the wind that entered through that Vatican window and exited through the front door is still being heard and felt.

Fr. Bob and his colleagues believed that the Cursillo was a magnificent tool for spreading and implementing the incredibly upbeat teaching that was emanating from the Council. The two fit hand in glove. The decrees on the Church and the Laity clearly spelled out that the laity were the Church, and the clergy were their servants. The apostolate of the laity was to be "thoroughly broadened and intensified," as Pope Paul VI had stated.

Cursillistas in Saginaw got the message. They were participants in every significant organization in the diocese. They were involved in state and national government at the highest levels. They were entrenched up to their eyeballs in the Civil Rights Movement of the 1960s, both for blacks and Hispanics. In the city of Saginaw they established and staffed a halfway house, treatment center, and job placement office for homeless men and women. Several middle class families moved into the inner city to work and be present for the poor. Others formed a group to buy houses on land contracts that they turned over to minority families who could not get conventional financing. Active Vincent de Paul societies sprang up all over the diocese, and old ones were reinvigorated. Cursillistas organized and promoted a diocesan-wide lecture series on the Vatican Council.

Unfortunately, enthusiasm scares people in general and threatens those in positions of power. The older clergy didn't know what to do with this new breed of laity. They thought they were trying to take over their church. The clergy hadn't heard that the Pope and all the bishops of the world had formally and clearly announced that the people were the Church and the clergy were their servants. The word that broke Bishop Steve's back was a message from a group of cursillistas that it would be a very beautiful and meaningful gesture to the poor if the bishop would consider vacating his mansion and become the pastor of a little Polish parish in the inner city that had just become vacant. One week later the Bishop declared a Cursillo moratorium. You no doubt recognize how closely that word is related to another, mortician. In the same decree, Fr. Bob was fired as diocesan director of the Cursillo movement.

The mortar that kept the bricks of leadership credibility together, both for priests and laity, began to crumble. For some years now the credibility walls have been tumbling down at an alarming rate and the ensuing dust has almost choked off the voice of Church leadership. The situation is similar to what happened to the priest Zacharias, the father of John the Baptizer. Because he refused to believe the message of the angel Gabriel that his wife Elizabeth would bear a son who would "reconcile families and bring back the wisdom of good people," Zacharias was struck dumb.

Zacharias changed his mind when his elderly wife gave birth to a healthy son. That was easy. But his speech did not return until he expressed a willingness to change custom and tradition and give his son a name that none of his family had ever had. The yet more subtle break with tradition was in Zacharias' yielding to the insistence of a woman, his wife Elizabeth, who held her ground against the patriarch and stated, "He must be called John." And the subtlest of all breaks was in yielding to the feminine principle in the Godhead, the Holy Spirit, Hagia Sophia herself, who put that whole show on the road.

That story had the happy ending of never too late. Even a very old lady can have a baby. Will the Council and the creative programs like the Cursillo that the Council generated survive and grow? Can the old lady, Mother Church, have some new babies? Sophia will win out in the end.

CHAPTER EIGHTEEN
SHEPHERDING IN THE ASPHALT JUNGLE

Sacred Heart was a German parish. It had been a prosperous place at one time. Its twin Gothic spires were the tallest in town. The high school and convent were old. The grade school and rectory were relatively new. In the 1950s the Germans in large numbers started to move to the west side of the river to make room for the blacks and Hispanics who were moving south. Bishop Woznicki sent Fr. Bob there as pastor with the hope that his German name might slow down the exodus a bit. Also, because of his identification with the blacks and Hispanics at St. Joe's, he would be a welcome sign to the folks who were moving into the area.

Fr. Bob arrived in late April and was received with mild suspicion. His predecessor was a distinguished monsignor who had been in charge of the matrimonial tribunal. As far as urban pastors went, Fr. Bob was a kid, the youngest pastor in the city. His only experience was at that "nasty" place down 6th Street near the foundry, St. Joe's. His dad's grade school classmate and now a priest in charge of Catholic Charities, Monsignor Ralph Richards, urged Fr. Bob to do nothing different for two years. He thought he would try that.

So Fr. Bob smiled a lot, carefully prepared his sermons, visited the children in school, the sick in the hospitals, and religiously attended every organizational meeting in the parish. In the first week of

Sacred Heart Church (photo courtesy Saginaw News)

June he presided over the high school graduation and his picture was front and center on the class photograph. When school was out he thought he would have some breathing time to tend to his three diocesan jobs, the Mexican Apostolate, the Rural Life Conference, and the Cursillo. No such luck.

A few days after the janitor locked the doors of the school for the summer, the state fire marshal knocked on the rectory door with orders to not only close the high school, but to tear it down. He stated emphatically that it was beyond redemption. The Bishop must have known that this was going to happen because he wasn't very surprised when Fr. Bob gave him the news. He simply directed him to the diocesan architect in order to have plans drawn for the second story of the grade school and to have the job bid out. When Bob indicated that this might be more than the parish could afford, Steve told him, "Just do it." And he did it.

About a month later when the bids came back for about $300,000, Bishop Steve jumped and said, "You can't do that." And Fr. Bob said, "Amen." Then the Boss sent Fr. Bob to see Olin Murdock, the superintendent of schools. Olin, too, must have been thinking about this for a while because he had a ready answer for Bob. "Merge the high school with St. Joe's. Move the junior high into the grade school building, and purchase six mobile classrooms for the grade school." Olin's response to Bob's inquiry about cost was, "about $100,000."

Bob's response was simple. "We can't do that."

"Tell it to the Boss," was Olin's answer.

Fr. Bob did. And what do you guess was the Boss's reply? You're right. "Do it." And Fr. Bob did.

There was a wonderful lady in the parish whose husband and son had made some nice money marketing wheat germ as a food supplement. With the mother's blessing Fr. Bob talked to the son about a loan. After assuring him that the Bishop's name would be on the note and that he would pay off the loan if the parish could not, the son loaned his old parish the hundred grand. So down went the old high school and two old houses to make room for the six mobile units. Water and sewer lines were installed as were yards and yards of more asphalt. Then to balance things off, up went power lines, posts, and rolls of wire fencing. Up went six mobile classrooms, and up went the debt, of course, and down went the collection. Why? Out went more Germans to the west side of town.

When Fr. Bob got his appointment to Sacred Heart it was with the stipulation that he continue his three diocesan jobs. He agreed to the stipulation on the promise that the Bishop would not take away the assistant pastor. Most of the other pastors in town had two assistants, so he didn't think he was asking for the moon. Fr. Ray Oswald hung around through the construction project and the Mexican Apostolate. School was underway and Fr. Bob was out of town conducting a Cursillo when Sacred Heart was robbed and Fr. Ray was episcopally kidnapped. On that weekend and several succeeding ones Bishop Steve sent his secretary, Fr. Jim Hickey, to Sacred Heart to assist with confessions and Sunday Masses. The bonus that Fr. Bob got out of that trade-off was to be able to brag in later years that the Cardinal Archbishop of Washington, D.C. was once his assistant.

The men in the Cursillo helped to solve Fr. Bob's personnel problem. Frank, Bill, and Dr. B. came to the rectory one evening with a proposal. There was a canyon in New Mexico where alcoholic priests were sent for rehab. The program was pretty simple. Manual labor and a holy hour everyday, a program something like the one at the old Walnut St. jail in Philadelphia run by the early Quakers. Solitude and Bible reading drove everybody nuts. This trio of "new" friends knew a priest out there that the Paraclete priest-directors thought was ready to go home. The only problem was his boss in another state didn't want him back. The trio, all longtime AA members, offered to fly this priest to Saginaw, and to help monitor his behavior. This sounded like a good deal, a chance to help a hurting priest and get some full-time assistance to boot.

John R. moved in a couple of weeks later. He was old enough to be Fr. Bob's dad, and he was exceedingly angry with his bishop. The AA guys visited him regularly and took him to meetings. They also helped him get a set of used wheels and some golf clubs. He was really a good golfer and playing was good therapy. He faithfully shared the duties of the parish, but he wasn't a happy camper.

John R. was old school and he had slept through the Vatican Council. He didn't believe in anything that Fr. Bob was trying to do and he found life in the busy rectory very frustrating. Before the year was out he was back on the sauce. People complained about him throwing empty jugs from his car onto their lawns. The state police fished him out of a ditch one night and drove him home. Something had to be done.

The AA guys and some other benefactors sponsored John at a high class, expensive treatment center near Detroit. He was there for two months. Things were better for about a year, but one night Fr. Bob had to rush him to the hospital because he had ruptured his esophagus. When John R. refused to be monitored on the drug antibuse, Bishop Steve called John's Bishop to notify him that he was sending him home. A few months later John R. died of a heart attack. A very talented but a very sick man. Priests, as you probably know, suffer from a very high incidence of alcoholism.

While John R. was away for treatment, Fr. Bob had to look around for help. Fr. Dave was a native of the territory and had been in the Navy during the war. He was about ten years older than Fr. Bob and had been a pastor in a small rural community for several years. Hard Navy memories, the death of his brother in battle, the loneliness of rectory life in the country, depressed him heavily. When he came out of intensive counseling no one seemed to know what to do with him. Fr. Bob invited him to come and live at Sacred Heart.

At first he was like a zombie from all the medication he took. He celebrated the 6:30 A.M. Mass daily and then returned to bed until noon. After lunch he faithfully visited the sick at the three local hospitals and got home for a short nap before dinner. After eating he watched a little TV and retired by 8 P.M. But slowly he came back to life, and it was a thrill to watch him come out of his cocoon.

Fr. Bob was a bit embarrassed by the rectory that he lived in. It was bigger and better appointed than any other house in the neighborhood. His way of dealing with this was to open the house up to the people who had paid for it. So on Saturday evenings he invited in a mixed group of six or seven couples for cocktails and dinner. After the meal they sat in the living room and discussed the issues of the community and the parish. Soon it was discovered that Fr. Dave was a gourmet cook and a master bartender. He fully enjoyed shopping, preparing the food, and serving the guests. He began to enter into the discussions and made insightful contributions. The children in school began to warm up to him. His Sunday homilies were warm and full of joy. He spent a whole lot less time in bed.

For a time Fr. Bob thought that Fr. Dave was falling in love with the ebullient Irish lady who did the books. He played cards with her after dinner and talked with her on the phone later in the evening. But Dave surprised everybody when he announced one early summer day that he was going to marry Michelle, the gorgeous young lady who was the organist. Michelle was an African-American. They soon had two beautiful daughters who seemed to have an overdose of Dave's chromosomes. Michelle would get seriously ticked when strangers on the street or in the store would ask if she were their nanny. When he got married, the people down town at the Chancery office thought that Dave had flipped out all the way. Fr. Bob thought that he had finally arrived.

As you no doubt have already noted, Fr. Bob did not follow closely the advice of Msgr. Richards. It was impossible to maintain the status quo when the environment around the status was exploding. He moved as rapidly as he could to explain and implement the ideas of the Vatican Council — Mass facing the people, full use of the vernacular, counseling rooms instead of confessionals, meaningful artwork and music, and especially involvement of the laity. Naturally he caught a lot of flak. He thought that a priest should be like Jesus — a sign of contradiction, an agitator, a questioner, a pest.

One of his early efforts at getting people to think came at Christmas time. Instead of placing a pinkish, blonde, blue eyed statue of Jesus in the crib, he placed a mirror at the bottom of the swaddling clothes. When people looked in the manger they saw themselves. The message was that Jesus is no longer a baby and his name now is John, Mary, Suzy, and Pat. Even old liberal Fr. Coughlin condemned Fr. Bob in his Detroit parish bulletin. So the following year Fr. Bob put a collage in the crib. There were Stalin, Tito, the Beatles, Jimmy Brown, Cesar Chavez, Carmen Miranda, Bob Hope, FDR, Golda Maier, and many others. In the background a Simon and Garfunkel tape played *Silent Night and the Six O'Clock News*. Nothing ventured nothing gained. You win some and lose some. He who hesitates is lost.

Local art students removed the hideous corpus from a huge crucifix in church and transformed it into a glorious, triumphant cross. Jesus didn't lose on Calvary, did He? He won and His

Fr. Bob (in sarape) marching on the Michigan state capitol, 1967

followers should celebrate with joy. Huge banners in church celebrated the feast of Pentecost with the theme "Burn Baby Burn," and the Ascension with "Sing, Jump, Dance, Get off the Ground with Jesus." The stations of the cross were replaced with pictures from the ghetto, the hospitals, the prisons, the factories, where the journey to Calvary passes in the 20th century.

1967 was the year of the long hot summer. When Detroit was torched the powers that were in Saginaw, 90 miles north, got nervous. It was announced on the evening news that the mayor had called an important meeting at city hall for the following day to discuss the situation with community leaders. Fr. Bob and other inner city clergy thought that this was an invitation to show up at the meeting and share their views on how to handle the volatile situation. When they showed up at the meeting they were turned away. They quickly learned that community leaders were GM executives and media folks.

A little angry and insulted the clerics left for home. On his way over to church for the five o'clock Mass, Fr. Bob got called to the phone. It was a black clergyman. He indicated that a number of black community leaders had decided to march from the ghetto to the main downtown intersection where they had invited the mayor to meet with them. In order to give the march some legitimacy and to help keep the lid on, he wanted to know if Bob could get three or four white priests to march with them. Fr. Bob called three guys, celebrated a three minute Mass, and made it to the starting point on Potter St. by 5:30.

About fifty people started marching, but the crowd snowballed rapidly. By the time the group reached the main intersection, Washington and Genesee, a half hour later, several hundred people had joined them. The police had been alerted and assembled at the intersection. The bridge over the river two blocks down Genesee was immediately lifted to seal off the east side. An officer announced that the mayor was not coming. So the group leaders sat down in the middle of the street and told the officer to tell the mayor that they were going to sit there until he came.

After about a half hour it became apparent that the mayor was adamant. The crowd was getting larger and more rowdy by the minute. A large contingent of police arrived. Urged by the black leaders, Fr. Bob went into the Bancroft Hotel on the corner, and called the mayor whom he knew quite well. He agreed to come, but on the condition that the meeting take place in the hotel and not on the street. It took the mayor a half hour to get there. It was too late

The riot was on. It wasn't anything like Watts or Detroit, but people did get shot and beaten and a lot of property was damaged. When the windows in Sacred Heart school were shattered, a Molotov cocktail thrown into the convent, and lethal weapons discharged in the parking lot, Fr. Bob knew that the blossoming relationship between some blacks and the white institution that he belonged to were dying and would probably never be resurrected in his lifetime. It was a sad frustrating day.

For Fr. Bob the riot symbolized a crushing failure of human relationships and the beginning of many disappointments. Until the riot his activities with minorities had been jokingly patronized by most of the diocesan priests. His presence at their gatherings was tolerated. Now the priests were openly hostile, especially those whose parishes were on the fringes of the ghetto.

At the Vatican Council one of the magnificent old concepts that was restored was that of collegiality. The concept means that the Pope and the Bishops are equal brothers. Collectively they are the Vicars of Christs. The Pope is only the Vicar of Peter and his unique function is to preserve unity. This spirit was also supposed to prevail at the local level with the bishop and his priests. In an effort to create this spirit, a small group of young, interested, and concerned priests began to meet on Sunday afternoons at Sacred Heart.

Cautiously and politely the priests began to suggest ways in which they might be able to participate and have a say in what, how, when, and where things were done in the diocese, especially in those areas that effected them personally. The response from the Bishop and Chancery office was silence. Finally, in exasperation, 37 priests signed their names to a list of proposals for action and requested a response within three weeks. Further ignoral would mean that the group would go public with their request and withhold religious services in their parishes on that third Sunday.

On Thursday of the second week, all priests of the diocese got a letter from the chancery urging them to attend a very important meeting on the ensuing Sunday afternoon at the seminary. The hall was stacked and so was the deck. A prearranged slate of safe people was presented to form a committee to take this matter under advisement. You know what a committee is, don't you? A group of people who individually can do nothing, and collectively decide that nothing can be done. There was only one negative vote to the proposal, and guess whose name was not on the slate?

As Fr. Bob walked alone out the front door, a brilliant classmate named Gradowski, groomed in Rome for the episcopacy, and whom Fr. Bob thought was the Bishop's fair-haired boy, approached him and said, "Pretty devastating, eh, Moose? I'm sorry." Surprisingly, Gradowski resigned a short while later. For Fr. Bob, however, this act of co-optation was like a vine that started to eat through the mortar and loosen the bricks in the wall of the Church.

About three weeks after this meeting, Fr. Bob got a letter from the man who had loaned Sacred Heart the money to put up the six mobile classrooms. He had been fighting cancer for some time, and now he wanted to get his accounts in order. He wanted his money back. The parish had been paying some interest but had no way of accumulating money to pay off the principal. So Fr. Bob sent the letter to Bishop Steve. His name was on the note.

The Boss immediately summoned Fr. Bob to the chancery and asked for his resignation so that he could send in a pastor "who could pay his bills." Fr. Bob told the bishop that he first wanted to talk the matter over with his church committee. The committee was infuriated and so were a lot of other people when the word got out. In a few weeks, the Bishop was going to celebrate his 50th anniversary as a priest and a big bash was planned at the cathedral. The committee wanted to plan a massive protest at this event.

In Fr. Bob's mind this was no way to run a railroad. He was running out of track, true, but there had to be a way to create a little space for everyone. So he went back to see Bishop Woznicki with a compromise. He would remain as pastor, but the day to day operation of the parish would be turned over to his assistant, Fr. Ecken. Fr. Bob would go to graduate school, but return on weekends to help with confessions and Sunday Masses. The bishop was so happy with this proposal that he even agreed to pay the graduate school expenses. The parishioners were also agreeable. A half of loaf is better than none.

The Bishop had a wonderful 50th anniversary. Bishops and priests came from all over the country. Not long afterwards, however, he became seriously ill and had to be hospitalized. Fr. Bob went to the hospital to visit him, and was cautioned by the nurses not to stay long and not to expect very much in communication because at times the bishop was delirious. This was a good day, however. Spiritual father and son had a warm talk together. As Fr. Bob, with tears in his eyes, was about to leave, Bishop Steve smiled and said, "Moose. You are the best fence walker I've ever met." No compliment could have pleased Fr. Bob more.

CHAPTER NINETEEN
TACKLING TOUCHDOWN TOWN

Going back to school was not a happy thought for Fr. Bob. He hadn't liked the main course of education from day one, and was extremely happy in 1956 when his seminary education came to an end. None of the seminaries that he had attended and none of his degrees were recognized by accrediting agencies. He didn't care. When the diocese started a program in the 1960s to get seminary degrees accredited he wasn't interested. Now when he was 38 years old and considering a larger playing field, he wondered whether the lack of accreditation had been a subtle means of social control. His options were seriously restricted.

When he negotiated with Bishop Woznicki on returning to school, he didn't have a definite program in mind. His initial intention was to go to law school. From hard experience he knew that you couldn't make charity toward one's neighbor a civil law, but it was possible to pass laws that gave people their civil rights, like open housing and equal job opportunities. Then once people became neighbors and enjoyed a similar economic base they might start loving one another. So he thought that maybe he should go back to square one and concentrate on the legalities and the politics of civil rights.

In the Spring of 1967 an interesting conference on celibacy was scheduled at Notre Dame. The venerable Fr. John O'Brien was the featured speaker. The mood among the clergy was that optional celibacy was just around the corner and celibates ought to start thinking about their options. So a carload of young Saginaw priests decided to drive to South Bend and hear what O'Brien had to say. The conference proved to be not only premature but also wishful thinking. Team Vatican decided that the lid was staying on.

The visit to Notre Dame, however, did prove fortuitous for Fr. Bob. At the conference he bumped into two priest friends from other parts of the country who had been involved in activities similar to his. They were now students in Sociology at Notre Dame. They seemed happy in their situation and convinced Bob that Sociology was continuous and supplementary to the activities that he was engaged in, so he applied for summer school to test the waters and was accepted.

Fr. Bob and John Sheehy from Grand Rapids rented an apartment on the edge of town. In early June Bob was attending three classes: Marriage and Family, Minority Group

Relations, and Cultural Anthropology. He was amazed at the amount of time he had on his hands. These classes only met three times a week. Nine hours of class and nine hours of reading left him with one hundred and fifty hours a week to do as he pleased. He almost went nuts. But Sheehy saved the day. He really knew how to play and the old Moose, his nickname was partially resurrected, was a quick learner.

Bob did well that summer. (The "Father" in his name started to get ignored in academia and clerical garb was traded in for sportier attire.) He got an A and two B's in his classes, and that convinced him that he could cut this mustard without a lot of sweat. So he enrolled for the fall semester. The course work got a bit more difficult with Theory, Methods, and Statistics, but it wasn't a schedule anything like the one he knew in the seminary. Besides he was a priest and this was Notre Dame. Also he was older than almost all of the students and a majority of the professors, nor had he totally forgotten the negotiating skills he had utilized in high school.

Like most people in the country and even most undergraduate Sociology majors, Bob had no idea what the discipline was all about. Most people identify it with Social Work, an area you study if you want to work with and help people. Sociologists, however, don't really want to do anything of that nature. They just want to understand what's going on among people. Like other scientists, their goal is to understand and predict, and their particular focus is on human interaction. Sociologists offer their insights to anyone who might be interested in doing something practical. They'll work for the government, the church, the police, or the underground, the Mafia, and the devil if these organizations will pay their fees.

What really gave Bob academic fits was Statistics. You no doubt remember the trouble he had with algebra back at St. Anne's. He had had only a geometry class since then and that was over twenty five years ago. He had extreme difficulty trying to figure out the least common denominator among a set of numbers.

It was an unique blessing of this course that the professor was a bona fide mathematician and he resented the fact that the administration was loading up his courses with social scientists who had no real interest in math and were there only to satisfy a requirement. It was his theory that social scientists were simply trying to legitimate themselves as true scientists by working out a nominal marriage with the math department. His way of coping with the unwanted numbers was to announce that everyone who passed the first semester course would get an automatic A for the second semester. The result was that everyone worked very hard the first term, and then let the professor do his unmolested thing with the math majors the second term. It was a great compromise, at least for Bob.

Bob drove religiously to Saginaw every weekend to help with the work of the parish. It was about a 500 mile round trip. It gave him a lot of uninterrupted time to think about what he was studying and what was going on in his life. It was also good to get back to his roots and see what was happening with the folks he had shared the world with the past dozen years. It was always a happy time.

One beautiful Sunday afternoon in the fall when a lot of folks were out looking at the leaves, Bob had a very unhappy experience on his way back to South Bend. More concerned about the colors than the road, a carload of elderly ladies swerved into his lane. To avoid a head-on collision he took to the ditch. Three rolls later Bob had a totaled car, but no personal damages. Seat belts really helped and somebody else must have been watching.

When John R. returned to his diocese and Fr. Dave resigned and got married, the Bishop sent in a young assistant by the name of John Ecken. John had been trained by one of the more conservative pastors in the richest parish in the diocese. At first he didn't seem too happy with his new assignment and was more than dubious about the programs that Fr. Bob was running. Bob gave him free reign to do whatever he wanted to do with the exception of returning liturgical practices to those proposed by the Council of Trent in the 16th century. When Bob left for Notre Dame, John was in charge. He enjoyed the new freedom and the direct interaction with the many fabulous people in the parish. The people loosened him up considerably and his growth in wisdom and age and grace became more apparent with every weekend.

In the spring of the year as new life starts to blossom, so did John. On a mid-May weekend he announced to Fr. Bob that he was going to marry one of the nuns from across the street and wondered if Bob would officiate at their wedding. He did.

1968 saw the largest exodus of American priests in history. Proportionately, the diocese of Saginaw lost more priests than any other diocese in the country. No one has ever thoroughly examined the variables that might have caused that Saginaw walk-away, and that's really too bad. It still could make very interesting reading and provide useful insights on how to deal with the future of the priesthood. If you had an historic home of great value and significance, and it started to collapse, wouldn't you call in some experts to take a look at it and see how it might be saved? What is even more upsetting, thirty years later priests are still leaving, even old ones. And no one seems to care enough to figure out why.

Bob went back to Notre Dame for the summer to take two courses and get ready for comprehensive exams and a master's degree. The diocese had a new coach, Bishop Francis Reh. During his first official visit with Francis, Fr. Bob was asked to resign the parish. He did, but only on the condition that his old buddy, The Hat Sikorski, be the new pastor. The Hat had just returned from the University of Louvain where he had been the spiritual director. Bob was neither asked about nor given another assignment. The message that he heard was that no one cared where he was as long as he wasn't in Saginaw.

The local seminary had been closed. There was no Catholic college anywhere close to Saginaw, and the diocese wasn't interested in research. So Bob began to seriously wonder about his future. Most sociologists survived by teaching. He wasn't sure that he wanted to teach. His advisor at Notre Dame urged him to give it a try to see if this is what he wanted to do with the next stage in his life.

After sounding out several small Catholic colleges in southern Michigan, a small girls' school called Madonna in Detroit made him an offer. He would teach three courses and be a part time chaplain. Housing and meals were provided. He would continue commuting to Saginaw on weekends giving the Hat assistance at Sacred Heart. Also, he planned to keep his ties to Notre Dame alive by taking a couple of readings courses during the year. When he discovered that the Madonna course load was not that heavy, and the Notre Dame connection was too fuzzy, he hustled downtown to Wayne State University and enrolled late in three sociology courses.

The school year of 1969-70 was extremely busy for Bob. He had fun teaching at Madonna. From the response of the students, he discovered that he had a talent for teaching at this level. Wayne State was a spread-out university. Classes were taught at a variety of locations in the metro area and at all hours of the day. At the end of July he discovered that he had accumulated 35 hours of credit. Along with his Notre Dame credits he now had enough hours for a Ph.D. What remained was the writing of a dissertation, and one didn't have to be on campus to do that.

It was major decision time. To be or not to be an active clergyman. His new knowledge about society, culture, institutions, stratification, and social change, was wonderful stuff, but the person and place to which he was "hinged" wasn't interested and to all indications would never be. Going back to Saginaw on a full time basis did not look promising. He was clearly a persona non grata with the ecclesiastical institution. Trying to implement his new sociological insights in a parish situation would only make things worse for everyone, the Bishop, parishioners, and himself. In an effort to clarify his thinking, on one of his weekend trips to Saginaw, he stopped to discuss the situation with his old mentor Ted LaMarre. To his chagrin he learned that this giant of a man who had given the diocese 25 years of intense service in the toughest spots in the territory was being pressured out. Case closed. If there was no room for LaMarre in Saginaw then sure as heaven there was no room for Bob.

Two questions remained — where to go, and alone or married? The first question was much more easily answered than the second. Bob went down to the placement office at Wayne State and worked through a folder of job descriptions from schools looking for professors. He sent out a pile of resumes and learned rapidly that he was not well-tuned to the educational institution. Most places did their serious hiring in the spring. He got a lot of thank-you -position-filled-notes. Finally in late August he got an invitation to visit Hanover College in southern Indiana. Their sociology department, two people, had just left in a huff and they needed somebody in a hurry. This was Bob's first attempt at negotiating a job. Eleven grand seemed like a lot of money to someone who made $100 bucks a month plus a few stipends. He took the job.

Chapter Twenty
JUMPING OFF THE ESCALATOR

When most people talk about leaving a job they use the verb quit. According to official teaching you can't quit being a priest. At ordination an indelible mark is placed on your soul and you become "a priest forever according to the order of Melchizedek." A priest can only resign. An exceedingly large number, 125,000, has resigned since the mid-1960s, about 25,000 in the U.S. alone. That's over half of the priests under 60 years of age.

So the big question that's on the table is why. There are no simple answers. The old Romans put it nicely: *tot capita quot sententia.* There are as many opinions as there are heads. Most resigned priests would need a long time to tell you specifically why they resigned. Some of them are still trying to work out an explanation in their own heads because all motivation is mixed and varied. It's a cumulative thing.

First off, it's very important to consider the social situation that surrounded these priests. Today a person is pretty much identified by his or her job. With your job goes about everything else, your status, your livelihood, your consumption patterns, your security, your future, and your mobility. Most priests were ordained in their late twenties and had invested a long time and a significant amount of income into their priestly preparation. Fr. Bob had spent eleven years in this preparation. Resignation came for the great majority after several years of ministry. It took Bob fourteen years before he made his final decision

The secular job market, as you well know, is not wide open for men crowding forty, especially if they have questionable academic credentials, and few marketable skills other than talking. How many corporations want a used preacher on their team? Sit yourself in a personnel office with a resume in front of you on your desk. Here's a near 40 year old man who has just quit a job with a fair amount of status, and his academic credits are in philosophy and theology. Now what color light is going to turn on in your head? Maybe yellow. Most likely red. The point to be made here is this. To pick up marbles at this juncture in life took a lot of time and courage. The situation in the lives of these priests must have been truly miserable for them to risk so much.

When people ask Bob why he resigned, he responds with a single word, prayer. With a quizzical look people answer,

"What do you mean, prayer?" Do you remember the chat about the Breviary — that long collection of Latin prayers that Bob had to recite every day? For him it was a real onus. Very rarely was he ever inspired by the recitation. Sometimes he was neither reverent nor safety conscious as he read it while driving his car around the state. Sometimes to beat the midnight deadline, he read it sitting on the ground in front of his headlights on the side of the road. At other times he read it on the john or during the ads while watching a football or basketball game, but he did it religiously for six years.

Then one evening about l0:45 P.M. a doorbell interrupted the final minutes of a basketball game that he and Fr. Ted were watching. They still had time for the Breviary. At the door he encountered a young couple who needed a referee for the fight they were having. So Fr. Bob invited them into the office, put the gloves on them, and told them to have at it. And they did. They hadn't talked about what was eating them for three years and they battered the life out of each other. When they finally ran out of ether, Fr. Bob tried to revive them with a little air on the spirit of love and forgiveness. Then he sent them home with the promise that they wouldn't talk about these things again until they came back the next night at 7:00 P.M., a more reasonable hour for clean fighting.

When he went back into the living room, the tube was off, LaMarre had gone to bed, and there sat his Breviary on the table. It was 12:15 A.M. and he had missed his obligation for the first time. He was a bit anxious and nervous. Should he have recited his Office earlier in the day? Did he commit a sin? He had the early Mass in the morning. Would celebrating Mass in a state of mortal sin put him in double jeopardy with God?

He had an up and down night and celebrated Mass without the roof caving in. At a reasonable hour the next day he drove across town to talk to his confessor. He was slightly shocked when his confessor told him that he had made a serious mistake. He should have asked the couple either to wait until he had finished his prayers or to come back the next day. Bob was doubtful whether the recitation of the Breviary superceded the law of charity, but he never missed again for seven years.

Many years later Fr. Bob was in Rome with a Cursillo team and they went to visit Fr. Bernard Haring at the Gregorian University. He was the top moral theologian in the world. A part of their conversation was about prayer and its importance in peoples' lives. Jesus had said that we should pray always. Of course He didn't mean that we should be reading and reciting and chanting formulae twenty four hours a day. He meant that we should try to live in the presence of God who is the Divine Guest within us as much as possible. Prayer is consciousness of who we are and how we relate to the universe, our neighbors, and our Creator. Prayer formulae are like an alarm clock that wakes us up to this realization. Once we are conscious, it's best to shut the alarm clock off because it will only deter or impede our prayer.

Then Fr. Haring said something that really got Fr. Bob's attention. "If the alarm clock that you are using doesn't work, then you ought to look around for another one." Immediately Bob inquired about the Breviary. Bernard, without hesitation replied, "If the Breviary is not a functional alarm clock for you, then try something else. The obligation is to pray and to live in the presence of God." Bob heard a heavy clunk in his head. A big brick had just fallen out of the wall of ecclesiastical truth. This was the beginning of the end. He never recited the Breviary again. What he did do was procure a pocket-sized copy of the Psalms in English and used it frequently and efficiently for an alarm clock. Many years later he still isn't a red hot prayer, but he's getting warmer.

A large number of people think that the major reason for the exodus of so many priests can be attributed to the mandatory celibacy rule that went into effect in the 12th century. This is the opinion of Team Vatican. The priests who left are weak and worldly. They can't take the heat and have fallen for the old traps, "the world, the flesh, and the devil." The flesh most of all. This, of course, is an oversimplification. In the 1960s, the world taken for granted got questioned at all levels. So a lot of priests like Fr. Bob began to ask, who started this business of celibacy? What were the reasons for making this rule? What is the significance of celibacy? What are the consequences? Does anyone understand and appreciate the symbol?

There is good historical evidence that celibacy was practised among Christians from earliest times, but it was never imposed on anyone, however, and it was never demanded as a condition for church office. In fact, the opposite was true. St.

Paul wrote to Timothy, "A bishop then must be married . . . If a man cannot manage his own household, how can he take care of one of God's congregations?" It is noteworthy that priests have been married for a longer period of time than they have been celibate. Four centuries longer, to be exact. If the Church survived for twelve hundred years without the rule, then it couldn't have been all that important. Then why was this rule mandated and made a condition for office?

There is also some historical evidence that celibacy was mandated to keep valuable church property in the hands of the institution, and out of the hands of emerging and powerful clerical families. A celibate priest could still have children, but by law they were bastards and could not inherit property. You had to have power to pull off a move like that. The Coaches of the Middle Ages had a lot of power in both realms, the temporal and the spiritual. They used it to their best advantage. They really only needed the temporal clout to pull off mandatory celibacy. It is now being frequently stated that it was their spiritual hammer which helped to disguise the real intent and that firmly nailed the rule to the wall.

This heavy hammering, overlaying, if you will, of "spiritual" significance gradually dominated Church teaching. One Coach, for example, without a shred of historical evidence declared that Jesus was a celibate. That belief became so strong that for centuries no one even dared to consider whether Jesus might have been married. Today there is strong evidence that in order to take on the role of teacher that Jesus did, he would have had to have been married, otherwise no one would have listened to him. In spite of all this heavy temporal and spiritual insistence on celibacy, clerics never fully accepted the program. Only a casual reading of history reveals violations on almost every page.

In reviewing the explanations that he was given for accepting the spiritual overlay or "the good" of celibacy, Fr. Bob recalls these basic ideas. One, he would be a walking sign of God, living proof that "with God all things are possible." Two, he would be set apart and closer to God for making this heroic sacrifice. Three, he would be freer and unimpeded in doing the work of God. Four, because of his unattached position he would be more objective and understanding in his dealings with God's people. Five, his reward would be great in the kingdom of heaven.

As Fr. Bob started to think seriously about this rationale many contradictions began to pop up. On the sign business, was he asking God to make a square circle? After all, when God put the human show on the road it was immediately declared that "it was not good for man to be alone" and a helpmate was produced on the spot. Was it the height of arrogance to demand a miracle of God everyday so that Bob could rise above his human nature? Is living alone more heroic than marrying and having a family? Doesn't the Bible state frequently that God is made most visible by the love of a married couple for each other? Is God's work limited to a formal ministry of the Mass, Breviary, preaching, and Sacraments? Does one become more insightful and objective by not participating in real life? Does God not treat everyone equally? Do ordinary people read any of this symbolism?

What has really gotten things out of whack is the distorted understanding of sex that has plagued Christians from the opening gun. When Christianity was born the culture of the Middle East was infected with Persian Dualism. This perspective on life framed peoples' thinking and permeated their language. Human beings were divided into bodies and souls. Their souls were good and their bodies were evil. To save their souls they had to mortify, make dead, their bodies.

In the very early years of the Church a bright, young North African lad went off the deep end and fathered a child out of wedlock. His mother prayed fervently for his conversion and her prayers were answered. What the world got was a righteous convert. He wrote and preached a lot and his ideas on sex have dominated and influenced Christian thinking until now. In his thinking, original sin was a sexually transmitted disease. To give you an idea how off the wall he was, he stated that it was OK if married people had sex to produce offspring, but if they enjoyed it that was at least a venial sin. Now Bob believes that St. Augustine is in heaven, but he'll bet you that Augustine's face turns crimson whenever that booboo is brought up.

What put a little bit of bounce in the shoes of 125,000 priests was the conviction that this teaching on the evilness and sinfulness of sex had to go. In their estimation, it is this false belief that is the foundation of the clerical state. Because clerics abstain from sex they see themselves as a separate and higher class. It is this false belief that has led many of them to choose power over love and service. It is this concept that is the source of the Church's very controversial teaching on birth control. It is the weapon that is used to subjugate women and deny them priesthood. Finally, it is the source of a mountain of problems that has troubled clerics for many centuries. Here's the start of a list that you can easily extend: The high incidence of alcoholism, pedophilia, and exploitation of females.

When the first priests lost confidence and trust in the leadership, the Vatican was relatively free in granting indults and allowing them to be married "in the church." Then things started to slow down, and finally came to a screeching halt with John Paul II. Recently, the process has opened up a little bit. But the process has never been gentle. To be liberated, the resigning priest had to be evaluated and recommended by a competent psychological authority. The priest had to write a personal letter to the Pope stating why he no longer could meet his celibate obligations. Many resigned priests believe that the thrust of the whole procedure was to label the resigning priest as "sexually sick" and thereby exonerate the institution of any blame. The procedure was also viewed as an attempt to make the hierarchy appear as kind and considerate toward the weak and wavering.

One day at Notre Dame, Fr. Bob chanced upon a faculty discussion where the great American scripture scholar, John McKenzie, was sharing his views. He made a very simple statement that changed Bob's life and helped to move him to resignation. McKenzie said, "The Church has as much control over you as you want to cede, and you have as much freedom as you want to seize." Wow! A bright light went on, and Bob seized his freedom immediately. Well, it wasn't quite as simple as that.

With the freedom seizure came a horrendous problem of conscience. He had made this solemn promise of celibacy and obedience. He occupied a position of reverence and respect with his family, friends, and thousands of people he had touched over fourteen years of ministry. He worried seriously about hurting them by scandal or abandonment. Many a night he went to bed wishing that he would die in his sleep. Almost every priest he talked to about his problem told him he was crazy and reinforced his guilt. They advised him to do exactly what he couldn't do, chill out and play it comfortably.

Here the study of sociology came to Bob's rescue and helped him to see through the smoke screen. He really wasn't crazy. He wasn't in need of serious counselling. He didn't need to die. The problem that he was involved in was not a personal one. It was a social problem and that made a lot of difference. If only a few hundred priests had decided to leave, then maybe their departure could be explained in terms of personal and psychological problems. Counselling assistance would then have been in order. But because 125,000 priests have resigned the problem is no longer personal, but social. Social problems cannot be solved by psychological remedies. Only change in the social structure will do the job. Bob's decision was that in monolithic institutions social change takes place very slowly if at all. He looked at his life-calendar and decided he didn't have that much time left. His call was on target. Thirty years later, Team Vatican is still backing away from the ideals they expressed so beautifully in their Council of the 1960s.

The conclusion that Fr. Bob and a lot of other resigned priests have arrived at is that they are not guilty of betrayal, but the victims of blind institutional thinking. They now see themselves for what they were and are — the courageous vanguard of Vatican II. It has been a long and torturous transition and paid for at a great price.

In reality, there is no shortage of priests in the world. There are 125,000 priests out there that Team Vatican doesn't want to use at this particular time. These men are too free and honest to be reinserted into the lineup. Jesus talked about the folly of putting new wine into old wine skins. With that idea in mind, resigned priests, infused with the fresh air of Vatican II, refuse to play the religion game with the antique balls (forms, containers) of the Councils of Trent and Vatican I. No game is worth playing when the balls have lost their bounce. Hope this doesn't sound too weird or vulgar. What resigned priests really dream about and pray about is that Santa Claus or somebody will bring them and Team Vatican some new balls. Literally and figuratively.

Chapter Twenty-One
INSTANT FAMILY

During Cursillos, a lot of jokes and humorous stories were told. Madolin O'Rourke, who went to California to make the Cursillo and became the first woman director west of California, told a classic story about an old blind horse. A man put up a sign to sell a horse. A buyer stopped, examined the horse's teeth, hooves, and limbs and then asked if the horse could run. The owner swatted the horse on the butt and he took off running, straight into a tree. The buyer asked if the horse was blind and got the response, "Hell no. He just doesn't give a damn."

Because she told the story quite frequently, Madolin became known as the old blind horse. In some ways, the appellation fit. She was an extrovert and an activist if there ever was one. But as you well know, people who do things make mistakes. She wrecked cars; she screwed up appliances; she broke dishes and furniture; she lost things; she wore a lot of band-aids and ace bandages; she was late for almost everything; she misplaced kids and got their names mixed up. She often gave the impression that she didn't "give a damn." Nothing could have been further from the truth. She was afraid and uncertain about a lot of things, but she wasn't a hand wringer or a worry wart. There wasn't any time for that. Because of her indomitable spirit and the constant demands for action she figuratively ran into a lot of trees. Like a Weeble, however, she always bounced back and ran again. Her enthusiasm and people skills were phenomenal. Her zest for life was contagious. When Fr. Bob got down to his last two dollars at the What'll-I-Do-Now race track, he bet on that old blind horse and became a figurative millionaire.

Bob had known Madolin from a distance for a long time. Over the years he had worked with her on the Mexican Apostolate and the Cursillo. She was a big honcha in the diocese, president of just about everything that was open to women. She also was the only female on the board of the Michigan Catholic Conference, and the National Secretariat for the Cursillo movement.

In junior high, Madolin became a part-time nanny for a family with four little boys. Then and there she decided that she wanted six boys. She got seven, plus two girls and two miscarriages. She was Catholic with capital letters. Whatever the Church said she did, sometimes with protest and lack of enthusiasm, but she did it. Her name was O'Rourke, after all.

The same was true with parental authority. When she was offered a scholarship to college, the family said no. Young girls don't go to college. They go to work and get married. She went to work and at age 19 went to church to get married. Before going in to the ceremony, she begged her father to get her out of there. He refused. "It would all work out," he said. It didn't.

Twenty eight years and nine children later, it was still not working. The matrimonial tribunal of the Diocese of Lansing examined the relationship and declared that it was dead on arrival, and that she was spiritually free to marry again.

When Fr. Bob was winding down his clerical career at Madonna College, he learned that Madolin had divorced and was living in nearby Ann Arbor with five of the children. The first four had already married and produced six grandchildren. Son Rick, child number four, was in law school at the University of Michigan and lived nearby. Bob knew Rick quite well. He had taught for a year at Sacred Heart in Saginaw, and together they had purchased a broken down sailboat that they refurbished and sailed around Saginaw Bay. So Bob drove over to Ann Arbor to do the Latino thing. He asked Rick if he would survey his siblings to see if it was OK with them if Bob dated their mother with the intent to marry. An affirmative answer came back quickly. They were smart kids and concerned that there might not be a lot of guys out there who wanted to take on a family of this size.

Seven months later, in spite of the July heat, Bob's feet started to get cold. So Rick and his wife Karen helped Bob. Like a whole lot of males at this juncture in life Bob knew what he wanted to do, but he just needed a little push. The date was set for July 15 and the place would be the Weber Inn in Ann Arbor. That was three days away. All of the kids were called and agreed to come. All except the oldest, Dr. Jeff, who was doing the M*A*S*H thing in Vietnam, but his wife and two sons were on their way.

Madolin and Bob got some new duds for the occasion, Bob's first civilian suit in twenty five years. Then they bought Bob a wedding ring at Kresge's for a dollar and painted it with clear nail polish to keep it from tarnishing. Rick and Karen took care of reservations at Weber Inn. Everything was ready, they thought. Then someone brought up the need for a blood test and a license which required a three day waiting period. Almost-lawyer Rick solved the problem by suggesting a probate license, an alternative for folks who want to keep their marriage a secret and which can be issued on short notice. Bob and Madolin got the paper just before the court shut down on Friday afternoon. They didn't have any secrets to keep. They were just hot to trot and so were the kids.

Madolin and Bob cutting their wedding cake, July 15, 1970

The gang all showed up at Weber's by six o'clock as did three of Bob's clerical friends who wanted to make this an official and ecclesiastical event of the first order. The entrance hymn was an original piece written, played and sung by Rick, entitled "Fiance." It was even more beautiful when the refrain was repeated in seraphic harmony with his brothers.

Bob selected and read a selection from Max Weber about an ethic of responsibility. The gist of the thing was that there comes a time in every man's life when he has to make a serious decision, and he has to do it in the face of criticism and rejection. Madolin told him later that it was a creepy thing to do, passing himself off like he was some sort of a gold-plated hero. She was right. Her selection was much more appropriate, St. Paul's Corinthian piece on charity.

Then the floor was opened to discussion. A lot of things, both heavy and light, were said during the next 25 minutes. Finally the voice of a child brought everyone back to reality. Three year old Paul raised his hand and asked, "Mom, can I ask a question?" When he got the green light, he asked, "When do we eat?" It's his favorite line to this very day, even though he's in his 30's, six feet four, and a controlled 240 pounds.

Before the exchange of spontaneous vows and rings, Rick and his choir sang the beautiful song, "Words." The rendition took everyone's heart away. After a simple Eucharist, all joined in a final song that has become a family theme, "My Cup Runneth Over."

Dinner followed immediately in a private dining room. The meal was frequently interrupted by spoon pounding on glasses. These weird kids wanted to see two old people kiss in public. Most of them also found the courage to get up and make short toasts and speeches. Twelve year old David gave a protest speech when his older brother Rob tried to cart him off to bed about ten P.M. David didn't know why he had to go to bed when "he was having some real fun for the first time in his life." The fun really came from his first public taste of fermented grape juice of which he had managed to sneak in more than a taste.

About midnight everybody crashed. Bob had frequently heard that most couples were so tired at the end of their wedding day that when they got to their honeymoon suite they just put out the lights and fell into bed. Period. Bob is proud to report that they left the lights on and fell into communicating with each other. The period came the following week and they were glad.

The following afternoon, having exhausted the extended checkout time, Bob and Madolin threw their gear into an old Winnebago Brave and headed through Canada to the Northeast for their honeymoon. Part of their gear was five kids and a dog.

Madolin and the "nifty nine," 1984 (from left to right) Paul, Doug, Dave, Madolin, Mike, Rick, Rob, Joan, Jeff

On the honeymoon the kids decided what they were going to call their new parent. They had known him as Fr. Bob, but that was more cumbersome than just plain father. They already had a dad and as luck or fate would have it his name was also Bob. As so often happens, wisdom comes out of the mouth of babes. Paul Andrew, the three year old, piped up, "Why don't we just call him Papa?" And Papa it was and is. The family now has five alliterated and sequential pairs — Jeff and Joan, Rob and Rick, Mike and Midge, Dave and Doug, and Paul and Papa.

When you look at car evaluations in the newspapers, in our town it's on Fridays, the description of hot numbers will let you know what kind of rapid pickup they have, such as 0-40 m.p.h. in 15 seconds. When people reflect on parenthood and learn that a couple has gone from wedding to child in nine months, eyeballs roll, heads nod knowingly, and sneaky, closed-lipped smiles appear. That's fast family! Well how about 0 to 9 kids and 6 grandchildren in less than 10 minutes? That's instant family!

The temptation for the guy in this type of situation, and maybe even for you, is to think that a knight in shining armor has arrived on the scene. You, remember, no doubt, that this new papa was far from a dead chauvinist when he read that sociological crap at the wedding ceremony. Bob's response to Fr. LaMarre's questioning of his sanity when informed of the marriage was also that of a magnanimous martyr. "Well, someone's got to do penance for all the birth control stuff we dumped on people."

Now please don't start thinking that Papa became an instant convert to sanctity and equal rights at the time of his marriage. He didn't. It took a lot of patience and education on the part of the family, as well as a lot of extended hindsight on his part to arrive at what he is going to say next.

How about the adjustments of a wife to the thinking and behavior of a forty year old celibate who thinks that he is God's gift to this family? How much does that cost? How about the children who are asked to open their lives to this stranger who has zero experience with family, wants to move them to another state, has no status, no possessions, and a piddly income? The long and short of all of this is that the family did as much for the "raising" of Papa as he did for them.

CHAPTER TWENTY-TWO
FROM PREACHER
TO TEACHER

Moving from Ann Arbor, Michigan to Hanover, Indiana was a major event. This newly blended family had belongings that were as numerous and as humorous as George Carlin's comedy routine on "stuff." To give you an idea, the parade was led by the largest U-Haul truck towing the largest U-Haul trailer. In that truck were seven sofas and seven beds. One for each person in the entourage. A second tandem made up of a Winnebago, and a Maverick followed that truck and trailer. Both vehicles were loaded to the ceiling with "stuff." A third tandem of a Pontic sedan tethered to a 20 ft. boat ferried more precious "stuff." Finally, a Ford sedan with a fully loaded trunk carried the remaining four people. Incidentally, this transfer of such an abundance of "stuff" was preceded by a huge yard sale and two trips to the dump.

The trip to Hanover was an eight hour ride. The troop had to sleep in a Madison, Indiana motel that night, for a crazy reason. The house that Madolin and Bob had agreed to purchase a month earlier was a long way from the agreed upon fix-up and cleanup. The deal was cancelled. So the next morning they bought another house and moved in that afternoon.

Happy to see new kids in the neighborhood, the youngsters from next door hurried over to say hello. One of the first questions asked related to religion. "Are you guys Catholics?" Midge answered for the Final Five, the handle for Madolin's five children still at home, "Are we Catholic? Our dad's a priest." The youngsters didn't seem to mind that, but were disappointed that their new neighbors wouldn't be going to their school.

Now you've been through a major move haven't you? The census indicates that just about one fourth of Americans move every year. Well anyway, the packing-moving-unpacking gets to you after a while doesn't it? After five days of this moving routine the teeth of this new conglomerate were on edge and getting sharper with frequent grinding. Remember! This was not only a different town in a different state but also a different house with a different floor-plan. Tentative designs for the location of people and the distribution of furniture had to be abandoned and new ones made. It was raining and 104 degrees outside.

The axiom has it that when the going gets tough the tough get going. So dictator Robert decided it was time for someone to take charge of this group and get the job done. His sociological mind coughed up his favorite aphorism, "predictability is the basis of human behavior." For their own comfort and security people need to know what is expected of them and what they can expect from others. Drawing on his experience at managing a staff of twenty people at Sacred Heart, he assembled the little group of seven and proceeded to make life predictable for them. That was not a good move.

Professor Keller, 1984

After Bob's autocratic presentation as to how the move-in was going to evolve and how the labor would be divided among the seven, Madolin called a time-out and made a terse little response. "That is not the way this family operates. You no longer have a janitor, nor a housekeeper, nor a secretary, nor a bevy of nuns to do your bidding. I and the children are not going to play those roles for you. We will allow you a little time to learn how a small democracy operates and we hope that you learn quickly." He did, but in a controlled simmer. He tended to pout a lot, and some say he still does.

By night fall the "stuff" was unloaded, the furniture positioned, the closets filled, the beds made, the rented equipment returned, and Bella's pizza delivered for sustenance. With a little grape juice, some fermented and some not, the new home was toasted and still simmering Papa was amiably roasted by the six. The beds were inviting. Thus began twenty-one years of life at Hanover.

Hanover College is a venerable Hoosier institution. Dating back to 1827, it is the oldest private college in Indiana. It boasts a distinguished collection of alumni. Woody Harrelson of *Cheers,* helped a lot to let everyone in the U.S. know where and what it is. The college is situated on a bluff overlooking the Ohio river in the southeast corner of the state. The natural setting is beautiful and the Georgian architecture is nicely coordinated and appointed.

What keeps the college alive and a thriving is its emphasis on family. A reasonable price tag for an excellent liberal arts education also helps. Over 80% of the faculty and administrators live on campus with the students. Parents are invited and encouraged to participate in a wide variety of campus activities. Faculty members meet frequently with parents, especially the parents of their advisees. If the "real world" is an exacting and demanding place requiring skills in communication, compromise, adaptation, cooperation, and bullet-biting, then Hanover is smack dab in the middle of it.

It proved to be a very wise thing for Bob and Madolin to move to Hanover from Michigan. They were not kids, and both were relatively well known in Michigan church circles. Most people who knew them were willing to bet that their relationship wouldn't last two years. Madolin and the kids were accustomed to a comfortable upper middle class existence. For Bob the question was how would a forty year old celibate adjust to this large instant family. The couple needed some quiet, some privacy, and a non-judgmental arena to work this out.

It is axiomatic in family theory that when you marry you don't marry a single individual. You marry a family. By marrying, Madolin and Bob severely fractured family rules in all directions. Divorce in Madolin's family was unheard of. Divorced Catholics were denied the Sacraments and there was a rule, not always observed, that they were to be shunned. At that time in history, because there were so few, most people didn't know how they were supposed to deal with a "spoiled" priest. Not many years before such men were publicly defrocked and fed to the wolves.

When the wedding was announced their families were cool at best. Surprisingly, the first and practically only one to congratulate them was Madolin's ninety year old mother. Being attuned to what is going on in the world is not necessarily a function of age. Certainly the two strong Catholic families were concerned about Madolin's and Bob's spiritual well-being. If the rules were to be believed, they were on the road to hell. Their behavior was scandalous for many of the people they had known and worked with. And how about the children involved? What kind of an example was this? Latently at least, the relatives must also have been thinking of their own reputations and status. How would they explain this deviation to their children and friends? Whose side should they be on when this subject was brought up for discussion?

Close friends and relatives beyond the immediate family found themselves in a tough situation. Most people don't like boat rocking. It makes them seasick. Bob and Madolin rocked a lot of boats and made a lot of people sick. Good people had to talk about things they didn't know much about. They were forced to do some thinking and some acting that made them uncomfortable. So it was beneficial for everyone that Bob and Madolin got out of town. If nothing else their absence cut down the number of times that questions would be posed and answers had to be given. A new environment also helped Bob and Madolin.

There were sticky problems for Bob and Madolin in their new environment. Jack Horner, the president of Hanover College, was a very good boy. But he was not content to sit in his corner eating plums from his Christmas pie. When new faculty and their spouses joined the Horners for dinner the evening before the school year got underway, Dr. Horner circuitously warned Bob and Madolin that they would be carefully watched. Simple sociologists were suspect at this semi-conservative Presbyterian school. A resigned Catholic priest sociologist would be observed with field glasses and microscope. Almost immediately, however, and to his great credit, Dr. Horner became a loyal supporter and staunch defender of his new Sociology professor.

Other strange things started to happen at Hanover. A few anonymous letters of dreadful condemnation showed up in Bob's mail box. These were balanced with promises of prayer for his return to sanity. Several invitations from small, outlying fundamentalist churches arrived inviting Bob to come and tell about his struggle with "The Whore of Babylon." These he politely refused but learned from them how closely he was being observed.

All things considered, however, Hanover was a wonderful place in which to be. The college had an excellent theology department. Bob had ample opportunities to experience alternative ways of thinking about and practicing religion. The school was a very ecumenical place. Both the faculty and the student body were religiously diversified. Surprisingly, Catholic students were in the majority on campus. Hanover had a strong liberal arts tradition and that fit like hand in glove with Bob's undergraduate education. He thoroughly enjoyed the interaction with the well-educated and congenial faculty. A cross disciplinary perspective on life was something that Bob badly needed in that time of transition. The institution staunchly defended academic freedom. That was new and different. Over the years Bob introduced a number of experiential and experimental programs, but never once was a whistle blown on his activities.

On the home front, major decisions had to be made about the religious socialization of the children. Bob and Madolin, it should be strongly pointed out, had zero beefs about the teachings of Jesus. Their discontent and frustration was with the human aspects of the Church. From the beginning Madolin had insisted on Catholic education for the children. The First Four had attended Catholic grade and high schools as well as Catholic colleges. The Final Five with the exception of three year old Paul had all been in Catholic grade schools. In this new environment the kids were given a choice of schools and very quickly chose the public schools.

Church attendance was another matter. Having been deeply involved in the liturgical movement and extremely conscientious about sermon preparation, Bob got turned off in almost every Catholic church he entered. After several weeks of getting acclimated to this new territory, one Saturday evening Madolin suggested that they try the neighborhood parish for Sunday Mass. Bob reluctantly agreed but on the condition that they arrive on time and find an inconspicuous pew. True to form Madolin wasn't ready on time and Mass had already started when they arrived. The only vacant pew was the front one on the left side. An usher with a scolding look led the group up the center isle giving everyone an unobstructed view of this new suspect family whose head was a resigned priest and whose children attended the public school.

A few minutes later, the elderly pastor ascended the pulpit to read the Gospel. With great seriousness he read the text, "If a woman divorces her husband and marries another she commits adultery." He reiterated the phrase several times in his ill prepared homily. When he finished, redheaded Madolin, from her far end of the pew, gave Bob, sitting on the isle end, a soft whistle and the thumb exit sign. Out they went never to return. At least they beat the Offertory collection and saved a few bucks.

Happy to be out of the parochial school, the kids were also happy to be out of boring, meaningless — their terms — church attendance. Madolin and Bob, however, were still convinced that some religious socialization had to take place. So every Sunday they created their own liturgy. Sunday dinner became a semiformal event. It was preceded by a simple Eucharist. The children took turns each week reading a section of the New Testament. For about fifteen minutes they talked about the reading, how the little story of their lives fit into the bigger story of Jesus' life. A brief ritual of forgiveness followed. Apologies for unkindnesses during the past week were made and the Lord's Prayer recited. "Forgive us our trespasses as we forgive those who trespass against us." Then, after a piece of bread and a cup of wine had been placed in the center of the table, everyone together recited the words of Jesus at the Last Supper, ". . . This is My Body . . . This is My Blood . . . Do this in remembrance of me." They passed the Bread and the Cup, offering each other this Special Food. A brief song made the transition to Mom's delicious cooking and a lot of meaningful and loving conversation followed. There was no pre and post test to demonstrate the effectiveness of this experiment. Today, however, the First Four, who had the complete Catholic treatment, show no significant signs of more intensive Christian living than the Final Five.

The first major lesson that Papa learned about marriage and family was the difference between love theory and practice. Most young couples learn this early in the game. It was harder for Papa. He was forty and you don't easily teach an old dog new tricks, especially one that thinks he already knows all the tricks that have ever been taught. Now in the USA people get married because they are in love. It's below American dignity to marry for money, blood lines, or convenience. For fourteen years Papa had been in the business of selling love, the theoretical kind. Basically, that's all he ever talked about. Love yourself. Love your neighbor. He had a stock-in-trade example of love that he used constantly. "If you want to know what love is all about, look at a crucifix." And for those who listened to him he also had a long list of ways in which they could implement the theory.

As an active priest, climbing into the pulpit and speaking to a church full of people was serious business for Bob. But it was from that location and that distance that he did his practical loving. He lived in an ice-cold castle where he was king and privacy was always available. He had a title and a uniform that set him apart. His relationships with people were always at a distance and on a rational level. The song of his life was played only on black key, sometimes sharps, but mostly flats.

The Hanover house, on the other hand, was small and seven people and a dog lived there seven days a week. The seven were all unique combinations of personality traits. They all had different needs and wants and experiences. They all saw the world and each other in a different perspective, but of necessity they all lived in very close proximity to each other. They shared a common table, common bathrooms, common recreational space. Bedrooms, vehicles, clothes, maintenance tasks were all shared. This was a primary group. Interaction was frequent, intense, and face to face. Love in this arena was a totally different activity. It was a foreign language and a foreign culture to Papa, the former celibate clergyman. He thanks God daily that he was blessed with six wonderful teachers. Papa now tends to believe that Jesus, from what he said and what he did, had to be a married man.

A second important lesson that Papa learned was the reciprocal nature of parent-child interaction. Parents and children both have needs that can only be met by each other. Children, for example, have a lot to do with establishing their parents' identity. Just as they go about as their parents' extension, recognized and computerized by their parents' name, address, characteristics, habits, and credit cards, so do their parents get catalogued and programmed by their children.

You've noticed, no doubt, that parents talk about their kids a whole lot. Some will just out with a detailed commentary on their kids' recent activity. The more courteous ones will ask about yours with the expectation that you will respond by asking about theirs, so your kids had better be worth talking about or you are going to be either embarrassed or turn into an improvisor and a prevaricator. It's the same deal with pictures. Folks ask to see yours so that they can show you theirs. Your kids better look close to normal or you're in trouble. This kind of parental competition goes on all the time, at school, church, athletic encounters, and you name it.

Madolin taught Bob that in order to get everyone's needs met in a peaceful fashion parents have to be direct and up-front in clarifying assumptions and defining expectations. It's very important for everyone to know where the fences are. Another caveat that Madolin inculcated concerned the use of manipulation, working the system. It's a talent that is almost second nature to some youngsters. It can quickly get to the point where parents are intimidated by their own children.

Starting in junior high, students looking for a little more space and status with their peers, will back a parent to the wall with statements like, "Are you afraid of what other people think and say?" or "The bourgeois attitude of this neighborhood makes me want to puke," or " I think the rules of our school and our church really suck."

Another favorite teenager ploy is to pit the parent against the rest of the neighborhood. "C'mon, Dad, everybody else in town is going." "Look, Ma, you're the only one in the area who thinks like that," and "Why don't you give us more options like the other kids have?" Papa got suckered into the option game and frequently got outflanked by the clever kids. Madolin quickly advised that options had to be very specific and limited or you were dead in the water. The kids could cook up a zillion options to everything if you gave them just a little time. Madolin's options were brief and either/or. "Do you want to walk to the movie or stay home?" and "Do you want to shut up or do you want to go to bed?"

Madolin was very clear and straightforward with the children. Her expectations for them were frequently stated and not debatable. Her reason for that was simple. She believed that practically everybody in the world was trying to sell her kids something or trying to tell them how to think and how to live. She couldn't prevent that from happening, so she believed that she had to lay out a strong meaning and value system that the children could use as a comparative base. She was their mother, she loved them like no other, and she had the primary right and duty to let them know what she believed in and stood for. She wouldn't screw them up and they would know that sooner or later by what she did for them. It worked.

On the question of higher education, for instance, from day one there never was a question about the children going to college. The only question was which college. From day one there never was any pressure to be anything but educated. For her that meant the experience of a liberal arts formation. That experience, she believed, if addressed with curiosity and enthusiasm would point out and prepare them for the future. All the children graduated from college in four years with only one illness exception, and seven have completed graduate school.

A third major lesson that Papa learned from this group could be expressed in the axiom, "The family that works together stays together." It's truly amazing what happens to people when they do physical work together on a common cause, like Habitat for instance. Too many people think that just plain talking is binding. It isn't. Like all hot air it soon dissipates. Some people say that money talks and binds, but that isn't true either. Money commands and divides. People are bound together by activity, by exertion, and by sweat.

To meet educational and recreational needs, the Hanover gang started a small construction company to restore historic homes in Old Louisville. When the First Four began to expand from apartments to starter homes, the entire clan like Amish barn builders converged on the scene to paper and paint and build additions. A lot of time and energy were expended, but that was like liquid nails that bonded this family into a loving and caring unit.

The cherry in the Manhattan of life at Hanover was the annual Thanksgiving reunion. It was a struggle for the First Four to get there with their young families and equally difficult for the Final Five to get things organized. Nonetheless it was the event of the year for everyone. The college campus, vacant for the holiday, was an ideal place for such an event. Almost everyone arrived on Tuesday evening. The earliest arrivees got the bigger and better bedrooms. Wednesday was given to hiking, horseback riding, roller skating, fire truck riding, basketball between the in-laws and the outlaws, swimming, square dancing, card games, cutting down and decorating a Christmas tree, home movies, and slides.

On Thursday morning everyone suited up in their best attire and walked to chapel for a homemade Thanksgiving liturgy. After an incredible meal that everyone seemed to contribute to in some way, the little ones took a nap while the big people got ready for the arrival of Santa Claus. He had gifts for all the little people and the big folks exchanged gifts according to lots. Except for the infants, Friday was a day at Churchill Downs in nearby Louisville. Believing in potlatch, winnings were put into a hat for a big family dinner at a nice restaurant. Saturday was a day for games, shopping, theater, rest and preparation for early departure on Sunday morning. The annual event was a strong and binding tradition that everyone treasured. It was a living tribute to Madolin's firm but loving way of doing family.

This was the general pattern of Bob's new life. From the family he got a free-flowing, give and take experience of joyful living. From faculty and administrators he found new peer acceptance and esteem, new ideas and new models of healthy living. From students he received intoxicating and genuine feedback that rekindled his defeated enthusiasm. It was at Hanover that he learned again to be a music maker and a dreamer of dreams. The Weeble was still wobbling, but the guilt was gone.

CHAPTER TWENTY-THREE
MADOLIN'S TREE

Have you ever noticed that there are some things in life that you would like to change and others that you would like to hold steady? Then when you do a reality check you find that everything changes and nothing remains the same. It makes life frightening, especially when you start thinking about your health and continuity. We start doing that pretty early in life. Things start breaking down and falling apart for us at an early age. We start with little boo-boos that gentle hugs and tender kisses cure. Then before you know it we get big boo-boos and need the doctor, and it's not long after that the "takerunder" starts up his backhoe to dig a hole for our box.

Why don't we like to think about that? No doubt it's because we haven't heard many clear answers to the questions about pain and death. So here Bob would like to share with you one of the most significant experiences of his life, the dying of his wife, Madolin. Maybe the sharing will be of some help to you in looking at your own mortality.

First of all, here are some basic principles about life and its purpose. When you open the box of life in any part of the world you will discover, as Joseph Campbell did, that the instruction manuals all say the same thing. The characters are different but the stories that contain the instructions are all basically the same, and have been since the beginning of time. This is what they say. One: we are all made in the image and likeness of the Creator — there is a spark of the divine in all of us. Two: we are all one family — we are all brothers and sisters. Three: Like all other creatures we belong to the universe, it doesn't belong to us. Living in sync with the universe is the only way to go. Four: Loving and forgiving one another will bring us wholeness and eternal life.

In 1985 Madolin was recruited by Our Lady of Peace Hospital in Louisville to head-up a new family program for their substance abuse unit, and that meant that either she or Bob would have to be a commuter. Because of Madolin's more intense work schedule they decided to purchase a home in Louisville and let Bob do the commuting. Madolin flourished in this new environment.

In the Spring of 1987, however, Madolin began to experience perpetual fatigue and stomach problems. As a partial solution, she encouraged Bob to buy a house that would make for one floor living. She had spotted a place that had been on

Madolin's tree

the market for a long time and which she thought could be had for a very reasonable price. She was right. They bought the property for the lot, not for the house. It was the dumpiest structure within a five mile radius. It looked like three beat up house trailers nailed together with each one set back from the other about eight feet. That made for semi-neat looking corner windows, but the termites had eaten up the frames as well as other significant parts of the house. So they built over and around this weird structure and ended up with a decent house.

The lot of course was the drawing card. There were fifteen large trees nicely scattered around this one hundred foot square lot. Directly in front of the entrance was a large maple tree that came to be known as Madolin's tree, a prophetic metaphor of life. In early May as the renovation of the house got underway, an odd and heavy snow storm hit Louisville. One of the major branches of the tree could not support the weight of the snow and split off, crashing on the driveway and leaving a large gaping scar on the trunk of the tree.

A tree doctor advised, "The tree won't survive. Cut it down."

"Over my dying body," replied Madolin. "Trim out the tree and paint the trunk. I'll do the rest. That tree will live."

"The rest" was fertilizing the roots and talking to the tree every day. It healed slowly, and by midsummer it was doing beautifully. Then came an August thunder storm.

It was an hellaceous water, light, and sound show. Power lines and trees were down all over the place. Storm sewers backed up. Traffic stopped in its tracks. Sirens wailed for hours. When the storm subsided, there was a second major branch of Madolin's tree split into large pieces all over the yard. A new tree doctor advised, "A tree struck by lightning like that one has been is a rapidly dying tree. Cut it down." Madolin's response was almost identical to her first one. Rather than trim the tree this time, she requested that the doctor cut the tree back almost to the trunk. He did so with impatience and disdain. Again Madolin fertilized and talked to the tree, and again the tree healed.

Next came the earthquake. On a Saturday morning in the fall of 1987, Madolin got a call from her doctor's office that they wanted her to go to the hospital immediately for a blood test. The test that she had at her regular checkup on the previous Wednesday did not look right, so the doctor wanted another one right away. The doctor's suspicion was strengthened by the second blood test. A bone marrow sample subsequently confirmed that she had leukemia, the worst kind, myelogenous.

Physically, Madolin resembled her mother who died at the age of 102. Her father died at 86, and she had brothers and sisters in their 70s and 80s. She had always been the most energetic and active member of the family, a very young 67. This was devastating news. The doctor indicated that the disease would go from chronic to acute in three to five years and when that happened there would be no remedies.

Back home in the family room Madolin went through Kubler-Ross's five stages of death and dying in about twenty minutes. Then she called the nine children to appraise them of her condition.

All of the children and grandchildren came home for Thanksgiving. During the formal meal of the day, Madolin urged the children not to worry nor be depressed. She announced that she did not intend to play the sick role; that life would go on as usual; and the way to handle this situation was to take it one day at a time. She repeated one of her many axioms, if life throws you lemons then make lemonade.

Madolin went on chemotherapy immediately and made frequent visits to the oncologists for blood counts and adjustments in the dosages of pills and shots. She did regular exercises in the neighborhood pool, walked often in the park, and even played tennis when the weather was suitable. She did tire easily and walking got increasingly more difficult, but she consented to an occasional use of a wheelchair only in the last two months of life.

During the four years of her illness, Madolin and Bob often visited the children across the country, went to workshops and conventions, took a cruise to Alaska, and visited European shrines during two summer tours.

Madolin's number one priority was healing. She didn't rule out a miracle, a complete cure of her leukemia, and she pursued this in every possible manner. She went to daily Mass, a practice she had observed for most of her life. She prayed fervently for the doctors and nurses who were treating her. To her they were direct and immediate instruments of God. Madolin and Bob together went to many healing workshops and conferences. They attended a lot of prayer meetings where loving friends prayed with her and imposed their healing hands on her ailing body. Bob administered the Sacrament of the Sick to her on a regular basis. Finally, they visited Marian shrines where thousands of people had been healed over many years.

The effects of these ceremonies and pilgrimages on Madolin's life were many and visible. She gained new energy to be active and engaged in life and an unbelievable amount of interior strength to deal patiently and quietly with the debilitating effects of the disease and the side effects of the chemotherapy. Hardly anyone ever suspected the extent of her pain and inconvenience. She also acquired a new zeal to serve others and profound insights and compassion for the clients she counselled right up to her final days of life.

Lourdes in Southern France, which Bob and Madolin visited in the summers of 1988 and 1990, was their favorite shrine. What truly moved them about Lourdes was the love and care of the sick expressed by the thousands of volunteers of all ages and from all parts of the world who came annually and at their own expense. They met the sick at the depot with stretchers, and brought them to the hospitals where they placed them in beds. They awakened and dressed them in the morning, fed them throughout the day, wheeled them to the chapel, the grotto, the baths, the processions, and prayed and sang with them. The young scouts and little children who participated in these activities brought tears to Madolin's and Bob's eyes.

For Madolin and Bob, this was the miracle of Lourdes, the strong members of the body of Christ serving the weaker members, who in St. Paul's language were "making up in their bodies what was lacking in the sufferings of Christ." Christianity was alive and visible at Lourdes.

Both years they were at Lourdes on the feast of the Assumption. The crowds were enormous. All activity at the shrine, however, was marked by dignity and reverence and priority of concern for the sick. The Eucharistic blessing of the sick, the stations of the cross, the candlelight procession, the mixed multitude and the variety of tongues, the spread of ages all reflected clearly the universal message of Christ, we are one in the Spirit and our goal is to live in love.

On their first tour, Madolin and Bob covered a lot of territory by Eurorail. They spent several days at three European shrines, Lourdes, Fatima, and Medujgorie. At all three places the message was the same: where charity and love prevail there is God. They didn't receive any new revelations about their faith nor witness any acts of extraordinary wonder. The experience of the shrines was simply a bonus, a strengthening of what they already knew. The wonder of these places is the people who go there with broken bodies and spirits and who become healed, sometimes exteriorly but always interiorly by the presence and the love of God living in people.

During her four years of suffering Madolin did experience two major incidences of physical healing. In the summer of 1989 she and Bob had flown to Vancouver to board a cruise ship for a tour of Alaska. In a motel room late in the night before they were to board the ship Madolin began to experience very severe pain from the enlargement of her spleen. After a couple of Bob's miscues attempting to secure some professional medical assistance, Madolin said, "Honey, why don't you just administer the Sacrament of the Sick for me and I think I will be OK." He did and the pain ceased. The cruise was a carefree experience for her.

In January of 1991 she had a very bad spell. The oncologists were convinced that the end was immanent and so advised her two children who were doctors. But Madolin wasn't ready to die and told them so in her ever cheerful and humorous way. When Bob started to insert conditional phrases into their daily prayers for healing, she told him to quit being so tentative. After a few blood and platelet transfusions and a switch to the drug Interferon, she bounced back. She hosted the big kids for the Kentucky Derby in May, travelled to Hatteras, Tucson, and

Salt Lake City in July and August, and made plans for the annual Thanksgiving reunion.

During the first three years of her illness Madolin had pursued inner healing with vigor. But now, after talking with her eldest son and the oncologists, she accepted the fact that her leukemia was for real and that some aspects of life are transitory. She then began to focus in earnest on the healing that is available for everyone and is critical for the enjoyment of eternal life, the inner healing of the spirit. She believed that if she healed her inner wounds the devastation of her leukemia would slow down or be transformed and the quality of her remaining days would be improved.

With the direction and guidance of a insightful counselor, she first wrote out a thorough inventory of her past. Because of the intensity and extended involvements of her life, the list of people and events that needed reconciliation and forgiveness was long. Systematically then she set out to heal those wounds by visiting, corresponding, telephoning, and praying. As she pursued this very difficult task the consequences became very real and rewarding for everyone involved. Her leukemia didn't go away, but it became a sacrament, a healing instrument for her and those around her. Life became a thanksgiving. Existence took on new dimensions. Fractured families were put back together. Relationships became much more open and sincere. Joy abounded where it had been absent for years. It was amazing what one person's quest for healing could effect.

In early November of 1991, Madolin was ready for her final journey. She and Bob drove to the clinic where she informed her doctors that she had had enough blood and platelets, enough Interferon and radiation, and that it was time to stop all that expensive stuff. She had the doctors sign and staff witness her living will that they were not going to do anything further to keep her alive. She said good bye and thanked all of them for their wonderful care and concern over the past four years.

Back home she asked Bob and a daughter-in-law who was a nurse to go with her to noon Mass and one last stroll through the neighborhood park. When they returned to the house she wanted to sit out on the patio for a few minutes to say goodbye to her trees, flowers, and animal friends. A short while later she danced a little jig with Bob as he helped navigate her to the bathroom and back to the living room couch.

By mid-afternoon the pain had intensified severely and it became necessary to switch from patches to direct shots of morphine and move her from the living room couch to the bedroom. The children started to arrive in the evening and whenever they entered the room she opened her eyes, smiled and kissed them. During the daylight hours of Wednesday and Thursday she would occasionally watch the grandchildren playing in the leaves outside her window and also check on the antics of her bird and squirrel friends.

The family passed the hours in the room with her singing songs, reading poetry, and telling stories. The prayers of the old Roman ritual weren't much help because of their emphasis on sin and gloom, so the group prayed spontaneously, assuring Madolin that they loved her and were grateful for the innumerable blessings and gifts that she had heaped upon them.

Because of internal bleeding it became more and more difficult for Madolin to breathe and the pressure on her bladder became intense. So she frequently tried to sit up. The children discovered that the most comfortable position for her was to have someone sit spread eagle behind her and assist her in sitting up. As they took turns doing this the symbolism became clear. It was in this position that she had presented these nine children to the world, and now it was their turn to present her to eternity.

At 10:30 A.M. on Friday, while the family sang the song that she had frequently sung to all of them, "Tell Me Why," she died, a valiant lady who complained very little and made a lot of lemonade.

In the evening, after the major details of the funeral had been taken care of, the eldest son made an exceptionally large batch of Manhattans, Madolin's favorite cocktail. Everyone quaffed a memorial Manhattan while they sang again, this time in harmony," Tell Me Why." The youngest daughter, her namesake, set the tone of their response to Madolin's death, "This (life after death) is what Mom lived for, so we shouldn't be sad. We should celebrate," and they did.

The day after Madolin died, her extended family gathered at the foot of her wounded maple tree for a simple liturgy. It was November and with the leaves off the tree, the scars of the storms past were fully visible. The tree could not have looked more ugly and deathly. For most of her life, Madolin was a beautiful woman. The ravages of leukemia drastically changed that situation.

One of the boys read the parable of the seed, "unless the seed falls into the ground and dies it remains alone." As the group sat there talking and reflecting, two of Madolin's favorite squirrels cavorted through her tree in a game of tag. Several cardinals, a blue jay, and a red headed woodpecker did several flybys. They came, no doubt, to remind the family that they too are parts of the universe and that the sooner the family would get in sync with the rhythms of life the happier they would be. Madolin, like her tree, still lives. Basic physics. You can't destroy energy. It doesn't go away. It changes and transforms and is with us "all days, even to the consummation of the world." We have to learn new ways of perceiving life, "fertilizing" and "talking to" all of the creatures with whom we share this universe.

A daughter read a verse by an unknown author:

Fear not that which is now

Fear not that which is to come.

Life, Death, and Being are one.

It is a circle. There is no

beginning and no end.

For that which is the beginning

is the end of the other.

And that which is the end

is the beginning of the other.

Surely the lessons of life are

the wisdom of death.

Those that live in the knowledge

of what the circle truly is

have peace beyond measure.

The funeral Mass was a beautiful celebration. It didn't start on time because Madolin was rarely on time for anything. The children managed to drag their feet long enough at the funeral home to delay the program for fifteen minutes. The entrance hymn was "When the Saints Go Marching In." The Offertory was particularly meaningful. The pastor invited all of the family to place a hand on the white draped coffin and to offer Madolin, God's gift to them, as their return gift to God.

The ceremony took a long time because there were thirteen homilies delivered, the pastor's, Bob's, nine children, and one representative from the spouses and one from the grandchildren. It was important for the family to tell friends and relatives what Madolin meant to them and what was the special lesson they each had learned from her. "The Battle Hymn of the Republic," was sung as a recessional.

Madolin was cremated. She didn't believe that it was necessary for her to have her own piece of real estate with perpetual care. In her immediate family she was referred to as Dad number two, a title she was particularly proud of. Her father, Patrick, was a fabulous, extroverted, engaging Irishman. So now her canister of ashes rests on his bosom in Flint, Michigan. The simple marker reads Madolin O'Rourke Keller, Oct. 29, 1920 – Nov. 15, 1991.

The ceremony was completed with the reading of a wonderful bit of verse written by an anonymous Native American.

> Do not stand at my grave and weep.
> I am not there.
> I do not sleep.
> I am a thousand winds that blow
> I am the diamond glint on snow.
> I am the sunlight on ripened grain.
> I am the autumn rain.
> When you awake in the morning rush,
> I am the swift uplifting rush
> Of birds circling in flight.
> I am the stars that shine at night.
> Do not stand at my grave and weep.
> I am not there.
> I do not sleep.

If Madolin is not in her grave in Flint and is not sleeping, then where is she? Can she be reached? Is it possible to communicate with her? The poem indicates some of the places where she lives, in the wind and snow, the sun, the rain, and the ripened grain, with the birds and the stars. Those are tangible, energy-filled places. But is her unique individuality, her playfulness, her enthusiasm, her deep love of little children, her passion for justice, and her incredible dedication, still alive and with us? For those who believe in the mystical Christ there are other places where the deceased live and where their presence can be felt.

For a long time Sacraments have been thought of as the gestures or actions of Christ. Because He now lives in the spirit world and we now live in a split world of spirit and body we need some help in bridging the gap between us. We need symbols that can tie or bind these two worlds together. It's not enough; it's not satisfying for us to live only in our spirits. Our bodies too want to be and need to be involved and centered. That's why there are Sacraments.

Fundamentally what Sacraments tell us is that all is one, God is one and we are one in God. Jesus put it very nicely, "All are to be one; just as you, Father, are in me and I am in you, so they, too, are to be one in us." Most people catch a glimpse of that truth when they share the bread and the cup, when a child is immersed in water, when a sick person is anointed with oil, and when other Sacramental gestures of Christ are sensed.

There is another significance to Sacraments that many people overlook. One of the deepest pains of human existence is that separation from loved ones that occurs at the time of death. Oneness appears to be severed and destroyed when the physical presence of the beloved is removed. But consider this equation. If we are one in Christ then wherever Christ is, we are, both the living and the dead. If Sacramental symbols make Christ's presence tangible, then they simultaneously make the presence of the deceased tangible.

One early morning while at Sacred Heart, Fr. Bob was summoned to the home of a dying parishioner to bring Viaticum and administer the Final Anointing. He knew this elderly man and his wife quite well. They had been married for over fifty years and were paragons of virtue. Inspiration moved Fr. Bob to suggest to Mary, the wife, that she give Peter his last earthly Communion. (Those were pre-Vatican II days when lay people were not allowed to serve the Eucharist.) Without hesitation Mary placed a portion of the host on a spoon with a little water and offered it to Peter. Then she consumed the remaining portion.

Mary never forgot this encounter. She became a daily Mass participant from then on and the Eucharist became for her a daily, tangible visit with Peter as well as with Christ. This experience calmingly carried Mary through the final years of her life and made her a sign of peace and love to the whole neighborhood.

Thinking symbolically like this is possible for all of us and offers answers to a lot of problems that stem from separation and loneliness.

We know precious little about life after death, because energy is not destroyed but transformed then life goes on. But where and how? Jesus told us, "There are many rooms in my Father's house. If there were not, should I have told you that I am going to prepare a place for you? It is true that I am going away to prepare a place for you, but it is just as true that I am coming again to welcome you into my own home, so that you may be where I am."

The doubting apostle Thomas responded, "Lord, we do not know where you're going, and how can we know what road you're going to take?"

Jesus responded simply, "I myself am the road."

That's about all we've got — a road that leads to a roomy house. But that's better than nothing, isn't it? The road is narrow and steep. And that, too, is better than nothing. There are a lot of nice people on the road in front of us, with us, and behind us. And that's better than nobody, isn't it? When folks build a road it usually goes somewhere. A roomy house is better than nowhere. Most roads have accommodations like gas stations, motels, restaurants, somewhere along the way. That's better than total desolation. Most roads have signs and directions every now and then. That's better than disorder, confusion, and going in circles. A good number of roads are at least partially lit. That's better than being totally in the dark. Jesus said, "In doing this, you will find your happiness."

Surely the lessons of life are the wisdom of death.

CHAPTER TWENTY-FOUR
THE CRYSTAL
BALL THING

GREETINGS!

Books make wonderful gifts. Journey Books of Louisville would be happy to send copies of this book to your relatives, friends, colleagues, employees, whatever. We will include a greeting card. Call us with names, addresses, re check or credit card # (MC or VISA), expiration date, and your phone number in case of any confusion. Autographs upon request.

Journey Books, 286 Persimmon Ridge Dr., Louisville, KY 40245

<u>Call</u>: 1 (888) 419-6443. <u>Call/Fax</u>: (502)243-0087 . <u>E-mail</u>: Kellerbook @aol.com

DISCOUNTS: 10% for 5 copies or more. (We will figure for #, taxes, & mailing.)

P.S. As for gifts, this might not be the season, or you''rpe lacking a valid reason, or your assets are in "freezen", but those factors should not prevent you from telling your relatives, friends, and associates about this book and where they can get it, should they? Thanks!

Over thirty years ago a fascinating article appeared in the *U.S. Catholic* magazine, November, 1965. It was written by the great Jesuit theologian, Carl Rahner. The article was entitled "Christian of the Future." The article really caught Fr. Bob's attention when he was pastoring Sacred Heart parish in Saginaw. The article, yellow, dog-eared, coffee-stained, heavily underlined, still sits on the top of his desk. It is like a crystal ball that he looks into from time to time to gauge and give relevance to his weeble-wobbling.

Rahner puts his thoughts in the category of a dream, perhaps a nightmare. He says that it doesn't matter when this dream will actualize, but he suggests maybe 20, 30, or 100 years. At that future date, he dreams, "Christians will be a little flock . . . gathered round the altar announcing the death of the Lord . . . They will know each other . . . They will form only a relatively small minority with no independent domain of their own . . . It will not be a Christian philosophy which is proclaimed as the official ideology of society."

Rahner says little as to how this transition will come about and what the process will look like. In effect he says, dream your own dreams. What follows is the dream or nightmare that Fr. Bob has been entertaining since he first read that article in 1965.

What Fr. Bob thinks Rahner implies is that the Catholic Church as people have known it for centuries is going to undergo some very radical changes in structure. Why?

1. Numbers. Mankind grows quicker than Christendom.

2. Numbers. The clergy is dying. The median age of American priests is around 65. New candidates are rare. The rate of priests ordained today is 70% lower than it was in the late 1960s. 25,000 priests have resigned and at the same rate for the past 15 years, 20% within 10 years, 35% within 15 years, 42% within 25 years. Parishes are merging, closing and being torn down all over the country. Close to 15% of U.S. parishes no longer have a resident pastor; the figure is over 50% world wide.

3. Psychology. Large scale religious organizations and institutions do not satisfy the basic religious needs of evolving human beings.

The center piece of the Catholic religion is the Eucharist. Just about all Catholic religious activity starts and ends there, hatching, patching, matching, and dispatching. Most of the Sacraments are or should be administered in the context of the Mass. Catholics are strongly obligated to go to Mass at least once a week. The Mass is one of only a few religious exercises that still requires the presence of a priest.

Strange as it seems, very few Catholics can tell you what really goes on at Mass. Just for the fun of it, why don't you ask a half dozen Catholics about Mass and see if you don't get a variety of answers?

Most of them will be able to tell you the order of things. After all they've been going for years and the procedure doesn't vary much from week to week. Others will tell you that it is their way of worshipping God, the Mass is a sacrifice, a gift that they offer to God, and that's a pretty good answer.

Now this is very important. The way folks perceive and deal with Eucharist, is going to determine the future structure of the Church. That perspective and consequent behavior has been drastically altered over the centuries and is being seriously rethought again today.

So why don't you dig out your New Testament and read what happened at the Last Supper. It won't take you long. In the four Gospels combined there are only 114 verses that pertain to the Supper. It's always good to start at the beginning.

Most of us have an image of the Last Supper that sort of replicates DaVinci's painting. Like Romans, everyone is reclined and only twelve males are present. Probably didn't happen that way. Chances are they sat and there were others there besides the twelve Apostles. Matthew and Mark state that Jesus sent disciples to prepare the place and to tell the owner, "I am going to keep the Passover with my disciples at your house." He had both male and female disciples, his mother and Mary of Magdala among them. How could he have excluded his mother from such an important event? Mark states only that Jesus "arrived" with the twelve.

Periodically, Jewish people have inserted new things into the Passover meal. That evening Jesus also gave the celebration a new twist. At the start of the meal Jesus did something that really shocked those in attendance. Like the lowest servant on a house staff, Jesus put on an apron and washed the feet of his guests. When he finished he told them, "I have given you this example so that you may do as I have done. Believe me, the servant is not greater than his master and the messenger is not greater than the person who sent him. Once you have realized these things, you will find your happiness in doing them."

Then the meal got underway. In the middle of it Jesus took some unleavened bread, broke it and said, "Take and eat this. This is my body which will be given up for you." Then he probably passed pieces of the bread in each direction around the table and the disciples fed one another like people in that part of the world still do today.

The Apostles and disciples must have been a little surprised at this. They knew it wasn't outright cannibalism. Jesus was still sitting there and he wasn't diminished as they ate the bread. Then Jesus took a cup of wine and told them, "Take and drink. This is the cup of my blood which will be poured out for you." Then he passed the cup which they all drank from in turn. They must have been a little shocked like any of us would be if someone asked us to drink their blood. Jesus didn't seem to go pale as they consumed the wine. Then he clarified what he was doing. "Now do this in remembrance of me."

Clearly this was a ritual that Jesus wanted his friends to observe so they wouldn't forget him, so they would know in their gut, to be literal about it, that they shared a very intimate relationship with him. That word, relationship, is a very important one. This wonderful and brief ritual was something like an adoption ceremony. How better and more simply could you tell friends that you wanted to be one with them, share your identity with them, than by asking them to eat and drink the food that you had sacralized and designated as yourself? We are what we eat and drink to a great extent, aren't we? It's basic physics. The energy that is in the food is transformed into us. There is only so much energy. It is never destroyed. It doesn't go away. It just moves around.

Luke then tells us, and this is hard to believe, right after receiving the Eucharist for the first time, the disciples began to "argue among themselves as to who should be considered the most important." So Jesus tells them again that they are missing the point. "Among the heathen it is their kings who lord it over them, and their rulers are given the title of 'benefactors.'

But it must not be so with you. Your greatest man must become like a junior and your leader must be a servant. Who is the greater, the man who sits down to dinner or the man who serves him? Obviously, the man who sits down to dinner — yet I am the one who is the servant among you." Then the group sang a hymn and left.

By the way, there is no indication in the Gospels that Jesus ordained any priests at that time or later and set them aside as a separate social class. The only reference in the entire New Testament to a new priesthood is in St. Peter's first letter and that priesthood extends to all people who believe, not just a few select males. Peter says, "You, (who believe) are a chosen race, a royal priesthood, a holy nation."

So now, how did we get from that simple family-like ceremony to the pomp and circumstance of today? Where is the foot washing? Where are the servants in their aprons, waiters who don't give orders but take orders? Where is the table that you can sit around and have a caring conversation? Where are the substantial portions of bread and wine so that your gut will know that you've had a meal?

Facts about the celebration of Mass, the Eucharist, are pretty sketchy in the New Testament. The second celebration took place on Easter Sunday. Two disciples, not from the Twelve and probably a married couple, walked seven miles with Jesus on the road to Emmaus and finally recognized him at the end of the trip when He "broke bread" with them.

The Acts of the Apostles and St. Paul's epistles are also sparse in their references to Eucharist. The Acts contain five verses and Paul has six. When things settled down and the little flock became convinced that Jesus wasn't dead and gone but living on a new level of existence, more basic physics, the disciples still retained their Jewish identity and observed the Jewish way of life. They went regularly to the Temple for religious ceremonies. When they got home, however, in small groups they observed "the breaking of the bread" to keep the memory of Jesus alive, that the kingdom of God was within them.

In brief, what the records tell us is that the celebration of the Lord's Supper was a small group event for probably a couple of hundred years. That's easily understandable. There weren't a whole lot of followers of the Way in the early years. Most of the Jews in Palestine thought that Christians were nuts. Even the great St. Paul had fun tracking them down and persecuting them. When Peter and Paul moved out to places like Antioch, Corinth, Ephesus, Rome, the Christians didn't multiply like rabbits. They experienced a lot of rejection and persecution. "The Way," as they were first known, was a small underground church for a long time.

Things changed drastically, however, in the fourth century. The Roman emperor Constantine had a vision that indicated he would conquer his enemies by the sign of the cross. "In hoc signo vinces," the vision stated. He did conquer and then converted. In 313, he issued the Edict of Milan and that day the Church went into the real estate business, climbed into bed with civil authority, and joined the establishment. It was probably the worst day in the history of Christianity. The disciples forgot what Jesus had said at the Last Supper to keep it simple. You've got to be waiters. Power, lording it over people, it must not be so with you.

Theodocius followed Constantine as Emperor and he proclaimed Christianity the official religion of the empire. With the support of the Emperor and the so called gift of an abundance of pagan temples, the Church entered the world of theatre and entertainment. The simple breaking of bread that memorialized Jesus and provided a tangible experience of the presence of God in self and others got buried and camouflaged in imperial buildings and ceremonies. Loving service, like foot washing, was traded for power and the real message of Jesus has been obscured ever since.

Early Christians and their leaders, for the most part, were working class folks. They were totally inexperienced at theatre. Liturgies were simple and in private homes. The leaders, following the example of Jesus, were servants. They told stories about the Master and presided at the "breaking of the bread." But the Emperor was surrounded by an abundance of talented people who knew how to salute and promote royalty as well as entertain the masses. Before his conversion Constantine was the god of the Empire and he knew how to treat a colleague. Consequently, the imperial ceremonies and garb of the Roman court gradually became the liturgy and attire of the Christian church. Funny thing about that. They still are.

The early church leaders who got caught up in this revolution can be easily forgiven for the mistake. After all, not a whole lot about basic human psychology was known at the time. And as for power, it must have looked pretty good to them after their long stint in the catacombs. Unfortunately, Lord Acton hadn't yet made his famous remark about the corruptibility of power. How were they to know?

As often happens, when you hit the big time you forget who or what got you to the dance. Loudly and clearly Jesus had repeated, "My kingdom is not of this world . . . The kingdom of God is within you;" in other words, it's not out there. He tried so hard to keep it simple. One commandment. One ceremony. He emphasized that temples were not necessary. Many of his critics were priests. He never played the priestly role and said absolutely nothing about establishing a new priesthood. The role that he played was that of a prophet, a pest. He was as anti-establishment as you can get. That's why he got killed, and by the same Roman establishment that his disciples were now taking as their bed partner.

Perhaps the most deleterious and far-reaching consequence of the marriage of the Church to the Empire of Rome was the conversion of "The Way" to an "ism." An ism is a system of laws, rules, hoops, regulations, formalities, hierarchies, proclamations, decrees, dogmas, divisions, and levels. The Romans were deep into that stuff. Catholicism became a head trip and a legal obstacle course, the exact opposite of what Jesus intended.

It is quite clear that Jesus came to establish a relationship with people. "I am with you all days, even to the consummation of the world . . . Where two or three are gathered together in my name there I am in the midst of them . . . I am the Vine, you are the branches . . . As long as you did it to one of my brethren you did it to me . . . Abide in me and I in you." Jesus wanted to be engaged with, involved with, communicating with people in an ongoing way.

Let's take a moment to think through that word relationship. The root word in Latin is *ferre* — to bear or carry. (The pluperfect participle is *latus*). *Re* means again. The significance of the word is that a relationship is not a one shot deal. It's an ongoing, back and forth exchange between people. That old song, *You tell me Your Dreams and I'll Tell You Mine,* says it pretty well. I carry my stuff to you and you carry your stuff to me and as we do so the ties between us grow and strengthen.

If you've got blood in your veins and experienced such an exchange you don't want it to end. As a recent Jack Nicholson movie indicated, "That's as good as it gets."

Now this is the heart of the matter, the basic question that has to be answered. How does one establish a relationship? Head trips we know. We've got schools for that. Establishing a relationship is a long hard process and most people are not very good at it. Look at marriage in our society. Year after year, in poll after poll, Americans overwhelmingly declare that their highest value is to belong to and have a "good" family. What they are seeking is a warm, enduring, productive relationship. Tragically, large numbers of Americans never succeed at building a permanent connection with another person. Note the exceedingly large number of divorces in the U.S. yet divorcees don't give up. Second and third marriages are common today because so many people are starving for a primary relationship.

Relationships demand conversation. A lot of it. Both words and gestures. Relationships take time. A lot of it. It takes time to build trust, to understand another's psychological makeup, to listen to another's words and gestures and evaluate their beliefs, and values, and dreams. It takes time to clarify one's own thinking and expressions. It takes time to know one's own typology and how it mixes with that of another. It takes time to work out agreements and compromises, how to be creative and productive, how to do things together.

You've hungered all your life for good relationships and you've burned up a lot of energy in the process, haven't you? Well, if it's tough building a relationship with someone like your parent, your spouse, your child, who is quite visibly present and lives in the same house with you, then how tough is it to build a relationship with Jesus who is not quite so visibly present?

As in buying real estate, the first question that has to be asked is "location." Where do you think Jesus is? Well shortly after the Church got off on its rational/legal trip with the Roman Empire, Catholics came to believe that Jesus was basically in three places. First of all, He was in heaven, a vague place where you can't go until you die and then only on the condition that you've been very pious. Second, He was in the tabernacle or bread box of every Catholic church that had a red candle burning beside it. Third, He was in the priest. All

Destruction of Sacred Heart Church (photo courtesy Saginaw News)

priests were called "other Christs." A few people thought that maybe He was in the Bible. And the Bible also contained some expressions that indicated that Jesus might be in other places, but none of this was taken very seriously.

Finally in the mid 1940s, Pope Pius XII wrote an encyclical letter entitled the "Mystical Body." The gist of what he said was that Jesus is in the community of people who have intentionally identified with him. It was a strong effort to get back to what Jesus had said: "Where two or three are gathered together in my name there I am in the midst of them." Most of the people who read the encyclical accepted it as another dogma or statement of belief. It stayed in their head and never got to their heart. Only rarely did it get into their experience and behavior. Do you want to know why?

Simple. There wasn't a mechanism in the Church to make that happen, and Team Vatican wasn't about to put things in reverse. Jesus had left a mechanism, the simple Eucharistic meal, but the folks who went big time with the Emperor took Jesus' mechanism, jazzed it up with pageantry and mystery, put it on the big stage, mandated attendance and started to charge admission. Do you think that after all the time, money and energy the Team had invested in setting up its own Broadway they were about to declare that it wasn't necessary to go to a building or need a priest go-between to build a relationship with Jesus? Heavens, no.

If in your lifetime you have succeeded in leveling with one other person, how long did that take? One year? Five years? Ten years? From that experience, do you think it is possible to build a serious relationship with another person in the middle of a Las Vegas dinner show? How about in a church with a thousand people sitting in tight rows and examining the hair styles of the people in front of them? No way, McKay!

Now if Jesus is in people, and you accept His offer of a relationship, "Come to me all you who labor and are burdened and I will refresh you," then you have to go out and level with at least one person who is identified with Him. Right? As my old friend Slatchakowski used to say, "If you want one dat is go where are they." Today, probably the easiest place to find such a person(s) would be in one of the many small Christian groups that come together for Eucharist in their homes, some with an official waiter and some without.

Another good place to look for such a person would be a 12 step group. That person might not even be what some people would call a Christian. But remember what Jesus said He was going to base the Final Judgment on? "I was hungry, thirsty, lonely, naked, ill, in prison . . . and you took care of me. Whatever you did for the humblest of my sisters and brothers you did for me."

Twelve steppers know suffering like Jesus did, so He really and truly identifies with them. Twelve steppers are all over the place and meet at a great variety of times. Most of them know pretty well who they are and how to communicate at a gut level. They come together to share their weaknesses and by doing that they have acquired great strength which they are more than willing to share, so check them out.

A third location for encountering the transformed Christ is a dream group. More and more people are coming to realize that there is more to dreams than simple indigestion. In the overwhelming number of cultures that have existed over the ages, dreams have been regarded as sacred. The Bible itself is a dream book. Simply put, a dream is the voice of God. You might deny it, but you are dreaming all the time. Have somebody check your REMs, rapid eye movements, when you're sleeping. When you go to bed it's more important for your health and sanity that you dream than rest. Dreamers are in touch with God and so is Jesus. You can meet Him at a dream group.

And finally you ask, what do we do about the parish plants, the real estate? First of all, let it be said loudly and clearly that what's going on in the parishes is not all bad. The major problem with the parishes is that they are running a second stage program for people who supposedly have already developed an intense personal relationship with Christ. The truth of the matter is that there aren't a whole lot of those folks around. Relationships are for psychologically mature people and the Church, until recently, has offered precious little for adults to grow in this regard. Relationships have to be experienced. They are not delivered on command at an one hour, imperial production on Sunday morning with fifteen hundred people in attendance.

The "Little flock of the Gospel," however, that Carl Rahner spoke of so eloquently some thirty years ago, is slowly forming and growing, and mostly outside of the institutional church. These little communities, scattered all over the world, need to know that there are others who share their experiences and their goals. They need one another's support and inspiration. From time to time they might need one another's cooperation for some needy project.

It is at this level that the old parish might play a transitional part by providing a space and an inspiring, overarching liturgy. Also, the buildings could be used for ceremonies like baptisms, weddings, and funerals that demand larger communal expression. The parish staff might also serve to further motivate the small groups, give them new information for collective projects, broaden their views on social issues, and advise them of new theories and methodologies for spiritual growth. Summoning the small groups in every week would be counterproductive. A general meeting every three or four months would be sufficient. In brief, this second stage activity should be instrumental, occasional, broadening, and celebratory.

The head servant, male or female, who coordinates this parish program should be a married bishop elected by the people in the small groups. The basis for that person's election would be service like Jesus recommended for leadership. St. Paul said that all bishops should be married. His or her role would be to model service and the assignment should be a temporary one. Service should also be the basis of leadership in the small groups, and again leadership in a Christian community is the opposite of power and authority. You don't "lord it over" the group. You take care of it and serve it in whatever way is required and needed. You take orders and don't give them.

The leader of the small group, selected only by the group itself, need not be a priest. It is the people who collectively share in the one priesthood of Christ who make the Eucharist "happen." It only takes a minimum of two people, remember? "Where two or three are gathered together in my name, there I am in the midst of them." In down-home language Christ is the cook of the Eucharistic meal. The leader is simply the waiter. It's the group that makes it happen.

The procedure for this small group liturgy can be very simple like what the first Christians did. They had a little potluck, sang songs, told stories about Jesus, meditated on them, and applied them through discussion to their daily lives. "Not by bread alone does a person live, but by every word that proceeds from the mouth of God." St. John says that Jesus is the Word of God, so it's imperative that we listen to his story and be "imitators of Him as He was of the Father." Then they broke the bread, ate it, and drank from the cup in memory of Jesus. Such a simple setting offers a much better opportunity for an experience of Jesus in God.

Is this really going to happen? Bet your bottom dollar on it. Along with the clergy, the old church is dying, and new communities sans buildings and sans clergy are popping up all over the place. Read some samples of what Carl Rahner, one of the great theologians of our age, had to say about this and see if you don't agree that radical change is on the way. Here's a small sample:

"Christians of the future will form only a relatively small minority with no independent domain of their own . . . They will be the little flock of the Gospel gathered around the altar announcing the death of the Lord . . . There will be very few hangers-on, for there will be no earthly advantage in being a Christian . . . It will not only be the case, but it will be clear and plain to see, that all dignity and all office in the church is uncovenanted service, carrying with it no honor in the world's eyes, having no significance in secular society. . . It will no longer constitute a profession at all in the social and secular sense . . . It will no longer be a worldly honor to be a bishop in the little flock . . . the office will confer no special social position, power, or wealth . . . In the actual details of life as well as in theoretical questions . . . the official Church will simply leave most things which involve particular concrete decisions, to the conscience of the individual . . .The Church is only what it should be if it is a community of loving brothers and sisters." (*U.S. Catholic,* Nov., 1965)*

*Reprinted with permission from *U.S. Catholic,* Claretian Publications, www.uscatholic.org, 800-328-6515

CHAPTER TWENTY-FIVE
IMAGES OF GOD

Several years ago when Bob began his studies of sociology, he was exposed to a book entitled *The Elementary Forms of The Religious Life* by Emile Durkheim. Reading it was a wall kicking experience. Because he wasn't allowed a bed partner and to keep temptations out of his head, Fr. Bob always read himself to sleep. His single bed in a Notre Dame dorm was crammed against a wall. Durkheim's ideas sometimes pleased and other times angered him. Both responses solicited a kick to the wall.

One night he read something to the effect that God did not create man, man created God. Loud forceful kick! Hole in the drywall. Every Catholic kid who cut his teeth on the catechism knew that God made him or her and for one purpose, "to know, love and serve Him in this world and to be happy with Him forever in the next." Who did this guy Durkheim think he was?

But Bob read on. He was going to become a scientist and one must have an open mind. As he read on he learned that Durkheim conceived of God as an ideal type. Ideal types are used for comparative purposes. They represent a collection of traits and characteristics taken from various sources and the type does not actually exist. Durkheim's thought went something like this. People would look around and see a person who was just. After some reflection they decided that they liked that virtue and believed that it would be good for their society if that virtue was widely imitated. They did the same thing with all the other forms of behavior that they found acceptable and functional — honesty, bravery, loyalty, and chastity, among others.

Then people started to wonder where these virtues came from. Gradually, the men who got better food, the thinkers, began to wonder whether these virtues existed somewhere in their perfect form. So over time these "good" and therefore acceptable forms of behavior got personified as gods. Eventually, these behaviors were collected and placed in one person and given the name God. In this way then men created God.

Durkheim's conclusion to this reverse creation is also interesting. He states that men started to come together to celebrate these virtues in a ceremonial way, and institutionalized religion was born. They did not come together, however, to celebrate God. They came to celebrate themselves and their way of life.

Celebrating was their way of reinforcing the behaviors that they wanted practiced in their culture. These virtues were the glue that gave them cohesion and solidarity. The bottom line is that religion is for man, and you don't need an objective God "out there" to explain the birth of the religious institution.

So what do you think? Is Durkheim nuts? Best way to find out is to ask yourself: What is my image of God? What do I know about God? Where did I get that knowledge? Now Bob's been in the God business for almost seventy years. He's listened to a lot of lectures, read a lot of books, dialogued with people from a wide variety of beliefs and practices, meditated and reflected on the topic for hours upon hours. This is his "ideal type," what he thinks the great majority of people in our Christian tradition think about God.

God is an adult, complete human being. God is male, Our Father whose Son Jesus is also male. He is handsome in his maturity. He has a deep but warm voice that seems to come from a long distance. Only a few people have ever heard it, however. God listens well to what people have to say, but He doesn't always respond the way people would like Him to. He knows all the answers, so we get what is best for us. He exhibits the full array of virtues. His kingdom, often referred to as heaven, is a perfectly run government somewhere in the tropics. The inhabitants are all good people and closely resemble those who are thinking about this place and planning to go there. No derelicts. No street people. Heaven, also, is a United Nations-type place where all races, tribes, and cultural groups have their own separate territory and maintain their differences. Borders, of course, are open for tourism and all differences are respected. The kingdom abounds in comfortable stuff — nice residences with beautiful gardens, good transportation, excellent food and drink, first rate artistic opportunities, perpetual leisure, all of the stuff that people struggle for in life but never quite acquire to their satisfaction. There is no stress, no struggle, no evolution.

Then how do we act or respond to this human image of God and his kingdom? We try to convert our environment into a holy picture world. We secretly long for apparitions of Jesus looking like a stained glass window. We pray before saccharine looking statues hoping to hear a melodious voice telling us that we are doing just fine. We pray ardently and try to make deals for miracles so that our problems and illnesses will go away and that the people we don't like will be destroyed or punished in hell. Unfortunately, apparitions and voices never come to the overwhelming majority of people. Our problems seem to get bigger, our illnesses multiply, and our enemies get stronger.

Jesus, unintentionally probably, got a lot of people thinking about this holy picture world when He said, "Eye has not seen, nor ear heard, nor has it entered into the heart of human beings the things that God has prepared for those that love Him." His statement was like a dare, and many of us have taken up his challenge. "Yes we can imagine and will never stop imagining what it must be like," we respond. Some of us even have the nerve to peddle our personal imaginings to other people. We really aren't any different from the people that Durkheim wrote about, are we? Our image of God and his kingdom is made up of the things that we like about ourselves, the things that we celebrate. In a real sense we have made our own God, too, haven't we? Some wag put it nicely, "God made us to his image and likeness so we returned the favor."

So how do we erase this holy picture world? How do we rise above narrow and shallow definitions of God? How do we respond to people who tell us with absolute certainty that they have the answers to all the questions? Where can we find the courage and the confidence to say to everyone else, "this is my trip and I have to do it and I can do it by myself."

The basic and fundamental fact that we have to latch on to and never let go of is that the kingdom of God is WITHIN us. This is a belief that has permeated every culture that has ever existed. It isn't a belief that people have accepted because a missionary from another culture came and told them about it. All people are born with the Divine Guest within them. Furthermore, people are born with a blueprint-map-menu that outlines what the will of God is for them, and all people have the necessary means for fulfilling that will. God spells out what is expected through dreams. Simply stated, dreams are the voice of God. If you want to find out if this is true or not, then start listening to and recording your dreams. Learning how to analyze them would also help.

The second task that we have to perform then is to learn how to think symbolically. Symbols are signs that stand for something else. They lead us to know something beyond themselves.

They spiral up to greater insights. They reveal the link between the visible and the invisible world. Words, gestures, things can all be symbols. One of the offshoots of the scientific age is literalism, seeing only what is obvious, observing the letter of the law, and dealing only with external facts. Most religious institutions, whether they are streamlined, mainlined, or fundamental are literalists. They seem to blow right on by the majestic opening verses of St. John's Gospel, "When time began the Word was there, and the Word was face to face with God, and the Word was God."

A word is a symbol. God is a symbol. Jesus is a symbol. So is the virgin birth, the Incarnation, the Crucifixion, the Resurrection, the Ascension, and the Descent of the Holy Spirit. The question that we never seem to ask is what knowledge, insights, links do these symbols reveal? For some reason or other we never seem to get beyond the historical records. Because old scholars canonized these records we read them over and over again. We keep looking back, trying to refine and clarify the records. What did Jesus really look like? What words did Jesus actually say? Where is the exact location of his birth? Did Mary have other children? How many people were present at the marriage feast in Cana? and on, and on, and on.

If we want to know God and what his will for us really is, it is imperative that we learn to think symbolically. That's the way God talks. God speaks to us personally everyday in our dreams. They are loaded with symbols that are tailor made for us. If we really want to know what God has to say we've got to deal with symbols. If we don't have the courage and can't find the time to do that then we end up with somebody's else's message and no assurance that it's true. It's like trading an El Greco original for an old black and white newspaper photo of the same painting.

Sure, we are going to need help. We've got to read and talk to other people who are on the journey. There is a simple test to determine whether the authors or the speakers are in touch with God and have anything worthwhile to say on the subject. That person will always play the role of a servant or a waiter. Waiters never give orders. They take orders. They will never impose their experience and knowledge of God on us. They will do everything they can to help us and guide us in our search for God and knowledge of his will, but the search is our task.

It's a trip that we have to take on our own. No one else can do it for us. In this regard we are all called to the monastic life. The Greek word *monazein* means to live alone.

A third step that we have to take if we want to know God and do his will is to get fully acquainted with nature. The "wholly" people of the ages have all talked about the *lumen naturae,* the light of nature. To those who look upon nature with a loving eye the fingerprints and footprints of Hagia Sophia, the Holy Spirit, the feminine principle in God, are everywhere. The trademark of her sacred geometry is stamped on everything, from stars, leaves, flowers, snowflakes to the 45 trillion DNA molecules that carry the genetic code in every cell of our bodies.

The lumen naturae — light of nature — is a mass of symbols that "spiral" up to greater insights about the Creator. Mother Nature, if we would only take the time to read her, writes more beautifully and explicitly about God than does all the literature of human beings combined. Somewhere along the line huge numbers of human beings got disconnected from nature. Most churches don't want their members to be natural. They want them to be supernatural, above that earthy stuff. Most churches don't foster symbolical thinking, linking the visible to the invisible world, the *unus mundus,* the one world.

Bob recently read an item in the Sunday paper that quoted the journal of a lady who had lost her home in a 1997 flood. It clearly points out the stance of the religious franchisers toward nature. The lady wrote, "It hurts, it hurts, it hurts. I can't fix it back . . . Damn you Mother Nature. The Lord wouldn't do this. Amen." Who taught that lady to separate God from His creation? Who taught that lady to believe that Mother Nature is evil and to be condemned? Who taught that lady to believe that God, "the Lord" is exclusively good and not a complex of opposites with a bright side and a dark side?

Now that's a God concept that we don't want to deal with. It's also a male concept that we don't want to deal with either. We know that we've got a dark side that we work hard to bury or keep hidden. We also know that an easy way to deal with that dark side is to project it on others and we can get very professional at doing that.

Most likely the reason why the franchisers have taken a dim view of Mother Nature is because she has a dark side as well as a bright side. Mother Nature was pretty amoral when that flood hit in 1997 and those Florida hurricances blew through in 1998. If Mother Nature is a reflection of God, then the reflection conflicts with our holy picture world and we cannot tolerate that. So, "Damn you, Mother Nature."

Maybe we ought to take a closer look at Mother Nature and while doing so we might get a better concept of what we are all about, because whether we want to accept the fact or not, we are a part of Mother Nature. And most importantly of all, we might get a clearer concept of what God is all about.

The most obvious characteristic of Nature that we will discover is that she is feminine. Feminine has nothing to do with gender. Femininity is a quality, a way of being that exists in both males and females. In males it is called the *anima*. Masculinity, the opposite, exists in both sexes. In females it is called the *animus*. It's a good word. You no doubt recognize the root in the verb *animate*, to turn on, get moving, inspire.

Now there's the best word of all — *inspire*. That's what the feminine principal is all about. The root of that verb is spirit, breath, life-giving, nurturing, gift, soul. In the Old Testament, spirit is conceived as a divine dynamic entity. In the New Testament, the spirit is called Holy and our idea of the divine personality is enlarged to that of Father, Son, and Holy Spirit, or the Trinity. In the Acts of the Apostles and other early Christian writings, the Holy Spirit is connected and associated with the Old Testament concept of Wisdom or "Sophia," who is also given the title of "Hagia" or Holy. For that reason many scholars say that the Holy Spirit is the feminine principle in God.

In the eighth chapter of Proverbs, Hagia Sophia, Wisdom personifed as a woman, states her case in a forceful and glorious manner. She speaks very loudly to our patriarchal age:

> On the hilltop, on the road, at the crossways,
> besides the gates of the city Wisdom takes her stand and cries aloud:
> O men! I am calling to you; my cry goes out to the sons of men.
> You ignorant ones! Study discretion;
> And you fools, come to your senses!
> Listen, I have serious things to tell you.

From my lips come honest words
My mouth proclaims the truth . . .
Yahweh created me . . . from everlasting I was firmly
set.
When he fixed the heavens firm, I was there . . .
When he assigned the sea its boundaries . . .
When he laid down the foundations of the earth
I was by his side, a master craftman,
delighting him day after day,
ever at play in his presence,
at play everywhere in his world,
delighting to be with the sons of men.
And now my sons, listen to me;
listen to instruction and learn to be wise, do not
ignore it.
The man who finds me finds life . . .
He who does injury to me does hurt to his own
soul,
All who hate me are in love with death.

Now those are strong words from a strong lady. She was with God from the beginning. She delighted Yahweh as she crafted the world with her sacred geometry, stars, snowflakes, pussy cats, and DNA molecules on the one hand, and floods, earthquakes, plagues, and tornadoes on the other. She is delighted to be with the sons of men to help them find life, but they better listen to instruction and learn to be wise.

Jesus learned quickly that His disciples would not fully understand what He was talking about. He also knew that there were a lot of timid folks around who would chicken out and refuse to take the solo trip that He was going to take on the cross, so He told His friends that He would make it easier for them. He assured them that he was going to add another and final act to the drama of life. This is what he said:

"I will ask the Father, and He will grant you another Advocate to be with you for all time to come, the Spirit of Truth (Sophia). The world is incapable of receiving Her, because it neither sees Her nor knows Her. You will know Her, because She will make Her permanent stay with you and in you . . . The

Advocate, the Holy Spirit, whom the Father will send in my
name, will teach you everything, and refresh your memory of
everything I have told you . . . She will conduct you through
the whole range of truth . . . She will announce the future to
you . . . She will draw upon what is mine and announce it to
you . . . you will do even greater things than I have done."

Now if the Holy Spirit is going to move disciples to do "even
greater things" than Jesus did, then what are we going to be
called, or more accurately, what are we?

Serious religious thinkers today are beginning to comprehend what Jesus intended when He promised to send the Holy
Spirit. They believe that what Jesus was saying was this: "Look
men! The show isn't over. There is another act, and the lead
role is going to be played in that final act by another person,
the Holy Spirit. Now don't stand around applauding me as if I
am the big hero of this show. The best is yet to come. I am just
a prototype of what is going to happen next. God incarnated
in me, but it wasn't a complete job because I 'was like all other
human being except sin.' Even my mother was conceived without sin. In the next act, God wants to incarnate in you, ordinary
human beings. Because you are imperfect like I wasn't, it will
be easier for people to understand the love of the Creator and
why they ought to love one another when they observe God in
you. Also, because The Holy Spirit will represent the feminine
side of the Creator, the other half of the human race, women,
everyone will easily understand that we are really all one. You
better believe it. When the Holy Spirit comes you will do greater
things than I did. You will be gods."

The original Apostles got that message. After the Ascension they hustled home to join the women, and as the Acts and
the Epistles indicate, after Pentecost they viewed themselves as
"temples of the Holy Spirit." They behaved themselves accordingly. They were enthusiastic, joyful, generous, warm, nurturing,
nonviolent, respectful, prayerful, playful, and all those other
feminine fruits and gifts that the Holy Spirit distributes. But then
the machine got put in reverse and stalled. When and why?
Probably when the Church joined the patriarchal establishment
in the fourth century.

In a letter to Morton Kelsey, an American Episcopal priest,
Carl Jung quite accurately described the current situation. "We
are still looking back to the Pentecostal events in a dazed way

instead of looking forward to the goal the Spirit is leading us to. Therefore mankind is wholly unprepared for the things to come. Man is compelled by divine forces to go forward to increasing consciousness and cognition, developing further and further away from his religious background because he does not understand it any more. His religious teachers and leaders are still hypnotized by the beginnings of a then new aeon of consciousness instead of understanding them and their implications. What one once called the Holy Ghost is an impelling force, creating wider consciousness and responsibility and thus enriched cognition. The real history of the world seems to be the progressive incarnation of the deity."

The new "Church of the Holy Spirit," as it were, is now emerging. The universe is now moving out of Pisces — Fish = Christ — into the age of Aquarius, a spirit sign. The menu is written in the stars, the lumen naturae. And what are those who walk in that light saying? It will be the age of the common person, divinized by the Spirit. Relationships, feminine activity par excellence, will become much warmer and nurturing, more primary because of the Spirit. Large institutions, especially religious ones, will shrivel. People will find meaning and strength through small communities of sharers. Only in small communities can people share their weaknesses and thereby learn to embrace and own their shadow. Only in small communities can people share their dreams and hear more clearly and accurately the voice of God, and only in small communities can people meaningfully break bread and thereby recognize the Lord, their prototype, and gain strength from Him on their solo journey. Finally, there will be a return to nature where people with loving eyes will walk awesomely in the lumen naturae and learn that they belong to the universe and it is one.

To put all this in a nutshell: if the Church is the Body of Christ, then the Church like Christ must undergo suffering and death. The signs of that are becoming more evident every day. A resurrection is happening as the Holy Spirit incarnates into the lives of individuals. This evolution of the God-image is not and will not be a collective transformation. It is happening within isolated individuals doing their own solo trip through suffering and death like Jesus did.

The prophet Joel described it this way:

In the days to come — it is the Lord who speaks —
I will pour out my spirit on all mankind.
Their sons and daughters shall prophesy,
your young men shall see visions,
your old men shall dream dreams.
Even on my slaves, men and women,
in those days, I will pour out my spirit.
I will display portents in heaven above
and signs on earth below.
Is this a dream? Yes, and dreams
are the voice of God.

CHAPTER TWENTY-SIX
END OF THE ROAD

Well, the Rock, alias Moose, alias Fr. Bob, alias Dr. K is getting down to the end of the road. His wobbling has been going on for almost seventy years and your final question probably boils down to something like, "Where is he now? What's the result of all this shaking and baking, jumping and jiving, and all those other expressions about coping with life?"

First of all, he has finally settled on a name. Some wit once remarked, "Once a man, twice a boy." When you get toward the end of the man stage, your long term memory seems to kick in and get stronger. Your memories of youth get fonder and more elaborated. In that vein of thinking, the aliases get turned upside down, and the one that now sounds most enduring is that of the Rock. Rocks are tough, solid, compact, firm, stable, weighty, real, genuine, and a whole list of other adjectives. The nickname is now up for readoption.

On his desk the Old Rock has a green and yellow weeble with the face of a red headed boy on it. It is a gift of his grandson Robbie who is a delightful red head. As the Rock sits pondering the issues of life, he frequently spins this weeble on his desk. True to form the weeble wobbles about making a rapid sound like ra ra ra ra ra ra. As it runs out of momentum and prepares to settle down on its base, the ra ra gets slower and louder. Then with one loud RAAAK it settles firmly on its base sounding and acting like a rock. That's very euphonic and meaningful for the Rock on his second trip through boyhood, especially since RAK are his initials.

Another axiom has also come true. "There might be snow on the mountain, but there's still a fire in the furnace." In 1992 the Old Rock married again. Madolin had given him a list of eligibles before she died, but before he had a chance to check any of them out, some friends introduced him to Kate, a "long, tall, brown-skinned gal" who convinced him to keep his Bible down. With her came three more adult treasures. His family now numbers 12 children, 24 grandchildren, 1 great grandchild, and counting.

The Old Rock calls Kate his angel, or literally, his messenger. Remember that stuff from chapter 17 about the Myers-BriggsTypology Index? On that index of preferences Kate and the Rock are exact opposites. Psychologically most people live in a four room house; they lock themselves into a narrow range of thinking and behaving. With a little study

Kate and Bob on their wedding day, December 27, 1992

and practice, however, any of us can live in a 16 room house. We can enjoy and benefit from all 16 thinking and behavioral preferences that are possible to human beings if we want to work at it.

By her presence, Kate is a walking, breathing, living message to the Rock that he is only partially awake and living in a very narrow space. By her oppositeness she models the behavior that can help him see, understand, and move into those unexplored spaces. A new and exciting kind of wobble!

And what is so wonderful, yet paradoxical about this MBTI business is that our avenue to wholeness, the spiritual, is through our least preferred function. In the Rock's case that is extroverted intuition. For a long time he didn't have a clue as to what that function was all about. Recently, it dawned on him that he has an Olympic class extroverted intuitive operating in his presence 24 hours a day. Now that's what angels are for.

In the summer of 1994 life for the Rock was nothing but dew and sunshine. He was 65 and officially retired from college teaching. Kate had quit her job and was completing a long piecemeal graduate program in Counselling and Psychology. Their thought was that completion of her degree was enough. Regular employment wasn't necessary. Their plan was to live up to their E-mail address, which they had named "Travelcats."

Something synchronicitous happened, however. One of Kate's professors that summer had some interesting things to say about Carl Jung. Then a friend told her about a North Carolina, "Journey Into Wholeness" conference in October that would examine what Jung had to say about Christianity. Kate thought that she would like to go to the conference and asked the Rock if he was interested. His response was that he was practicing cerebral hygiene. He thought that it was time to quit putting new stuff into his head and start sorting out what was already there.

For the sake of peace, good will, and compatibility, however, the Rock agreed to go. If nothing else this was a chance to be a travelcat. His noble martyr position was that if he got bored and disinterested, he would contentedly walk in the woods or read while she attended the lectures. The first lecture that he attended was given by a tall, formal, Jungian analyst from California by the name of Robert A. Johnson. He talked about dreams. Over the years the Rock had had a recurring dream about looking for a functioning toilet in church without success, and a lot of hot and sexy visionary creations that as a confirmed celibate he thought originated with the devil.

Kate and "The Treasured Three," Edwin, Elizabeth, and Katherine

Robert started his lecture with the plain comment that if we were ever going to hear the voice of God it would be in our dreams. That was different and quickly grabbed the Rock's attention. For at least 60 years the Rock had been anxiously waiting to hear something that God might want to say to him but never got a message. Robert talked for about an hour and never had the Rock heard a more logical, sensible, and meaningful talk in his life. He had a dream that night that he still vividly remembers. He's now hooked. Dreams come now on almost a daily basis and his morning prayer is recording and analyzing his dream.

From that introduction the Rock moved on to a better understanding of the human psyche, the ego, the Self, the personal unconscious, the complexes, the shadow, the collective unconscious, and the archetypes. What particularly thrilled him in Jung's explanation of the psyche was a fleshing out of what Jesus taught regarding the indwelling of the Holy Spirit and what St. Paul explained as Christ living in us. For Jung, the Self is the Divine Guest living in all of us, and the cross that all of us have to bear is bringing our ego into the service of the Self.

Jung's ideas are complex and profound. They don't break down to popular jingoes and flip aphorisms. The cerebral hygiene remark still sticks in the Rock's throat. What an arrogant person he was thinking that he had acquired enough knowledge to go coasting into eternity. That Journey conference that Angel Kate got him to convinced him that there was more to think about and experience in life. When the Rock lines up all of the experiences and insights now garnered from about twenty conferences, he can only conclude that Journey Into Wholeness is a wonderful remedy for arrogance, a superlative antidote for senility, and a challenging ride into the afterlife.

Back in 1959 when the Rock made his first Cursillo in Spanish, one of the many things that impressed him was a talk on Piety. A large, gruff man by the name of Nicolas spoke. He had a tremendous story to tell that shook the other men there to their foundations. He ended his rollo by loudly stamping his heel-plated shoe on the floor and shouted "Hay que pisar fuerte en la vida." You've got to go through life with a firm step. Jesus said something like that. "I wish that you were either hot or cold. But since you are neither, I intend to vomit you out of my mouth." Today we would say, "No pussy-footing around. Grab the bull by the horns. Come down hard like a rock. Take charge of your own life."

Recently the Old Rock had a delightful visit with his brother, the Old Curly. He's further down the road of life by two years and four months. That's something else to hang on to. Whether you're a kid or an old fogy there are some people out there that you will never catch. Just prior to the visit, Curly and his wife had gone to their parish church for Sunday Mass. The relatively new pastor, foreign import with meagre English language skills, announced that all those who had not attended Mass on the holy day of obligation that had occurred during the previous week were forbidden to go to Communion at this Mass unless they had been to confession.

Curly and his wife had not attended Mass on that day for some reason or other. His wife was infuriated by this pastoral pronouncement. She would have walked out, but Curly was functioning on that day as lector, song director, and Eucharistic minister. (He could have run the whole show if they would have asked him. He does just about everything else in the parish.) So when Communion time came, while his wife remained in the pew, Curly was the first to line up to receive Communion.

Arlie and Gen's 60th wedding anniversary celebration, 1986 (rear): Curly, Rock, Joe, Jim (front row): Gen, Arlie, and Mary LaBlanc (Gen's Matron of Honor)

The first question the Old Rock asked Old Curly was, "How did you make that decision?" Curly responded," It was easy. Fr. Joe Simon taught us a principle in high school that makes all those decisions simple. He said that the individual's conscience is the final arbitrator in those kind of situations. I knew that priest was wrong and I just ignored what he said and went to Communion without any guilt."

That response really tickled the Rock. He had never heard that principle articulated by Fr. Joe, even though he was in the same religion class with Curly. Of course there were a whole lot of other things he never heard in school. Also, he never learned that principle in the eleven years he spent in the seminary, nor in the early years of his ministry as a priest. It wasn't until almost the end of the Vatican Council in the mid-1960s that he learned that this was a principle that has existed since the early years of Christianity.

Needless to say, that principle has been the guiding light in most of the Rock's wobble with God. What it all boils down to is this. One ought to seek guidance and advice on religious and moral issues, and God knows there is an abundance of such guidance and advice out there. More, in fact, than most people can cope with. But a lot of it goes well beyond the scope of guidance and advice. It ends up being heavily authoritarian, dictatorial, all or nothing, life and death, and just baloney. Religious leaders keep forgetting what Jesus said, "Your leader must be a servant." Servants don't give orders. They take orders. Wobbling through life is ultimately a solo deal. Everybody has to say and do, "Hay que pisar fuerte en la vida."

One of two things happen when people get authoritarian advice. Some see the religious package as too much for them to think about, so on someone else's word they buy the package and turn into robots. At the other extreme, others look at the package, note the disregard for the primacy of the individual conscience, personal responsibility, and chuck all religious and moral systems. Somewhere in the middle lies sanity and wholeness.

And that's what the Rock is trying to do, be sane and whole. He listens to what all religious leaders are saying. Basically and surprisingly they are all saying the same thing. He attends religious exercises when the Spirit moves him, studies what scientists, especially physicists, biologists, and mathematicians, are discovering and saying. Finally, he participates in activities that promote the oneness of humankind and the care of the universe. Four principles motivate his thinking. One: The universe doesn't belong to us. We belong to the universe. Two: Cada chango por su mecate — every monkey on his own rope. Three: In all moral decisions the individual conscience is the final arbitrator. Four: Beware of premature closure on any topic. Change is inevitable. Nothing is permanently set in concrete.

The little redheaded boy on the front of the Rock's weeble has a tightly rolled up scroll in his hands. On his backside are two stuffed pockets. If that little boy were alive and wobbled like this toy does, the scroll would spin out of his hands and be unraveled and his pockets would empty out. It is hoped that as you have wobbled through this book the scroll of your life has unraveled a little and your pockets have been emptied of a lot of encumbering stuff. Please don't be afraid of wobbling. It'll keep you young and make you whole.

Be happy in your faith at all times. Never stop praying. Be thankful, whatever the circumstances may be. If you follow this advice you will be working out the will of God. (1 Thess.)